MORTAL ENEMIES

A GLANCE TOWARD the pinnace showed the two vessels were drifting apart. The pinnace was damaged, but nothing beyond repair.

Leckenbie was aboard there. Rafe Leckenbie, of all people! I stared after his boat with almost a hunger in my heart. Never had I wanted so much to fight a man, to meet him face to face . . . to end once and for all what lay between us.

For with him alive, I would never know peace. Always I must be on guard, certain that he would strike at me in the way I could be most hurt. For Leckenbie, to kill was never enough. He enjoyed making other men suffer.

And now I was vulnerable, for now I loved . . . and neither of us could ever know safety as long as Rafe Leckenbie lived.

"Pursue them," I said. "We cannot let them escape. . . ."

Bantam Books by Louis L'Amour
ASK YOUR BOOKSELLER FOR THE BOOKS YOU HAVE MISSED.

FAIR BLOWS THE WIND

Louis L'Amour

To Bob and Roberta . . .

FAIR BLOWS THE WIND
A Bantam Book

PUBLISHING HISTORY
E.P. Dutton edition published April 1978
Bantam edition / October 1978
Bantam reissue / August 1996
Bantam reissue / April 2005
Bantam reissue / October 2007

Published by
Bantam Dell
A Division of Random House, Inc.
New York, New York

This is a work of fiction. Names, characters, places, and incidents either are the product of the author's imagination or are used fictitiously. Any resemblance to actual persons, living or dead, events, or locales is entirely coincidental.

Photograph of Louis L'Amour by John Hamilton—Globe Photos, Inc.

Bantam Books and the rooster colophon are registered trademarks of Random House, Inc.

ISBN 978-0-553-27629-9

Printed in the United States of America
Published simultaneously in Canada

www.bantamdell.com

OPM 61 60 59 58 57 56 55 54 53

FAIR
BLOWS
THE WIND

CHAPTER 1

MY NAME IS Tatton Chantry and unless the gods are kind to rogues, I shall die within minutes.

My two companions are dead, and those who came to this shore with us have fled, believing me already killed. Their boat bobs upon a gray sea flecked with the white of foam and soon they shall be alongside the *Good Catherine*.

I am alone. I am left without food, without a musket, with naught but the clothes in which I stand ... and a sword. I also have its small companion, a knife.

But what man can claim to be alone when he holds a sword? A man with a sword can bring a kingdom down! Many a man has a fortune who began with no less and no more. I stand upon the outer edge of a continent, and who is to say that continent cannot be mine?

But first, I must live ... and to stay alive I must be brave, but more than brave, I must be wary.

Crouched at the base of a gnarled and wind-racked tree, I wait with pounding heart. For they will come now, for me. My two companions are dead, and they must know that I am alone. One against many.

My lips are dry, and my tongue keeps seeking them. Am I, then, a coward? Death hangs over me like a cloud. Am I, whose blade has sent so many others to their deaths, afraid to die?

How easy to be brave when others stand round! How many a brave man is brave because he is watched, because he is seen. But none can see me now. I am alone. I can be a coward.

I can flee. I can hie myself down the beach, running until they bring me down like a frightened hare.

A Chantry flee? True, the name is not mine. I have but claimed it, used it, found it helpful. Dare I dishonor it? Dare I be less than the name deserves? I have carried it proudly. Therefore if die I must, I shall die proudly, even though the name is not mine and I die unheralded at the hands of savages.

Need this be the end of all my dreams, my struggles, my boasts? Am I, the son of kings who reached the heights and descended to the depths, about to die upon this lonely, far-off shore?

They have killed some of those who came with me, but was I seen? Is it possible that I escaped notice? Do they know that I am here? Do they delay killing me only to despoil those already slain?

If they know I live they will stalk and find me, and surely, then, they will kill me. Nor can they fail to discover me if they but look, for the belt of brush and dwarfed trees that borders the shore is sparse indeed. Beyond me lies the open sand and then the sea.

We had come ashore for fresh water. Our casks were filled, all were aboard the ship's boat but we three, two of the hands and myself, and we had lingered to look about. They started back at the call, but I saw a corner of something projecting from the sand, and paused.

The savages came then, with a soundless rush, charging the boat which lay yet along the shore, and they struck down my two companions, which delayed them long enough for the boat to shove off into deeper water.

Arrows struck the boat, doing I know not what harm to its crew, and spears were thrown, but most fell short. Then some good lad fired a musket.

The ball caught a savage in the face and he fell, his head half blown away. Shocked, the savages stopped their rush and the boat gained the current and was gone, downstream and to the sea.

Then the savages were stripping the two dead men, muttering and exclaiming over what they found.

Now a faint breeze ruffles the leaves, and I crouch, waiting. Cold sweat beads my brow, trickles into my eyes, and I dare not move for fear my motion will be seen. Very still am I, for they are but thirty yards away and often within plain sight.

My fears are with me. For I know that when they come—as soon they must—I shall charge among them and cut and slay until they kill me. Death is to be chosen above capture if all one hears of their tortures be true.

Is this to be the end of me? Of Tatton Chantry? The last of his line, the first of his name?

There lies the ship; the boat is now alongside. How I wish I were on it, to climb aboard! How many times since the voyage started have I wished to be ashore. And now ashore, how I long to be safe aboard once more!

The water casks are being hoisted aboard, and finally the boat itself. Before long my companions will be relating the story. Soon they will sail, and I alone will remain upon this barren shore. Alone, but for the savages...

In the ship's small cabin our captain will dine by himself tonight, for I, his companion at table, and a merchant venturer aboard this ship, will not be present.

What of my goods? What of my small share in the voyage? In the hold of yon vessel lies all I have earned until this moment, all that from boyhood I have managed to put together, that which I hoped would be the foundation for a new fortune for future generations of the family I will call Chantry.

Will the good master take it for himself? Or put it in trust for my heirs, of which, God save me, there are none? Or hold it a decent time against the chance of my return?

I wait and watch.... Now the sails shake free, the wind takes them and the *Good Catherine* moves. Something within me dies. I have never been one to weep, nor to bewail my fortunes, which God knows have been ill enough, and I cannot find it in me to don the mantle of Job. Perhaps it is that I am Irish. We Irish wear the cloak of adversity with style.

And being Irish, how can I be downcast or without hope?

Cold winds may blow, rains may beat upon my body, hunger gnaw at my belly, but am I not Irish?

The trouble is that no one has thought to tell the savages yonder.

I wait...the sails of my ship drop below the horizon. The squabbling of the savages has ceased.

They will come now. I shall meet them as my father's son should meet them, sword in hand. If I am to die, being the last of my line, let me go well that my ancestors need not feel they bred in vain.

Let cowards scoff at heroes because in their secret hearts they fear they could not measure to the standards of men. Let them cower and bend their backs to the lash. But I was bred on stories of Hector, Achilles, and Conn of the Hundred Battles. I straighten up, stretch my legs, hold my sword at the ready. They do not come.

Very well, then! I shall go to meet them! If there be lives beyond this, let them make ready. I shall go to meet them now.

They are gone! Did they despise me, then? Did they think me too meek a man for their killing? Or did they simply not know I was here?

The two dead sailors, good men both, lie horribly cut about the face and body... mutilated.

To them I doff my plumed hat in silent tribute, for they did what they were set to do on ship and shore, they lived and died as men. Yet had they been even the lowest of scoundrels I would have wished them alive and with me, for now I am alone.

How complacent we become when we sit secure, hedged round by laws and protections a government may provide! How soon we forget that but for these governments and laws there would be naught but savagery, brutality, and starvation!

For our age-old enemies await us always, just beyond our thin walls. Hunger, thirst, and cold lie waiting there, and forever among us are those who would loot, rape, and maim rather than behave as civilized men.

If we sit secure this hour, this day, it is because the

thin walls of the law stand between us and evil. A jolt of the earth, a revolution, an invasion or even a violent upset in our own government can reduce all to chaos, leaving civilized man naked and exposed.

As I am now....

It had been better were I born a lad of forest or farm, but for these past years I have been a creature of cities crowded about by men, and sometimes, God save me, by women.

Would it were so now!

What am I, Tatton Chantry, to do, marooned upon this shore with nothing?

I am, and have ever been, a superior swordsman. I have more than a modicum of knowledge as to tactics and fortification, and I have some knowledge of herbs, medicine, and magic—if they be not the same.

I could, on request, conduct a siege or a battle, or I could train a legion. I could negotiate a truce, a surrender, or a ransom for a king, but how can I find a meal upon this desolate shore? What use is my knowledge now?

It has been said of my family that we are descended from Irish kings, that our family came to Ireland with the Milesians. That I was born to the velvet. Yet I remember only that I was son of an Irish chieftain living in what passed for a castle on the rocky shores of Ireland.

As a boy I roamed those rocky shores, fished and swam, hunted too, seeking out all the caves and crannies.

They came hunting us then, the British did. Like wolves they hunted my family down, driving us one by one to the wall. My father and my uncles died, fighting bravely, and at the end my father told me to flee. "Go!" he said. "Go the way you know, and live, that our blood shall not die, and that our name shall live, if only in our hearts! Go now, my son, for I love thee well and would not see you die! Live well, live as a gentleman born, as a man bred, and as an Irishman always!"

And so I went....

A boy I might be, but the British would still have cut me down had I not fled. But I had nimble feet and a nimble brain and the wish to live long enough to see them die.

It was then my knowledge of the crannies and caves served me well, for I led them a chase down the rocks. I went through cracks where they could not follow, being so much larger than I, and I taunted them with it.

One tried to follow and became wedged between two boulders, trying to get a pistol up with a free hand to shoot me. Before he could fire I bashed him on the skull with a boulder, grabbed his knife from his belt, and fled down a tunnel under the rocks which none of them knew. Thus I left the body of my father and the ashes of my home.

There followed months of dodging and hiding, of stealing a bit of milk here or begging a scone there until I came at last to the sea again. I was not the first to flee my island home, nor would I be the last.

There were cousins of mine in armies abroad, and could I but reach them....

CHAPTER 2

BUT ALL THAT was long ago. Now I stood alone upon an empty shore, my ship gone, and I myself given up for dead. My small fortune was gone, nothing left for me but what I could win with my wits and a sword.

Now the sea was empty, and empty the shore as far as eye could reach. It was a gently curving shore falling away to the west and south, for where our ship had put in lay in a wide bay between two capes, the one still visible to the east.

We had come ashore in the dawning, and it was not yet midday.

Far away to the north, a half-year of walking, lay French settlements. To the south were Spanish settlements, and one of these was said to be on the Savannah River. My choice was a simple one: stepping from the brush, I turned right and started to walk.

Soon my strides shortened, for the sand was deep. My boots and my jerkin were heavy and the weather was warmer than that to which I was accustomed. Pausing at last, I removed my plumed hat and mopped my brow.

Far away to the south I thought I could make out the topm'sts of the *Good Catherine*. All I possessed was aboard that ship, carefully saved and treasured to make my venture. Had I remained aboard and the trade gone well, I might have returned a wealthy man.

On I walked into the blue and white afternoon, a blue sky above me, a blue sea on my left, and a long white beach before me, stretching away to infinity. I walked now with a certain swagger, for my depression was ended. After all, was I not the son of kings and cavaliers? And best of all, I had my youth, my strength, and all the wide world before me.

How, in such fine weather, could a man be anything but in humor? True, there was no tavern around the corner to which I might repair for a bit of a dram, or a cold bottle and a bird, if the thought came. There were savages about who might take my life—but take it they must for I would not offer it freely. How could I feel the less because of this? I had strength and a sword, and a man has been known to conquer a world with no more.

This thought I kept with me, for what small nurture it would be, during the darkest hours. My enemies, if such they were to be, had bows and arrows, with a far greater reach than the point of a blade.

Arrows and a bow? What was I thinking of? Had I not, as a lad, used an English longbow? And had I not made one or two of my own?

When I had walked the sun down, my eyes were restless for a place to sleep, some shelter, some haven, some corner away from the eyes of those who might come seeking.

Fortunately, in the loose sand my boots left no defined print. I slowed my pace. The sea was empty still, yet there were ships along these shores, the ships of several nations, and it was possible I might come upon one such to which I might signal. Ships came hither to trade for furs or pearls, to seek for gold, to take on water, or just in passing from the Spanish seas back to Spain itself. Dutch, English, and French ships were also here, and not a few of them. But now, when I needed the sight of one, there were only empty seas.

A moment! What lies yonder? Some dark mass, extending from the sea's edge inland, piled high...tangled. Roots, old casks, broken spars...a stove-in ship's boat.

Here in a tight turn of the shore, the sea had swept itself of debris and piled it, thrown ashore by wave and wind.

Warily, I circled the heap. My route led past it—which meant that I must go inland around it—but here, I thought, lies shelter. Surely, amidst this piled-up drift from the sea, there must be a corner away from the wind.

Removing my hat to spare the plume, I ducked under an overhanging root thrust like a tentacle from the root-mass of a great up-torn tree. I stepped over a smaller trunk and found myself in a shadowed and secret place, a cave half-covered and all hidden. Hanging my hat and jerkin upon a root, I gathered great slabs of bark from the drying trunks and placed them overhead to shelter me from rain. I gathered others to form better sides, and in a matter of minutes had a tidy little home, lacking but fire and food.

Almost a hut, as thick-sheltered overhead as though thatched. What more could be wished by man or beast?

How simple are the wants of man! How much at

ease he can soon become! Yet my stomach growled, protesting my good spirits.

"Be still, beast," I said cheerfully, "you've naught to gain by complaining. This day you'll do without, and perhaps many another, so let you be silent and endure."

The sea was out there. With the coming of day, and with some ingenuity, I might rig a pole and line, cast into the surf, and catch a fish or two. Yet to do this I must stand bold against the sky, visible for some distance, an invitation to any scalp-hunting Indian. Better a growling, protesting stomach than one ripped open to the blowing sand.

And so . . . I slept.

M Y STOMACH AWAKENED before my eyes did. Some vagrant odor, some sweet aroma . . . broiling meat!

I sat up.

Morning had come while I slept. The sun was in the sky, the waves rustling on the beach . . . and again, that smell of broiling meat. I got up swiftly, banging my skull on an overhanging limb. The sea had been a good builder but a poor architect. Brushing off my clothing, I rearranged my jerkin, shook the sand from my hat, fluffed the plume, stepped out upon the sand.

Nothing.

To my left and right, nothing. Before me the forest, behind me the sea, all else was sand. Yet the smell of broiling meat was fresh upon the breeze.

My stomach growled anxiously. Indians? I hoped

not. White men? Unlikely. There was no ship within sight, and no place one could well be hidden.

My eyes adjusted to the change of light and caught a faint drift of something that might be smoke above the trees. I started, cautiously, in that direction. I was no hunter, but chose what cover I could find. Suddenly, I came upon tracks in the sand at the forest's edge—several people with heels—I followed the tracks.

Soon I heard voices. Pausing, I listened. They spoke in Spanish. The Spanish were enemies of the English, but there were Irishmen in the armies of Spain as there were in the armies of France, Austria, and several other nations. I had lived, briefly, in Spain and spoke the language fluently.

Again I looked to the sea. No ship. No sign of boat or barge, nor was there any obvious cove or inlet where a ship might be hidden. Yet I knew enough not to trust my eyes on that score. Many such places are invisible until one is close upon them.

I had been told that there were outer islands that sheltered inland seas, islands many miles long, thin bars of sand crested by brush. Was I on one of those? It seemed likely.

Walking through the trees, I found myself at the edge of a small clearing. And there, gathered as if for a picnic in the forest, were a dozen people. Three were women—at least one of whom was young and lovely.

Some of the men appeared to be gentlemen. The others were soldiers, or sailors. They were roasting meat. There was also another odor, very pleasant . . . it brought memories of Constantinople.

Coffee! Only a little of the delightful brew had

come to England, by way of Arabia and Turkey. The brew was discovered, it was said, by a goatherd who found his goats remaining awake all night after eating of the berries.

Stepping through the last few trees, I paused. Dramatically, I hoped. Their eyes came to me and I made a low bow, sweeping the grass with my plume, and greeted them in their own tongue. At the sight of me the men's hands went to their weapons, the women's to their bosoms.

"Señores and señoritas, I greet you! May I ask what brings you to my humble estate?"

CHAPTER 3

T HEY STARED AS well they might. One of them, a young man with arrogant eyes, black mustaches, and a pointed beard, replied sharply. "*Your* estate?"

"But of course! Do you see anyone else about?" Replacing my hat, I walked toward them. "I am Captain Tatton Chantry, at your service."

"An Englishman!" he almost spat the word.

"An Irishman," I corrected, "and I bid you welcome. If you are hungered, feel free to kill what game you need, and please drink of the streams. The water is fresh and cold."

"By what right—"

Before he could continue the question which might have proved embarrassing, I interrupted: "I do not see your ship. Is it close by?"

"Our vessel sank. We have been cast ashore." It was an older man who spoke, a fine, handsome gentleman whose hair and beard were salted with gray. "If you could lead us to a place of safety we should be eternally grateful."

It was not my intention to reveal my own destitute condition, for at all times it is best to deal from a position of strength—or seeming strength.

"Unfortunately, there is no such place near here.

My own people are not close by." I paused. "You were bound for the Indies?"

"For Spain," the older man said. "I am Don Diego de Aldebaran. You speak excellent Spanish, Captain."

The pretty young woman interrupted. "Will you join us, Captain? I fear we have little to offer, for we escaped our ship only in the nick of time."

I bowed. "A pleasure, I assure you!" Well, that at least was honest. Little did she know how much of a pleasure. "Your vessel sank, then?"

"She was sinking. There was little time to take more than the merest clothing, and a little food."

Yet all the men were armed with swords and cutlasses, and an occasional pistol and musket were visible. Both Don Diego and the arrogant young man, whom I now ignored, carried pistols in their sashes.

Another young woman, an Indian servant by her appearance, brought me meat, bread, and coffee. As we ate, for the others dined also, they talked. Wisely, I kept silent and listened.

It became immediately apparent that they suffered from a divided command, with differing notions of what was now to be done. Don Diego wished to go north, believing another ship would come along which they might signal and which might take them aboard. The arrogant one, whose name proved to be Don Manuel, wished to go south to the Spanish settlements in Florida. Just how far distant they were, he obviously had no idea. I did.

"Of one thing you must be warned," I offered. "The Indians are not friendly. Two of my men were killed yesterday, only a few miles from here."

They were startled. That aspect of their situation

had not occurred to them. Living as they had been accustomed to, in well-protected cities, they had no true understanding of what might lie out in the wilderness.

"You will frighten the ladies," Don Diego warned.

"Señor," my tone was cool, "they would do well to be frightened, and so would you all. The danger is not to be exaggerated. I would suggest a smaller fire, and that you remain here no longer than you must."

"Do not fear," Don Manuel said contemptuously. "We are alert."

"I observed that," I commented, "when I walked into your camp."

He put his hand to his sword hilt. "I do not like your manner." The menace in his tone would have amused me at any other time.

I merely shrugged. "So? If you wish to fight, do not fear. You will have many chances before you reach your people. *If* you reach your people. Now let there be less fire."

One of the soldiers stepped forward and began drawing sticks from the flames by their protruding ends.

They ignored me then and began a casual, desultory conversation that had to do with clothing, the difficulty of walking, and whether they might have to sleep out another night.

The coffee was excellent, and I ate the bread and meat, savoring each morsel. My years of soldiering had taught me to rest when opportunity offered, to eat whenever there was food.

The man who had taken the sticks from the fire, obviously a soldier, stopped near me. He was a broad-shouldered, powerfully made young man, at least five inches shorter than I. Under his breath he whispered, "I am glad you are with us, *Capitán*. Save for the soldiers not one of them has ever slept out, carried a pack, or walked, except on well-trodden paths."

I had lived too long not to have an eye out for the main chance. One lives, one survives, and if one is wise, perhaps one gains a little. "Your ship sank?"

He shrugged an eloquent shoulder. "She was afloat when last I saw her but she was making water fast."

"Too bad. There might have been food aboard her, and more weapons." A thought came to me. "You came ashore in a boat? Where is it now?"

"Yonder." He pointed through the trees. "She was damaged in launching. We barely made the shore."

But they did reach shore, and there was a boat. Boats could be repaired. I made the suggestion.

"Who knows? It might be done, but Don Manuel was all for marching."

Little by little, as we ate, I drew information from him. He called himself Armand, the Basque. He had been a soldier in Peru. Don Diego had been governor of a province, Don Manuel an official of some kind, reputed to have influence in high places. My informant knew little more than shipboard gossip.

Don Diego was guardian of the lovely one, Guadalupe Romana, now en route to Spain to be married...maybe. There was more than a little mystery about her—or so I gathered from listening to Armand, the Basque.

I glanced toward her. She had been looking at me and her eyes slid away as mine reached hers. She *was* lovely, very much so. Large, dark eyes, rimmed with long lashes, a proud, beautiful face with a touch of sadness in it and a hint of something else—

Don Diego was coming over. "You have experience of this country?" he asked me.

I did not wish to lie. I did wish to survive. So I would not lie; neither would I admit to no prior experience of the country. For one thing I knew: Without guidance this lot would not survive the week.

"Enough to know there is great danger. My advice would be to return to your boat, repair it, then sail south to your settlements in Florida."

"Who knows how to repair a boat? We are gentlemen and soldiers, not workmen. Boats are for fishermen and sailors."

"You wish to die, then?" It was a time for brutal honesty. "A few years back a ship was wrecked on the shores of southeast Africa. It was Portuguese. The only way the people could survive was to walk, but they were mostly gentlemen and ladies who had never walked. One man was so fat he could not walk and had to be carried. The few sailors carried him only a little way, then refused to carry him further. They left him sitting on the sand. He died rather than make the effort."

"But the boat is damaged! We scarcely made the shore!"

"If it brought you this far the leaks cannot be so great. It is my thought to repair it. Believe me, the journey will be easier, and safer, than if you go by land."

"But who could do this, Captain? A gentleman such as yourself would not have the skills—"

"I have lived in your country, Don Diego, and

know that a gentleman there does not work with his hands, but we Irish... we do what needs to be done."

Guadalupe Romana walked over to us and stopped beside Don Diego. She was looking at me and her gaze was disconcerting.

"Don Diego, if you attempt to march north now, you will surely encounter the Indians who killed my men. Dangerous as the sea may be, it is preferable to the land, especially as you have women along."

"We have seen no savages," Don Manuel interrupted. "Nor do we fear them."

"If you do not fear the savages," I did not wish to offend him more, so tempered my language, "you might ask yourself if you and the women are prepared to swim the mouths of rivers. Or to cross swamps infested with snakes and alligators."

Don Manuel did not like me. What he might have said I do not know, but a fourth man now approached us, and spoke. "Señor Chantry speaks truly. On my last voyage along this coast, we came close inshore and sailed past the mouths of several rivers. There are miles of swamps. If the boat can be repaired, I would recommend it."

Don Manuel turned on his heel and walked away, disdaining to talk longer. Don Diego lingered, then followed Don Manuel, and they stood together, talking, with many gestures.

The third man remained beside me. He was a man perhaps ten years older than I, with a stern, confident way about him, a man of substance, I thought, a man who knows himself.

"Tell me," he said, "do you think we could reach Florida?"

"It is not far . . . I have heard there is a colony on the Savannah River, which is even closer." I hesitated, glanced at him, and then said, "I do not know the situation there . . . or here, but I have a feeling all is not well. Perhaps you would know better than I whether it is safe to go to Florida."

"Your feelings do not lie, Captain. Don Diego and Don Manuel have agreed to the marriage of the señorita. Her marriage is to a creature of Don Manuel's, through which both hope to profit. Now there is trouble."

I waited.

He glanced at them, but they were concerned only with their own affairs. Señorita Romana was standing by herself near a tree. "There is trouble, indeed," he said. "Don Manuel now wishes to marry the señorita himself, and this Don Diego does not want. For if she marries Don Manuel she is out of his hands, and he will get nothing more from her. If she marries this man to whom they take her, both have a hold upon him."

"And she is but a pawn in their games?"

"A very pretty pawn, Captain, with millions at stake."

"Millions?"

He shrugged. "If the story is true. I believe but a part of it, myself. The point is *they* believe it, or enough to gamble upon it, and there is much at stake."

"And you?"

"A chance bystander, who knows more than either of them but has no chance of making a penny from it. Nor would I try." He smiled wryly. "Captain, to be an honest man is not easy, but I fear that that is what I am. It is an affliction of mine that tries me sorely. Yet...what can a man do? I want only what is mine, and not to trade upon the happiness or unhappiness of others."

"It is a fault we share, señor. To a degree." I smiled. "My friend, I have been many things in my life, and when at the end they speak of me I fear all they can say will be: 'he survived.' "

"So must we all. The rest comes after."

"You are of their party?"

He shrugged. "I was a passenger upon their ship. I am a man whose honesty has defeated him. I commanded soldiers in the armies operating from Lima. I was ordered to take my men against a foe I knew to be too formidable. I replied I would be taking the men to destruction. I was told I had no choice, to do as I was told or resign my command and return to Spain. I knew the Araucanians, Captain. I could beat them but not as they wished—"

"You gave up your command?"

"What else? And in doing so I gave up all. I am no longer a boy who can play games with fortune, Captain. I will not have another command in the armies of Spain. I have no other trade. But I do have a wife and a son."

"There are other armies."

"Of course. That has been much in my thoughts. And you, señor? Have you fought elsewhere?"

"I am Irish. At home we have no future, so we of good family have become like the wild geese. We fly away to whatever army will employ us. We are everywhere."

"And now you are here. Why?"

"I saved a little, and made a venture. It brought me here. I had a dream, you see. I fled my own land after my parents were killed, yet I love it still. I thought to win a fortune abroad and then return and buy the old place again ... buy what is rightfully mine anyway."

"It is a good dream. I wish you good fortune."

"And Guadalupe Romana?" I suggested. "What of her?"

"What, indeed? Somehow she must escape their designs. Somehow, I believe she will. She is beautiful, but make no mistake, there is steel in her, too. When we reach the end of our journey, she will be there still. She may be the strongest of us all."

Suddenly his mood changed. "Come! Let us look at the boat."

We started, and as we passed Guadalupe Romana she fell in step beside us. "You are going to the boat? May I come?"

"Please do," I said.

It was only a short distance to the stream where the boat lay. Twice along the path, snagged by brush, I found threads from the clothing of the women. If I found them, then so might the Indians.

The boat was of a common enough type, built to carry twenty men easily and a few more under crowded conditions. I walked around the bow, looking at the damage and the contents, about which I offered no comment.

There was a mast and sail, unused on the trip ashore, three sets of oars, a water cask ... empty ... a sea anchor, and a few tools.

Obviously, the boat had been banged about in the launching or afterward. A plank near the bow was splintered and a shirt stuffed in to stop the leak. I removed the shirt—well worth saving under the circumstances.

Someone moved up beside me. It was Guadalupe Romana. She looked at the boat. "What do you think?" She spoke softly.

"It can be done," I said.

She looked at me, right into my eyes. "Are you then good for something?"

I liked her, and I smiled. "It is a matter of opinion, but *that* ..." I indicated the damage. "I can do."

"We must pray for good weather. Still, it will be better than walking along the shore." She looked up at me. "They are such fools. I could not believe they would contemplate such a thing. One would think they had never traveled along a shore."

"And you have?"

"I am of Peru. We lived in the mountains at the jungle's edge, but sometimes we came to the shore where some of our people had lived long ago."

"I would like to have known Peru," I said, "in the time of the Incas or before."

She shrugged a shoulder. "It was different then, but I do not know that you would have cared for it. The life had dignity, and it had a kind of splendor."

She looked at me suddenly. "Our civilization did not begin with the Incas. It was old before they came." She shrugged. "They had a kind of skill ... like your Romans."

"*My* Romans? I am Irish, señorita."

"You are European. It is enough."

"And you also. You are part Spanish, are you not?"

"I am. But I do not think like the Spanish. I am of

Peru, Captain, and it is a little different. I am of my mother's people."

"And now you go to Spain?"

She turned sharply around. "It is not of my choice, Captain. Had I a way—"

"The others are coming." My voice was low. "You spoke of a way. Perhaps we can talk later of that."

She turned on me. Her eyes were scornful. "Do not think I am any maid whose head can be turned by words, Captain. I have my own way to go.

"They want me because they think I know where there is gold. He, that one who calls himself Don Manuel, wants me also because I am a woman, but at the last it is the gold they want."

"They *are* fools," I said.

"And you, Captain?"

"I, too, am often a fool. Were it not so, I would not be here. Were it not so, I might have become a man of means. The men of my family are romantics. We have common sense, but we have heart also, señorita, so we end up with many thanks and empty pockets."

She laughed, and it had a lovely sound. Armand, the Basque, had come down and engaged the others in conversation, so for a moment longer we were almost alone.

"They believe I am an innocent, that I do not know why they take me to Spain. It is not only for the marriage, Captain. They believe the splendors of their court will put me in such awe of them that I will tell them what I know . . ."

"What do they think you know?"

She was facing me now, her eyes intently upon mine. "Whether there remain some hidden places where the old life goes on, where the old ways persist. They think I am a child who can be persuaded or frightened, but they waste their time, Captain. I shall tell them nothing."

"Bravo," I said softly. "I hope you do not."

"And you, Captain? You do not wish to know?"

"Señorita, I live to know, to understand, and if possible, to see. Yet it would be enough for me to know there is such a place as you suggest . . . somewhere . . . and that the old ways persist. I would not have the old ways die, for all people in their own way find a path to wisdom. Each way can be a good way. Each has something to offer the world."

"Then, if you could, you would help me?"

"That I will, but you must let me know what it is you wish. I must first understand. Then I can think and plan."

"They would kill you, Captain."

I smiled. "I cannot remember a time when someone was not trying to kill me, señorita. Perhaps I shall live long enough."

"But you are alone!"

"There is Armand."

"He is one of them!"

"Is he? Armand is a Basque, señorita, and the Basques have their own way of thinking. It is he I will get to help me repair the boat."

Suddenly Don Manuel was there, his features pale with anger. "Señorita! This is no place for you! Come!"

Without a word she turned from me and walked to him, her submissiveness puzzling in a girl who seemed of such an independent mind. Yet it was not my business. True, I had offered my aid, such as it might be, but what she might have in mind, I knew not. Nor did I know the whole situation, or just what or whom I must save her from.

My concern at the moment should be with returning to England and putting in a claim for my portion of the *Good Catherine*'s trade—if she survived the voyage and if there were any profits.

At the moment the boat was my stock in trade. I could repair it, and I could sail her to the Savannah River settlement, or on to Saint Augustine, if that be necessary.

With Armand I walked back to the fire. He left me and went to join the others. Was I contaminated, then? Or was he merely wishing to avoid a controversy?

Don Diego called over to me. His voice was cool. "You have examined the boat?"

"I have."

"Can it be made seaworthy? You can make it so?"

"I can . . . on the condition that I accompany you. I wish to return to Europe."

"Of course. You can do the work tomorrow?"

"If I have one man." I indicated the Basque. "We have talked about it. Together, I think it can be done."

"Very well. In the morning, then."

Darkness had come, and their fire burned just as bright as before. No sentries had been put out. I accepted the food Conchita, the Indian girl, brought to me, and I ate alone in silence.

It was just as well, for I had much thinking to do. They had come ashore on a galleon. That galleon was still afloat when they left her, and it might not have sunk. Such vessels often carried treasure, and certainly a marketable cargo.

It was sinking, they said. But had it actually sunk? Nobody had seen it go down, and even so, how deep would the water be?

I had seen no ship off shore, so it might be in the waters that lay behind this long island on which we were...or *believed* we were.

I, Tatton Chantry, a young man of family but no fortune, nor of any position now that all was lost in Ireland, I might have access to a fortune greater than any my family had known in these last hundred years or more.

Perhaps a galleon loaded with silver and gold from the mines of Peru? For long had I dreamed of such a thing, of finding my pot of gold at the foot of my own rainbow.

This could be it!

CHAPTER 4

M Y KNOWLEDGE WAS of armies and cities, although more than a few times I had sailed upon the seas. A man who has nothing must follow chance wherever it takes him. Although I loved the far places of the world, my wanderings were dictated more by the circumstances of employment than choice.

At least I knew enough to gather leaves and make a bed of sorts. I chose a place alone, well back from the fire and under the edge of brush that would serve both a windbreak and hiding place. Watching the others, it seemed the only ones who had any conception of how to prepare for a night in the wilderness were Guadalupe, Armand, the Basque, and the strange captain whose name I had not heard.

My thoughts returned to the boat, yet there was little to think of there. The splintered portion could be replaced by a slab of thick bark, easily obtainable and easily fitted.

The ship, their ship, held my thoughts. I tried to visualize how she might look and where she might have drifted, if she had not actually sunk. Above all I must give them no inkling of what I was thinking...even planning—if all proceeded as I believed it might.

Before the day broke I was up, pulling on my boots and brushing my clothing free of leaves. Then away I went to the inland shore.

Here the trees grew down almost to the water. The channel inside the islands, if such it could be called, appeared to be shallow. It was also narrow. There was no sign of a ship.

Rounding a small point by climbing over drift-logs, I startled a great flock of egrets and herons, thousands of them who flew with a great flapping of wings sounding much like applause from a vast theater. As they flew away, their wings caught the pink and rose of the rising sun. I stood a moment, in awe of their beauty against the morning sky.

Changes in the color of the water led me to believe there was a deeper passage leading westward into the land, or nearer to it.

A thought came to me that I had stupidly over-looked. What had become of the rest of the crew of the ship? Were they by chance still aboard? Had they taken another boat and gone elsewhere? Or were they still about? What had really happened aboard the ship? Had it simply started taking water? Or had there been a mutiny? The master of the vessel was not among them, so where was he?

I didn't like the situation. I must speak with Armand. I paused, scowling, and studied the movement of the water. The deeper channel was there, I was sure, and the tide might have taken the vessel deeper into the channel, beaching it somewhere on a bank or shore—if it had not sunk.

Nearby was a mound, low and long. Kicking a boot toe into it, I exposed a thick mass of seashells. Obviously, savages had long lived here, taking their living from the sea. We ourselves might profit from their experience, for the great number of sea birds could only be attracted by great numbers of fish.

From the sand I picked a broken arrowhead, beautifully made by chipping away flakes of stone. It reminded me again that I must have a bow.

After glancing all about, I sat down on the shell mound. Nearby, there was an old log that had sloughed off some great sheets of bark. They might be too brittle for my purpose. It would be better to peel fresh bark from a standing tree, but I would take this, just in case.

I walked over and picked up the bark, and came upon several other arrowheads. These were intact, and I pocketed them for future use. As I straightened up with a sheet of bark in my hands, I saw her.

Rather, I saw a bit of the poop beyond a wall of leaves. Squatting on my heels, I looked again. Only from that position could I see the vessel.

———

IT WAS TIME I returned to the boat, where they would be expecting me to be, and then to the camping area, where I might find food.

All was still at the boat. Placing my bark on the ground, I looked about, measuring the trees for a better selection of bark. Nearby was another and more recently fallen tree that looked better than what I had, but the bark I'd brought back would prove a convenient excuse for my absence—if one was needed.

I found a small canvas-wrapped bundle of tools in the sail locker and went to work. Trimming off the end of the plank, with a hatchet I cut a strip of bark of the size needed. I made holes and with an awl stitched the bark into place with cords drawn through the holes. As I worked, I considered my situation.

Don Manuel disliked me, that was obvious enough. Don Diego had been polite, but no more. The third man, whose name was still unknown to me, was in no position to do more than register an opinion. I trusted none of them.

As for Guadalupe Romana, she was but a pawn in the game, and I had seen how quickly she showed submission when Don Manuel spoke. Was she genuinely obedient? Was even her fear genuine? Or was it part of a pretense she was carrying on?

With the job half-done I walked back to the fire. They were moving about, and Conchita was at the fire. She threw a quick glance my way and seemed friendly. I walked to the fire and extended my hands. "I shall soon have the boat fixed." I spoke only for her ears. "Let Armand know."

"*Sí.*" She was squatting, Indian-fashion, at the fireside. "*Cuidado!*"

Be careful. Aye, I would that.

Don Manuel looked at us suspiciously, although he could have heard neither of us. He came to the fire.

"The boat is repaired?" His tone was brusque.

"Soon," I said. "It will be makeshift, but it will serve if we are not pushed against rocks, and if we keep to quiet waters."

He ignored me, paying no attention to my comments. Suddenly he asked, "You have experience of boats, Captain?"

"As a lad I fished in waters off our coast. They were often rough waters."

"You could take us to Florida?"

"With God's help. First it would be wise to see if there are people on the Savannah River. We might even find a ship there. There was a French fort, but I believe your people captured it."

"Don Diego!" He had joined us. "I suggest what food we have be rationed. It must last us at least a week, perhaps two."

He smiled at my ignorance. "You jest, Captain. We have food for a day, perhaps two."

"But your packs! I have seen large packs—"

"Clothing, Captain. You would not expect us to dress like beggars? When we again appear before civilized people, they must understand who and what we are. We could not appear in poor costume, or clothes soiled by travel. It would be most unbecoming."

For a moment I was speechless. "Don Diego," I spoke carefully, "you must face reality. It cannot be much less than *four hundred* miles to Saint Augustine, although I do not know its exact location. Even the Savannah is far, and I am afraid you will be very hungry before you arrive... *if* you arrive."

"You jest, Captain. I do not think it—"

"I do not jest, and the sooner you understand the situation the better. To the north of us there is nothing, although there are rumors that the English have tried a settlement there.

"To the south of us...somewhere...are Spanish settlements. Between here and there are savages who have often been badly treated by the Spanish and who will not be friendly. This is an unknown coast with many shoals, few bays or coves. Trouble is everywhere.

"We can catch fish from the sea. We may even kill a deer, but only at the risk of attracting enemies.

"There is no one to help you, no one to save you, no miracle we can expect. You have no servant you can command to bring food, and nowhere to bring it from if there were. The clothing you so carefully brought with you is not even likely to clothe your bodies at burial, for the savages will take it."

Don Diego's face was stiff with shock, I suspect not so much at the facts I laid before him as my manner of speaking. In many ways these people were children, for always before there had been a servant or a slave to do their bidding, and no need for them to lift a hand. It was simply a fact: they disdained any sort of physical labor, and disdained those who did it.

Don Diego was not accustomed to having facts so cruelly thrust upon him. His dignity was offended.

He stood speechless. His lips worked with unframed words. Guadalupe seemed wryly amused.

"What had you planned to do?" I asked, at last.

"Planned? There could be no plan. The ship was sinking. We seized what we could and got into the boat. We did not think of food. Why, we..."

They simply had not thought, or believed it necessary.

"What happened to the others? To the sailing master? To the rest of the crew?"

"I do not know. There was another boat, I believe. I do not know what happened to it."

"Well, my friends, you will now have decisions to make, work to do, and much hard travel. Whether you live or die will depend on you."

"I think not, Captain," Guadalupe said, sweetly.

"It will depend on *you*. After all, Captain, we have had someone to think for us and care for us because we have been able to pay. If we ask you to do this for us, what will we have to pay you?"

For a moment our eyes met. Slowly, I smiled. Her eyes widened and became wary. Perhaps she feared what I might say, but I merely bowed. "I will do what can be done, and all I ask is passage to Europe. If, that is, you want my assistance."

"We can kill deer!" Don Manuel was contemptuous. "We are skilled at hunting."

"At killing, you mean? I doubt not that most of your hunting was done on game preserves where beaters drive the game close to you to be killed. It will be different here.

"Here you must stalk your deer, get very close, and be sure of your shot. Then you must butcher the deer, clean it, and remove the cuts of meat you will need. You must also skin the deer, as the hide will be useful for making moccasins."

"*Moccasins!* We have our boots!"

"How long will they last when you wade streams, struggle through swamps and bushes? And what of the women? Their slippers are suitable for ballrooms, but not for walking in the forest."

Don Diego brushed aside my objections. "We have the boat, Captain, which you are so kindly repairing."

"The boat?" I shrugged. "Much can happen in four hundred miles. This will not be like floating upon a lake. There will be times when we must get into the water and drag the boat through shallows or over sand. We do not know what lies before us."

They simply stared, then turned away unable to

grasp what had happened to them. The reality they faced was utterly grim, and they had no pattern of behavior with which to meet it.

What had become, I wondered, of the old breed? Of the Pizarros, of the Ponce de Leons, the Balboas and the Alvarados? They were hard, fierce men, many of them survivors of the Moorish wars. Bloody men in a bloody time, but in their own way they had been ruthlessly efficient. Nothing had stopped them.

These people before me were the latecomers, the courtiers, the politicians, skilled at intrigue and the use of family and political connections, who had outwitted the *conquistadores* at court, robbing them of the fruits of their hard-won battles and taking the profits for themselves. But the lions had made the kill, and the vultures now ate the meat.

Ours was a time of radical change. The world was in ferment, yet so it must seem in any period of growth, for growth is ever accompanied by pain.

Men had crossed the sea and ventured into new lands, discovered new things, new peoples, new religions, new gods. Luther had led a break with the Church, and her vast domains had dwindled, and with it, something of her power. England, North Germany, and the Scandinavian countries had broken free and set up their own churches. Even the domains Spain claimed in the New World had been invaded by the French, English, and Dutch.

Yet there were many like Don Diego, no doubt a good man as such men went, who lifted no hand to do anything for themselves. He had been a competent governor of a small province, ruling by regulations already in force. He was a diplomat, a courtier, able enough in his own world, but helpless outside it. Like others of his kind, he despised physical labor and depended on work done by others. And now there were no others, only Armand and the soldiers—and to these Don Diego and the others had become a burden.

My years were but twenty-eight, yet seventeen of those years had been spent in bitter struggle to survive in a world of wealth and privilege, when I had neither. They did not like me, but for the time I was needed. Already I knew what a Spanish prison could be like, and I also knew that gratitude is rare, especially from such as these.

When Conchita brought me coffee and a sturdy piece of ship's bread, I spoke for her ears only. "Armand is a good man, I think—one of the best."

She gave me a quick smile and hurried away, but now there was understanding between us, a certain sympathy. I would need all the friends I could get.

I spoke to him. "Armand, tonight we must watch. You and I."

"Felipe," he said quietly, "is a strong one."

Felipe was the youngest, not more than seventeen, I thought, but a strong-looking lad who seemed close to Armand. The others seemed a sullen, lazy lot.

Wearily, I went to my place away from the group and burrowed into the sand, using a strip of bark as protection from the wind.

My eyes closed. The wind stirred the leaves, and along the shore the waves rustled upon the sand. I thought of my home, and how the sea would rumble and growl among the worn black boulders, licking with hard tongues at the soft places among the rocks.

Tatton Chantry... a borrowed name belonging to a man long dead, a man from where?

Who had he been, that first Tatton Chantry, that stranger who died?

I remembered him from my father's time, remembered the night we had lifted him from the sea, a handsome young man, scarcely more than a lad.

Dead now... yet living in me, who bore his name. Had he family? Friends? Estates? Was he rich or poor? Brave or a coward? How had he come where we found him?

A mystery then, and a mystery still.

He had spoken to my father, yet what had he said beyond the name itself? Had he really said anything? I only know that my father leaned close as the pale lips struggled to speak.

He died there, in our house by the sea, and when desperately I needed a name other than my own, his had come to mind.

It was my name now, for better or worse.

In all the years since, I had come upon no man who knew that name.

Yet it haunted me then, and it haunts me still.

CHAPTER 5

ARMAND AWAKENED ME with a light touch on the shoulder. My eyes opened on stars shining through the trees. It was clouding over, but here and there a star still shone through. Slowly, my mind cleared itself of the dream-stuff that lingered and brought me to reality.

I was on the shores of America, I was with a party of people who were not my friends, and the future was doubtful. If there was to be any future at all.

"All is quiet," Armand whispered.

Felipe had taken the first watch, Armand the second. Now it was my turn. We had not involved the others as I trusted none of them.

Armand and I walked together to the outer edge of camp, but he seemed reluctant to leave. He sat down near me where we could watch along the shore and around the camp.

He was silent, and I waited, knowing there was something he wanted to say.

"I think we have much trouble," he said, at last. "These people, they understand nothing, yet there is much that is wrong here. I feel it."

"You are a Basque, Armand. Were you a fisherman?"

"Sometimes . . . a herdsman, too. My family owned a boat, but we had sheep on the mountains near the sea. The sea troubled me. I kept wondering what was on the other side."

"So it was with me. I, too, wondered." I indicated the mainland. "I wonder what is there. Someday I shall know."

We were silent, and then, choosing my words with care, I said, "Armand, I agree there is trouble here. There will be more trouble. We will be stronger if we know this, and if I know I can depend on you, and you on me.

"There are savages. I have seen them. We have far to travel, and to survive will be difficult. Also, there are Conchita and the Señorita Romana to consider. We must see that they are safe, always."

"*Bueno.*"

"You are sleepy now?"

"No, *Capitán,* my mind is alive with thoughts."

"Then do you watch a little longer. I wish to look about."

The boat worried me. Now that it had been repaired after a fashion—although I intended to seal the seams even more carefully with resin—I feared somebody might come upon it. It represented our best chance to escape. Without it we should have to travel overland, a journey that would require weeks rather than days.

The boat lay undisturbed when I came to it, and I stood for a few minutes, listening. Once, I thought I caught a distant sound. Unwilling to return by the same trail, on which I might encounter enemies, I followed the creek to the shore, then swung around and started up the shore so that I might approach Armand from the sea and in plain sight. Several times I had to walk around formidable piles of driftwood, and to crawl over logs.

I paused to catch my breath, and looked out over the still water. I thought I heard voices, but the sounds whispered themselves away and left nothing.

It was on such a night—dark, still, and with gathering clouds—that I had landed at Bristol. Behind me lay all that I had known; before me, loneliness, uncertainty, and a life among a people who had destroyed all that I had loved.

The fisherman who brought me over was a rough, kindly man. "Leave the shore," he advised, "and go inland away from it. There be many accents in England, and away from the coasts of the Irish Sea they'll not know yours from any other.

"Be a quiet lad, and try to learn a trade, and you'll do well. Folks be not travelers now, y' ken, and most have been no distance from their homes. They have heard of your country but it is little enough they know. Be wary of the lads, for they can make it hard upon a stranger."

That night had been dark, too, and there was little enough movement along the key, and as I started to walk ashore the good man handed me a bundle. "There's a change of shirt for y', lad, and a bite to eat, but dinna stop until you're far from here. Bristol is a canny town. Some would be friendly, but a sight more would not, so get y' hence."

He was a good man, but I never knew his name.

I never saw him again. But here or there, time and again, I gave some friendless one a hand because of what he had done for me, a homeless lad.

Truly, my life had two beginnings—the one when I was born, and the second when I walked away from that fishing boat. The delivery was made on the Key of Bristol, and I walked away into the world.

Now, seventeen years later, on the shores of America, I was facing another beginning... or perhaps an end.

It was time I was getting back. Armand would be waiting, and now I knew the boat was safe. I went along up the shore, meeting with no more obstructions.

Stepping through the last curtain of trees and brush, I emerged into the clearing.

The fire was there, burned down to coals, but there was nothing more.

They were gone... and I was alone again.

My first instinct was to get out of sight and I did so, stepping back quickly into the darkness under the trees. The faint reddish glow cast by the fire lit the clearing just enough for me to see that it was empty.

After the first shock of discovery, I stood very still, listening. I heard nothing. Yet they had vanished, disappearing into the night as if they had never been.

No, the fire was there. There might even be tracks, but I was no red Indian to read a story from the dust. There would be tracks, of course, but how to tell those of the Spanish party from the newcomers... or were there any newcomers? Perhaps they had left to be rid of me. Don Manuel's outright dislike had been obvious from the start, and even Don Diego had been offended by me.

Inspecting the scene more carefully, I saw near the place where Guadalupe had slept something dark, seeming with a shade of red... a cloak, perhaps.

Holding to the edge of darkness, I worked my way about the clearing, recovering the blanket, for such it proved to be. A blanket or a robe... I could use that.

Then, near where Don Diego had slept, I saw a package that contained the food.

Little enough was left, yet sufficient for a meal or two for the lot of us.

No Indians had taken them, then, for they would surely have wanted both the robe and the food. On the other hand, it was unlikely, if they had left to be rid of me, that the blanket and the food would be left behind—unless they were simply careless, and that I could well believe.

If they were taken, how could eleven people be captured without noise? I had never been further off than three hundred English yards, always within hearing of a cry or shout. And I had heard nothing.

They must have left me freely and of their own accord.

So be it.

I picked up the robe and the package of food, which was heavier than I'd have believed, and walked back to the boat. Shoving off, I scrambled in, got up the sail, and left the creek, the clearing, and the red coals of the fire. With a light wind blowing, I moved out across the sound—if such it was.

At the moment I had room in my thoughts for but one destination. The Spanish galleon.

Yet I found myself scowling and perplexed. Why had they not taken the boat? And if they merely wanted to be rid of me, why not simply tell me so? I should have gone. But even had I refused, they had firearms and I had none.

It made no sense.

If they had been taken by force, why was there no evidence of a struggle?

There were no ships about. There had been no evidence that anyone but ourselves was in the area.

Yet how much evidence had *we* left? Would anyone have known that we were ever present?

My attention reverted to the water across which I was sailing. It was still, yet I could sense some movement, some current. Was there a river flowing from the mainland?

There was a faint suggestion of gray in the eastern sky. The water had the sheen of metal except where the shadow of some great tree fell across it. Working in along the shore, I glimpsed the dark bulk of a galleon's hull. I lowered the sail and moved in toward the shore, sculling the boat with an oar until I was close alongside. I listened, but heard no sound aboard the ship. Lines trailed from the side, evidently where the ship's boat had been lowered. Making fast to one of these, I caught another, gave it a test yank to see if it was fast at the other end, and then I went up the rope and swung to the deck.

All aboard was confusion. Lines lay about, scattered clothing, even a sack that proved to be filled with food, apparently forgotten in the haste to get free of the vessel. Carefully, alert for anyone who might still be aboard, I worked my way around the ship's deck.

She lay where the tide had left her, yet she seemed to lie on an even keel—and would float again, I believed, when the tide was right.

All was dark and still. The vessel seemed haunted. And although I had always accounted myself a brave man, I shrank from going below. Even an empty ship is not lifeless, for it seems to stir, to creak, to yawn, even to whisper.

She was a relatively small vessel, and I went aft. Dagger in hand, I entered the passage. All was still. Before me lay the great cabin, and I stepped in.

The room was in turmoil. Astrolabe, sandglass, and cross-staff lay upon the table along with some hastily bundled up charts.... Was ever a vessel abandoned so heedlessly before? All they might have needed was left behind.

There was a pistol also, and I picked it up. It was loaded. I thrust it behind my belt, just in case. Adjoining this room was another, and much smaller one. A faint perfume lingered... without doubt the cabin of Guadalupe Romana.

Then I saw an incongruous touch. In a corner of the room was a small chest. It must have belonged to her. The top was thrown back, as though its contents had been ripped from inside. No woman would have been likely to leave it so, for these chests were used to store keepsakes, the little things a woman treasures.

No... there was but one likely explanation. After Guadalupe Romana had left the cabin, somebody had entered here and searched... for what?

I took another look around... I would return later.

When I came again to the deck there was a faint pink in the sky. I went forward. The vessel was lightly aground, but the tide would float her free. Perhaps she would work free, anyway, if there was a little current here, some movement of the water.

The vessel was simply abandoned, deserted by passengers and crew, fair game for any who came. And I was here.

The sack of foodstuffs found upon the deck I dropped into my boat. I also collected some further gear, a coil of line, some canvas. I found a cask of powder, a bullet mold, several bars of lead, three muskets, two more pistols.

I returned to the cabin of the Señorita Romana and carefully repacked the small chest. Then I gathered what I could find of clothing and packed that into another leather chest.

As I kicked aside some of the fallen bedclothing that lay in my path, I heard a faint tinkle.

I looked down and saw a small medallion of peculiar shape and design. Putting down the chest, I took it up. On one side was some odd lettering—or what seemed to be lettering—of a kind I had not seen before. On the other was a strange design of twisting lines and half-circles. It was not a coin, but it seemed to be very, very old and worn. I dropped it into a small bag I carried in my belt.

On deck I completed loading the boat, going to the pantry for further food.

It was broad daylight by the time the last items were aboard, and I stood by the bulwark looking all about me. Nowhere was there any sign of life save the occasional flocks of birds that flew over, or a fish jumping out on the sound. Lying close in to shore as she was, there was small chance of the boat being seen.

Again I went below, but this time into the hold. There I saw a full cargo—casks, bales, and bundles of I knew not what—but not, I knew, what I sought. Suddenly I came to a door, heavily timbered and locked.

For a moment I looked at the door. I looked at the lock. It made me smile. To one who had wandered the high roads of England, France, Spain, and Italy as I had, locks were no mystery. In less than a minute I had picked the lock and opened the door into the room.

There were several stacks of something covered with sheets of canvas. I lifted one—silver bars. I hefted the nearest. Not less than thirty pounds. Stepping back, I judged the sizes of the piles.

Eight . . . perhaps ten tons of silver!

The silver was neatly piled, with cross-beams of oak to hold it in place so the cargo would not shift.

Beyond, in a smaller cabin or locker, was what I hoped to find: not one chest, but three. I tested the weight. Heavy . , . very heavy, yet I was a strong man, and such weights had once been common enough for me.

One by one I carried them into the main hold, then closed the door and locked it once again.

Back on deck, I rigged tackle over the hold and hoisted the boxes, one at a time, to the deck. Then I lowered them into the boat. Although the boat could carry twenty men and their gear, she was well down in the water when I loosed my painter and shoved off.

I saw the name on the galleon's stern—*San Juan de Dios.*

My heart was beating heavily, and I was perspiring, but not from the work I had done. I had no need to examine the chests. I knew what was in them.

If I could only get away with what I had here beside me, there need never again be hunger, thirst, or cold.

I would have my fortune. . . .

CHAPTER 6

HOLDING AS CLOSE to the shore as was practical, I rowed the heavily laden boat westward. Along the shores were great stands of cypress and swamp gum festooned with Spanish moss. Behind the clumps of trees in some places lay swamp or shrub bogs covered with evergreens, all low-growing.

Somewhere I had to find solid ground, or a river leading inland, up which I might take my cargo. Now that I had a boat loaded with supplies and wealth, I was a worried man, for fear that I might come upon Indians or even pirates, many of whom haunted these shores, lying in wait for Spanish vessels.

As I moved, I kept alert for whatever might come, yet a part of my mind worried over yet another question. There had been but little water in the ship's hold that I could see, and not much damage that was visible—surely not enough damage to cause the passengers to abandon ship in such a quiet sound. Something or somebody must have frightened them. There could be but one reason I could think of: They wanted the ship's treasure.

If such was the case, then I could expect them to come searching for the ship ... and soon.

The wind was rising, yet I hesitated to hoist my sail.

With the sail I could move faster and easier, but my boat would be more visible.

I worked the boat among some small islands, most of which were strips of sand and mud covered with low growth. Many of these, I suspected, would be temporary, to be flooded out by the next big Atlantic storm, with heavy rain or snow. Yet now they offered concealment, and a sort of backwater where I might feel safe a moment.

My eye caught a break in the end of an islet near me. I moved up around the end of the island to see that it was cleft from the end almost to the middle. The cleft was walled to the water's edge by a thick growth of willows and swamp gum. Deliberately, I trailed one oar and pulled on the other, turning the bow of my boat into the cleft.

The green walls closed about me. Catching at branches, I eased the boat to a stop before it hit into the mud at the bank, then I made it fast to a small tree. Now, unless someone came right past the end of the islet, I was hidden, lost to the world. Filling a shot pouch and powder horn, I checked the loads on another pistol and a musket, and stepped ashore.

Now to find a place to hide my fortune, if such a place could be had. Hidden well, and above high-water level.

Catching hold of a slim tree, I swung myself ashore. The islet was no more than a hundred yards long, perhaps less, and like its neighbors it was covered with low brush and small trees. Near the upper end of the islet there was a mass of driftwood, a tangle of roots, branches, and bark that had floated down the river and piled up here. Several of the logs offered a convenient bridge to the next little islet and from there it might not be difficult to get ashore.

I returned to the boat and found bread and cheese, enough to make a meal. Slipping a few squares of ship's biscuit into my shirt, I crossed to the neighboring islet, then waded through the shallow water to the shore.

For an hour I walked steadily inland—or what I believed was inland, for with the number of water courses, streams, and swamps, it was impossible to be sure. Yet finally I came to higher ground and a thick stand of cedar giving way to pine. Turning to look back, I found only a few steps from me an edge of the forest with a view of the sound from which I had come. At first I saw nothing, and then I did ... *the ship was moving!*

She had somehow worked herself free of her position and the wind and tide were moving her inland toward the shore. Slowly, gracefully she moved. She was down in the water, all right, but not very much, and the tide, coupled with the rising wind, was moving her along. I watched her, thinking of those tons of silver, yet I had no way of moving them.

Still. . . .

Watching her, my eyes caught something else, something closer to me. I shifted my gaze. Had I been mistaken? There was nothing. Yet even as I turned away my eyes caught the movement again.

A moment I waited, looking. Faint ... yes, it was smoke. Only a suggestion, and it was some distance off, perhaps two or three miles, but there was smoke.

Savages? Perhaps. And perhaps, too, it was my former Spanish acquaintances. My excitement caused me to consider. After all, what were they to me? Had they not left me, abandoning me to my fate?

They were no business of mine. None at all. What I imagined was a mystery about Guadalupe Romana was nothing to be concerned about. She was to be married. She was probably looking forward to it with some excitement, even though she did not know the man. And she had protectors . . . of a sort.

Yet I could not completely convince myself. Suddenly I became aware that I was walking, I was already headed toward that smoke.

"Feet," I said aloud, "you lead me to trouble. For as surely as I go back to them, there will be strife."

Yet, when I stopped to think of it, when had I not known trouble? And was not struggle the law of growth?

It took me more than an hour to get close to the smoke, though it was little more than a mile away.

The camp was on high ground among the pines, and I could see their fire a good hundred yards before I was expecting it. They were less than careful, which did not surprise me, but they had company, which did.

I paused behind some brush and looked them over carefully. At the distance I could only make out the fire, some smoke, and several more people than I had expected to see. I had started to approach closer for a better look when I heard, close by me, a faint *chink* of metal on metal.

Instantly, I was immobile, my hand on my sword. The brush was thick, so I squatted to peer through the stems where there might be fewer leaves.

I found myself looking into a pair of squinting

brown eyes belonging to a man who was crouching not six feet from me.

"Captain Tatton Chantry," I said, "and may I be of service?"

He blinked. He had the advantage of me, for his blade was in his hand. "That you may," he replied grimly. "I'd like to know who the bloody hell you are and what you think you're doing?"

"Merely a passing wayfarer," I replied cheerfully, "left ashore by the ship the *Good Catherine* when we were attacked by Indians. And you?"

"The *Catherine* was a ship, y' say, and not a woman? 'Twould not be the first time a man had been left high and dry by a woman."

"It was indeed a ship, and carrying all I owned it was. Gone now, and here I stand."

"And here you *squat,* y' should say, because that's what you're a-doin'. I am wondering if your story's a true one."

"Do you question my word? If so, stand up like a man, call me a liar, then make your peace with the Lord."

"Ah, you're the cocky one, aren't you? Ready to fight, are you? Well, I am not. Unless cornered, that is, or there's gold in it. I'd fight then. Once I'd have fought for a woman, but no more. They aren't worth it.

"Fought for 'em often, I did, until oncet the two of us stood to our weapons nigh an hour with no benefit one side or the other, and when we stopped to draw breath, be damned if the woman had not gone off with a man not half of either of us. It shows a man. It shows him."

"You have the advantage of me. There's a woman

by the fire yonder I'd fight for. Now, tomorrow, or any day."

"Ah? That fire? That woman? Well, you'd have to fight, my friend, but you'd lose. That man yonder who stands beside that fire is a *swordsman*. He's one of the best."

"Only one of the best? Then perhaps we shall see what 'best' is where he comes from."

The man slowly stood up and unlimbered himself. He was a good two inches taller than I, and perhaps twenty pounds less in weight. He had a long, haggard face and half an ear missing. His hands were extraordinarily large and his feet as well. He was clad in rags, the merest remnants of clothing.

"Who am I, you ask? Just a poor sailorman who's been ashore these past months, dodging redskins an' keeping a weather eye out for a ship, any kind of ship to take me back where there's Christian folk."

"What about those people?"

"A bad lot! A mighty bad lot, if you'll be takin' my word for it."

Had he seen my boat? If he had not, I was wishful that he would not, yet such a one as this might easily stumble upon it where a larger party would have small chance of doing so.

"You've been down to their camp?"

"That I have not, nor shall I, for they're a bad lot, as I've said. They're folk to fight shy of."

As briefly as possible, I explained how I came to be here, and what my intentions were—as far as I knew them. "Aye," I said at the last. "It is a ship I want, too, and a means to get back to England. But there's a girl yonder that worries me. I think she is in trouble."

"Hah! It's the youth in you speaking! In trouble, is she? I'll warrant if she's not she will be. Trouble goes with women, walks hand in hand with them, and he who goes among them shall expect nothing else."

"I believe she'd like to be free of them," I said, irritated.

"Did she tell you that? Is it her husband she'd be free of? Well, I'm not surprised. The trouble with women is they're always looking over the fence where the grass is greener."

"She would not be looking at me then," I replied, "for I've nothing more than what you see. I'd put by a bit, and made a venture with the *Good Catherine,* and it is lost to me . . . gone."

"Aye, y'll see nothing more of that cargo. The good captain of the *Good Catherine* will add your portion to his and grow the fatter for it."

He glanced at me shrewdly. "The girl is it? The Injun girl or that proud and devil-be-damned Spanish lass?"

"It is the Señorita Guadalupe Romana," I said, with what I hoped was dignity. "She is a lady, and a lovely one."

"Oh, I doubt it not! Them's the worst kind! She'll invite you to come forward in every way a woman has, then scream if you put a hand on her! I know the kind."

"You do not know her," I replied stubbornly, "but we'll get nothing done standing here. Go you about whatever it is you do. I am going to see if that girl needs assistance."

"Now what would I have to do in this godforsaken place besides saving my skin? What, I ask? You'll not be rid of me so easy as that. I think you've a means to a ship, so I'll stand hard by. And I'll listen t' your troubles, I'll share whatever it is you eat, I'll drink at your wake, but I'll have nothing to do with your fancy women!"

He turned his head, looking for all the world like a big bird, and then shook his open hand at me. "Don't get me wrong! I like a woman as well as the next man. But find them, have your hour with them, an' leave them, that's what I say! If they speak of love, put your hand on your poke and keep it there. If they start worrying about you catching cold or not eating right or drinking too much, catch the first vessel out of port. Believe me, when it comes to women, I know them! Oh, do I know them!"

My gesture indicated his sword. "Can you use that thing? Or is it just hung there for show?"

"Show, is it? Aye, I can use it! Well enough, I can use it! I've fought my battles by sea and land and used every sort of weapon, and I am alive to see this day. I've been a rich man twice, left for dead once, twice a slave, and many times a prisoner. I know when to fight and when to run—and run I will if the time is not right or the numbers too great." He glanced at me. "Don't look for me to be a hero. That I am not. I will fight as long as it looks like winning and if there's a bit to be had, I'll fight the harder, and longer, too!"

"Do you have a name then? I've told you mine."

"Captain Tatton Chantry, he says. Now there's a name! It has a sound to it, all right. Well, mine does too, for I'm known as Silliman Turley."

"All right, Turley, come along with me if you wish,

but if trouble comes, you stand to that sword or I'll have no part of you."

"Well now! *Captain,* he says, and captain he acts! So be it. You lead and I will follow and you'll not find me lacking. But if you fail me, I'll be off, and you can lay to that."

My attention had been on the camp as we talked. We were some distance off, and had kept our voices low, but I didn't want them to know we were about until I had some idea of what was happening.

It was clear enough what my intentions should now be: to find a ship, or some way in which to return to England and open proceedings that would establish my claim to some of the profit from the voyage of the *Good Catherine.*

A thought occurred to me. "Turley, how long have you been here?"

He shrugged. "Two years...I think. A man loses count of time when the days are alike and he has no need to be anywhere at a certain moment. It was a late summer when I came ashore, and there was a winter, then another winter."

"No trouble with Indians?"

"Aye...with some of them. Mostly I keep shy of them." He pointed. "I've a place in the swamp... deep inside."

Moving with infinite care, we edged closer to the camp. Turley was like a ghost in the woods. His body seemed to glide between leaves and branches, or under them, stirring scarcely a leaf in the passing. I was more clumsy, yet watching him, I learned to do better. Soon he paused, lifting a hand.

There were voices, a faint smell of smoke. First, I

saw Armand and Felipe. They stood together, off to one side.

Don Diego and Guadalupe Romana stood together; Don Manuel sat on a log not far from them. A large man was facing them, a huge, enormously fat man but one who moved with that curious ability some fat men seem to possess.

"Do not repeat to me this fiction, this romance! I do not believe in your mysterious Englishman! I think he is a lie, but no matter! Tell me this only: where is the *San Juan de Dios?*"

"I repeat," Don Diego replied, with dignity, "the galleon was sinking. Don Manuel acted quickly, getting us into the boat and away. Without him we all might have been lost."

"Ah, yes! *Don Manuel!* Very heroic, no doubt! But do you not ask yourselves *why* he hurried you? Was the vessel actually sinking? Was he saving your lives or merely getting you off the ship and away?"

"Of course, she was sinking!" Don Diego protested. "She was lying well over when we made the deck."

"I acted to save them." Don Manuel replied coolly. "As for the *San Juan de Dios,* she undoubtedly lies on the bottom of the sea."

"Hah!" The big man turned in such a way that I could see a part of his face. It was a bearded but brutal face, the face of a strong, ruthless man, but an intelligent one—or such was my immediate estimate. "Very neat! Very tidy, indeed! And does the distinguished Don Diego know that your own vessel, the *Santiago,* is soon to sail up this coast?"

"Is that true?" Don Diego spoke in a lower voice and we could scarcely hear the words.

Don Manuel shrugged. "But of course! It was to sail to Florida, then to come along up the coast to spy out the presence of any French settlements. Or any English settlements, for that matter, for our people in England tell us that Sir Walter Raleigh is planning some such venture. It is a service to the King."

"And you?" The big man spoke with sarcasm. "Were not you to be here to meet your vessel?"

"I would have been in Spain," Don Manuel replied. "I took passage on the *San Juan de Dios* expecting it would take me to Spain."

"But you are not in Spain, Don Manuel," the big man said, "you are here, a galleon loaded with gold is near here, and your rescue ship is coming. How very convenient, Don Manuel!"

CHAPTER 7

FOR A MOMENT there was silence in the camp, then the large man turned abruptly away from the dons and gestured to two armed men who stood nearby. "They are not to leave camp. They will be guarded every minute, and if either escapes—"

The guards obviously understood the uncompleted sentence. Ignoring Guadalupe, the fat man strode across the camp to confront Armand and Felipe. "This Englishman . . . you spoke with him?"

"We did."

"Who was he? What was he?"

"A man cast away. He had come ashore for water. His party was attacked and he was abandoned when the others fled."

"Ah, yes. So he *said*." He paused, as if thinking. "This captain . . . what sort of man was he?"

"A gentleman, and unless I mistake not, a swordsman."

"You mean he was a man who carried a sword?" The big man's tone was contemptuous.

"I mean a *swordsman*. He had the movements and the manner, the style, if I might say so."

"Ah? You speak as one who knows. Do you?"

"I do. I worked in the armory at Toledo. I was a maker of swords, and I have observed many swordsmen. I have seen the best."

"A swordsman. All right, I accept it. And a captain, too? A captain of what?"

"I do not know."

"What has become of him?"

"He went for a walk along the shore. I believe he wished to see if any ships were about. He did not come back."

"Any ships? Or one particular galleon?"

"Who knows?"

"So he did not return. Did he join others hidden nearby, perhaps? Did he seem interested in the galleon?"

"No," Armand lied. "He knew only that we had escaped from a sinking ship, nothing more."

The large man turned sharply on Felipe. "Is that true?"

"I believe so. He seemed interested only in getting something to eat. He was hungry, I think."

"Why do you think so?"

"I have been hungry, señor. I observed his attention to the fire where the food was, and how he ate. He was hungry, señor, even though he claimed this land—" Felipe waved a hand, "—as his estate."

The big man changed the subject. "The *San Juan de Dios*... where is she now?"

"I do not know. We were ordered to the boats. When I looked back... she was down in the water. But where or when she sank, who knows?"

The large man, whoever he was, seemed to know what he was about. That worried me. He was no man to trifle with, and it was obvious his sources of information were excellent. Yet where was *his* ship? If ship he had.

Now he was giving orders to several men and they were moving out.

"We'd better get shy of this place," Turley whispered, "they're comin' for a look around, I'm thinking."

We moved back, taking our time and trying to make no sound or movement. From the slight rise from which we had first viewed the camp, I glanced back.

The original Spaniards were all there, but there were a number of other men moving about. There must now be at least twenty in all.

There was something disturbing about the large man, something that made me feel that I'd seen him before. Another strange man, a man lying on the ground with his back to us, had also seemed familiar.

Suddenly we heard the big man speak again. His voice was loud. "No man or woman is to leave this camp but by my order. Do you understand that? He or she who tries to leave will die, and I do not exaggerate. I don't care *that*," he snapped his fingers, "for any of you."

Don Diego replied, his voice strong and clear. "Señor, if harm comes to anyone here, I will see that you hang for it, and your comrades will hang beside you!" He paused then and said, "Do you remember who I am, señor?"

The large man bowed with a sweep of his hat. "Who does not, Don Diego? But let me remind you that the seas are wide and a man with a ship can go where he will. And I shall go where not even you can follow, and where the might of Spain is less than a whisper in the night. I will do what I please, Don Diego, and when it pleases me to do so I shall slit your noble gullet with my own hand, and feed what remains to the fish.

"Do you understand me, Don Diego? You are nothing here... *nothing!* I have the power now, and I alone!"

We moved away, finding our way back to a cedar-clad knoll where the waters of the sound could be seen, and much of the area around.

There was now no sign of the *San Juan de Dios*.

Had she sunk, at last? Or found some other place to rest until another tide floated her free? Search as I might, I could see nothing of her.

We went down off the knoll and into a deeper thicket of cedar. There we found a place where the earth had been hollowed, perhaps by some bear, long ago, at the base of a cedar, but close against the trunk where it was covered by thick branches. There was room for two there, and we took shelter. From the packet inside my shirt I took some ship's biscuit and shared it with Turley.

Night was shading down and we settled ourselves for sleep. Turley, with the ease of his years in the woods, was soon asleep, but I lay long awake, disturbed by memories of my youth. Why they had suddenly come upon me now, I could not guess, but lying back and looking up at the cedar, enjoying the pleasant smell of the crushed needles, my mind strayed back to my boyhood.

My father had been a bookish man, quiet in manner and gentle of voice. He loved to walk the lonely beaches as I did, and to climb among the rocks. Often when resting he told me stories of the Milesians who had come to Ireland from Spain, long, long ago, and how the Irish were then called Scots from a Milesian queen named Scota. She had been a daughter of Pharaoh, ruler of Egypt. He told me tales of Conn of the Hundred Battles and of the old kings who ruled from Tara, and of the Druids who had been their teachers and advisers.

He told me the story of how the Danes had settled Dublin. In Gaelic it was *Dubh-Linn,* or the Black Pond.

One morning he took up his stick and said, "Come, lad, I've a thing to show you," and he took me out along the shore and up among the rocks to a high place where the ground was suddenly flat, rimmed all around with the ruins of an ancient wall.

"It was a castle once," he said, "a fortress of a sort. It commanded," he pointed the path, "a way up from the sea, yet it was a rare raider who came this way. Most often they came from the east coast and attacked the people who lived there. Only now are we in grave danger here."

"We are?"

"You bear an old name, my son, as do I. Our name is a symbol, and so it has been for many, many years. Yes, one day they will come. Somehow we must get you safely away."

"I want to stay with you. I can fight." I said this with more hope than honesty, for although I had learned to ride and to shoot, to fence and to duel with the quarterstaff, I had never fought except with my fists against the village boys.

"No . . . you must not fight. You must escape, and then one day you will come back here and claim what is truly yours.

"The name must continue to live, even though it must live in hiding. This castle," he gestured about him, "was built of huge timbers once. Twice it was destroyed, and then it was built of stone. Again it was destroyed and again rebuilt. The last time it lay as you now see it, but if the stones are down and the walls are gone, *we* still live. You must come back here, my son. Someday you must come back."

A few short years later, he was dead, killed by the invader, and I was a fugitive, hunted through all the counties of Ireland.

My mother's people were of the *Tuatha De Danann*, who ruled Ireland before the coming of the Milesians, a wise and strong people, noted for their arts and knowledge. So my people were doubly old in the land, and my name was known throughout Ireland.

Hard had been the years of my flight! Hard the very days after I landed in England! The village folk stared at me as I walked through, and the dogs barked and ran snapping at my heels, but frightened though I was I did not turn, but walked on through the village and away into the land.

That night I slept in a corner of a stone wall, and in the morning started on. The bit of food I'd brought from the boat lasted me through the day. Twice I turned down lonely lanes and then reached a muddy road and passed an inn. I'd a bit of money and my belly demanded attention, yet I hesitated for fear of stirring curiosity at a lad going his way alone.

Most inns would not wish my custom. Yet my hunger was such that I turned from the road and went up to the door.

It was an impressive place, with timbered galleries,

a courtyard, and stables. I went into the common room, glancing into the kitchen as I passed the door. It seemed to glitter with copper kettles, brass candlesticks, and a row of pothooks at the wide fireplace.

There were evidently few travelers on the road, for there were but four men within the common room, one of them a stout, older man with gray hair who shot me a quick, appraising look out of kindly blue eyes. A pair of men who might be locals were sharing a bench and drinking to each other from the same tankard, as the custom was. The fourth man was slim and handsome, a man with prematurely white hair and lean features that might have been carved from marble, so white they were, and so expressionless—save for the eyes. The eyes were very large and almost black.

He had glanced up when I came in, then paid me no attention.

I had slept in my clothes and they were rumpled. I must not have looked well, for the tavern keeper, a burly, brusque sort of man, came forward. "All right! We'll have no—!"

Young I might be, but I'd not been born to a castle for nothing. "Ale," I replied coolly, standing my ground, "and a bit of bread and cheese. If you have a slice or two of beef, so much the better."

I pointed toward an empty table near the stout old man. "I'll have it there," I said and, ignoring him, I walked over and seated myself.

He hesitated, taken aback by my manner, so unlike a lad from the lanes or the farms. He started to speak. "I have little time," I told him. "I am expected."

He left the room and a maid came quickly throwing me a curious glance. She hit the table a swipe with a cloth and then put down a tankard of ale. "A moment, sir, and we'll be having the rest." Then under her breath she whispered, "If you've naught to pay with, better run now. He's a fierce hard man!"

Placing a gold coin on the table, I heard her gasp. In a moment the tavern keeper was there and he reached for the coin. "Leave it," I said. "When I've eaten you can take of it what is necessary."

The white-haired man in the blue coat had turned his head and was regarding me. The last I wished was to draw attention to myself, but neither did I intend to be robbed or bullied. It was little enough I had, and each penny would be needed.

The tavern keeper turned from the table, his face and neck flushed with angry blood. He liked it not, being spoken to so by a mere lad, and had there not been others present it might have gone hard with me. Yet he was worried, too, for my manner told him what sort of person I was, and he wanted no trouble.

The food came soon, and I ate slowly, taking my time. Every morsel of food tasted good, and the ale did likewise. After a bit the old man got up, bobbed his head in a brief nod to me, and went out. A moment later I heard the creaking of a cart and glimpsed them pass the door, a covered cart drawn by a donkey. The old man walked alongside and a big dog trotted behind.

The tavern keeper came in again. "That'll be sixpence," he said.

The man with the white hair was gazing out the door. "Fourpence," he said, absently.

The tavern keeper started, glancing swiftly at the

white-haired man. "It'll be sixpence," he said under his breath.

"Fourpence," the white-haired man repeated.

The tavern keeper took up the gold coin and left the room. I waited and waited, but the white-haired man waited also. Finally, my host returned and placed a stack of coins upon the table.

"Count them," the man with the white hair said.

"Is it that you think I'd cheat the lad?"

"You would," the man said. He got to his feet. He was not a tall man but lean and well set up.

My coins were a half-crown short. I held out my hand for it, and with ill grace, he put the coin in my hand. "Now be off wi' you!" he said gruffly.

"I shall," I said, then added, "The ale needs a bit of aging."

Once outside, the man with the white hair stepped to his saddle. He lifted a whip in salute, then rode away. Hastily, I made off down the road in the opposite direction. I had gone no more than a few yards before the two locals who'd been drinking in the tavern came to the door and looked up the road.

It was lucky for me they looked the wrong way first, for I saw them, knew what they were about, and ducked through the hedge. Once on the other side, I legged it along the back side of the hedge, then across the corner of the field and over a stone wall.

Behind me I heard a shout and knew I'd been seen, so crouching low behind the wall, I ran not away from them but back toward the lane. I heard them crashing through the hedge, but I reached it on the road above them, ducked through a hole, and crossed the lane and ran swiftly away from them.

A low wall loomed before me and I took it on the run, ducked behind a haycock and then a barn. There a dog saw me and began barking furiously but I kept on, knowing they'd be after me now. I'd no doubt the tavern keeper had put them on me.

Small though I was, I'd had practice in running these past months, and in dodging and hiding as well. I came out on another, smaller lane, and ran along it, holding to my own direction.

There was a village somewhere ahead, but I knew not whether that be good or bad, simply that it was there and I must consider it.

Then the village was before me but I went around a haycock along the back side of a barn and down a wild bit of hillside away from the village. Now I ran no longer, but moved from cover to cover, keeping an eye out for them.

I'd lost them, or so it looked. I came to another lane and followed it away from the village. But the lane suddenly betrayed me, taking a turn around a low hill within sight of the village. For there they were, the two of them, and no chance for me to get away.

They spread out a little and came at me.

CHAPTER 8

TO FLEE FROM them was impossible, for their legs were longer than mine. It was a sunken lane with stone walls on either side, and as they closed in toward me, I suddenly bolted between them.

One grasped wildly at my shoulder and my shirt tore under his hand. Yet I was briefly free of them and I went up the bank and swung over the wall, sprawling on the earth beyond. My hands closed over dirt and I came up quickly, frightened. They came over the wall at me and I flung the dust into their eyes.

One man let a fearful yowl out of himself and both men grabbed for their eyes. At that moment I saw a stout stick, a twisted branch broken from the hedge nearby. Catching it up, I swung hard on the nearest man and caught him alongside the jaw, and he went down. Then I closed in on the second, whose eyes were busy blinking the dust away. He threw up a hand as I swung my cudgel but I brought it down, striking him on the kneecap.

Then I ran.

Across the pasture into which I'd fallen, past a barnyard and into the lane beyond. On I ran until I thought my lungs would burst, when suddenly before me there loomed a patch of woods bordered by a wall. I went over that wall and into the woods, pausing, my breath tearing at my lungs, to look back. There was no one in sight.

I plodded on into the forest. I was sick of running and desperately worried, for in all this broad land there was no friend to whom I could turn. Nor had I a place to go. It was lonely and tired I was when at last I seated myself on a fallen tree and began to cry.

Shamed am I to confess it, but so it was. Lonely and sick with the fear of all that was about me, with enemies all on every hand, I cried. My dear father was in my mind, and my lost home, and the knowledge that I'd no place to go nor anybody to go to anywhere that was friend to me.

"Are you hurt?"

It was a girl's voice, and I sprang to my feet, putting a hand across my eyes to wipe the tears.

She was standing there, not a dozen feet away, with a great dog beside her, a huge bull mastiff with great jowls.

"I said, are you hurt? There you sit, crying like a great booby. What sort of boy are you, anyway?"

"I was not crying!" I protested. "I was tired."

"What are you doing here in my forest?"

"*Your* forest?"

"Yes, mine it is, and I did not invite you here. You are nobody I have ever seen. Are you a gypsy?"

"I am *not!*"

"Well, do not be so proud. I think it not a bad thing to be a gypsy. I have often thought it would be a great thing to go riding about in a red and gold wagon, eating beside the road. I would have white horses, four of them, and I'd have Tiger with me, and—"

"Who is Tiger?"

"My dog. Tiger is his name."

"It is a cat's name. Tigers are cats," I said scornfully.

"It is not! Tiger can be a dog's name, also! My father said it could, and my father knows. Anyway," she added, "Tiger does not know it is a cat's name."

"He's a large dog," I said. And then more politely, "I am sorry I am in your wood. I—I wanted to rest."

"You are not poaching? If you were and the gamekeeper found you—"

"I do not poach," I replied proudly. "I am sorry I disturbed you. I will go now."

Yet I did not go. I did not want to go. I had talked with no child of my years in many months.

She was a pretty child, with large dark eyes and soft lips.

"Have you come far?" she asked.

"From very far away," I said.

"Your shirt is torn," she said, "and you have skinned your knee."

Looking down, I saw that my stocking was torn and my knee bloody. "I fell," I said.

"Are you hungry?" she asked.

"I—I have just—" I stopped in time. If I admitted to eating at the tavern all would come out, and for all I knew the tavern keeper was her friend. The tavern could not be that far away. Suddenly I realized they might still be searching for me. "I must go," I said.

"It will be night soon," she said. "Where will you sleep?" She looked at me curiously. "Will you sleep in a haycock? Or beside a hedge?"

"It does not matter." I edged away. "I must go."

I turned and took a step, then stopped. "It is a nice wood," I said. "I did not mean it harm."

"I know you did not." She stared at me. "I think you are frightened of something, and I think you should talk to my father. He is very brave." And she added, "He was a soldier."

"I must be going."

I started away and then stopped, for there was a man standing there. He was a tall, slender man with fine features and brown eyes.

"I do not know that I am very brave, my dear," he said, "but I always hoped to be. Who are you, lad?"

My eyes went down the way through the trees by which I had come. I needed to be away from here. I did not want to answer questions, nor to have them discover there had been trouble at the tavern, even if it was none of my doing.

"I was just passing by," I said, "and wished to rest. It seemed better off the road than on it."

He was regarding me very seriously. The girl came up and stood beside him, taking his hand. My father had held mine just that way, sometimes. The thought made tears come to my eyes and I brushed them away quickly and turned to go.

"Wait." He did not speak loudly but there was command in his tone. Involuntarily, I stopped. "I asked who you are."

"I am nobody," I said. "I was just passing. I—I must go."

"Where is it you go to?" he asked. "My daughter is concerned."

"To London," I said, desperately, wishing to be away.

"I do not think you will reach London tonight," he said quietly. "You had better come along with us."

"I cannot."

He waited, just waited, saying nothing. At last I said, "Some men at the tavern are looking for me. They will rob me."

"*Rob* you?" He smiled. "Are you rich, then?"

"No. I do not think it matters if one has much. They would take whatever I had."

"Who were these men?" he persisted.

Reluctantly, I explained what had happened, and how the man with the white hair had stopped the tavern keeper from overcharging me.

He frowned thoughtfully. "A young man, with white hair? Was it a wig, perhaps?"

"It was his own hair. His face was white, too. Like polished marble. Only his eyes seemed alive."

"And *he* spoke for you?"

"Do you know him then?"

"I do not. I think I know who he might have been, but why he is here, in this place, I do not know. That he even was moved to speak to you, or act in your favor is amazing."

"He did not actually speak to me."

The man changed the subject. "Come with us, lad. At least you can have some supper before you go. And we have a good woman here who might do something for that knee."

"But if they find me—"

"Do you think they would come to my house? Lad, do not mistake them. Thieves they may be; cowards, also. Fools they are not...at least not so foolish as that."

He turned and started back, his daughter beside him, and I walked along with them. A bird suddenly flew up.

"What was that?" the maid said.

"A goldcrest," I replied, not thinking.

"Do they have them in Ireland then?" Her father spoke so casually that I replied quickly:

"Yes..." then realizing what I had said, "and in Scotland as well."

He was amused, and it angered me. "The goldcrest likes a place where there are evergreens. He chooses to nest among them."

"Are you a Scot, then?"

I did not wish to lie, and suddenly I realized I did not have to, for long ago were the Irish not called Scots?

"It is a loose term," I said, quoting my father. "For some Scots were Pictish and some were Gaelic, and some—" I stopped suddenly, and was silent.

We had come to the path's end in an open place covered with gravel where horses could gather for the hunt.

The manor before us was old, but gracefully built, and I liked it much. Great old oaks and beeches stood about, and there were stables to one side.

They started toward the great steps but I hung back. The man turned and beckoned me on, but I shook my head. "I cannot," I said, "my boots are muddy and I am not dressed—"

"It is my house," the man replied quietly. "Do you come then. You are my guest."

"I am obliged," I replied.

He turned and glanced at me. "Now that you are here, will you dine with us?"

"My clothes—" I continued to protest.

"That can be arranged," he replied. "If you will permit me. I have some clothes here that would fit you, I'm sure. You are a strong-looking lad. Yes, I believe they would fit."

To accept charity was not my way. I started to protest, and then realized this was no time for such false pride. He was not offering charity; it was courtesy, and I would do well to accept it as such.

"Very well. If it is no inconvenience."

He led the way himself. Up a wide, winding stair to a hall above and to a room with yellow walls, a blue bed with blue bed-hangings, and much blue-and-white porcelain about.

He opened a chest and took from it some clothes, a shirt, breeches, hose, and a coat. There were boots also.

"Water will be sent you," he said, "and the clothes, I think, will fit." He paused just a moment. "They were my son's."

The question came to my lips, but I did not speak, not knowing what to say.

"He went off to sea," he said quietly, "and was lost there ... we think."

"You do not know?"

"Does one ever, when sons are lost at sea? His ship may have been taken. He may be a prisoner. We know not. He may be a slave now, in Africa, where many of our sons have ended."

"I am sorry."

"Do you bathe now, and dress. In an hour we will

dine...and talk." He turned away, and then paused. "I do not know who you are, or where you come from, and I have no need to know, yet I know what you are. And if my son came to another man, I should wish him cared for."

He left me then, and soon after a maidservant, a brown-haired lass who shot me quick glances, brought hot water and linens.

I made shift to bathe then, and relished the doing of it. Then I donned the clothes they brought me, and when I was fully clad I glanced at myself in the mirror and was pleased with what I saw. And surprised, too, for it had been many months since I had a mirror at hand.

The boy I saw there was me, but a changed me. I was darkened by the sun, leaner somehow, and I looked older. I glanced at myself once again, then went out and closed the door behind me.

It was a quiet meal we had, the father, the daughter, and I, the homeless boy.

Her name was Evelina, but she was called Eve most of the time. His name was Robert Vypont. The house in which they lived was an old manor, built strongly and well some hundred years before, yet a house with much grace and style within.

We talked lightly, of this and that, and then toward the close of the meal, he said, "What do you now propose to do?"

"I shall go to London-town. It is a large place, and there I might find some way to live."

Vypont shook his head. "There are many boys of your age there, good lads some of them, rascals most. You would find it hard, I think."

"I must earn my way. I have no fortune, nor hope of any but what I can make of my own wit and strength."

He studied me gravely, shaking his head. "You are young for that. The apprentices of London are rough lads themselves, and apprenticeships must be purchased."

He watched while the maidservant refilled our glasses with ale. Then he said, "You have traveled much and are no doubt tired. Would you do us the honor to be our guest for a few days?"

I hesitated, dearly wanting to agree, yet wary of it. I didn't know this man, and although he seemed generous, I was not sure of his motive. Moreover, I was now accustomed to the rough way of living and growing daily more so. Might not living here make me soft again?

"You know naught of me," I said. "There was trouble at the inn, yonder, and it might bring grief upon you and yours. You have been kind, but much as I should like to remain, I must be about my business."

"You will stay the night?"

"If it pleases you, I should be delighted."

He paused a moment. "Forgive my curiosity, and I know I have no right to ask, but a lad of your obvious background...there should be a place for you." He looked at me again. "You have obviously gone to good schools."

"I have never been to school. My father was my teacher."

"Ah? A man of rare education, no doubt."

"He was that. He read me from the writings of Homer when I was very young, and from Virgil, too.

He taught me much of history, and not of our country only, but others as well.

"We walked much together, and he instructed me then. We also talked with visitors—"

"Visitors?" Robert Vypont spoke casually, yet I knew the question was an effort to learn something of my background.

"There were few visitors toward the last," I said, "and mostly from the Continent." I had no doubt he knew where I was from, for I had the brogue, although not much of it.

"Were they enemies of England?" he asked mildly.

"My father," I said, "was enemy to no man, and wished harm to no man. He was a scholar who wished only to be let alone."

"I am not a scholar," Vypont said. "Would that I were! I have many interests, and much desire to learn scholarly things, but for too long my activities were directed elsewhere."

My father had talked to me of his many interests, talked to me as though I were a man grown, discussing not only our bookish interests, but others as well. Often of a night I had gone to the shore with him when he would show a light to guide some of the returning "wild geese" safely to shore, for it was wild geese we called those young Irishmen of family who went abroad to join the armies of France, Spain, Italy, and others. Having no future in Ireland, not permitted by England to have an army, and not wishing to serve England, whom they considered an enemy, they fled overseas, usually aboard some smuggler's craft.

Often in my father's house I heard them talk of

politics in foreign lands, of wars, battles, and courtly intrigue, of music, art, and letters.

They came by night, and they left by night, catching short visits with friends and relatives, then off to the wars once more. Mayhap when I was older I could become one of them—or so ran the thoughts in my mind.

Yet Vypont was a kindly man, and wished me well. He was hungry for talk with one of his kind, and Eve was also. Two days I remained, eating too well, talking, riding, and walking with them both.

On the third day we had come to the bottom of the steps for a ride when suddenly there was a clatter of hooves and into the yard came three red-coated soldiers, and with them one of those who had tried to rob me at the inn.

"See? What did I tell you? There's the Irisher!" he shouted, pointing at me.

The soldiers started toward me, and I sprang to the saddle. My life long I had ridden, for my father was a horseman ever, and those fine Irish horses of ours! Ah, how I missed them!

Turning the horse, I raced around the house, leaped the low hedge, and went down across the lovely meadow and into the old beeches beyond. Under their cover, I turned sharply back, circled a haycock and another barn, and was into the lane. My horse was running hard.

Wild was the riding, and beautiful the movements of the horse beneath me, but he was Vypont's horse, and I must free him. There was a place where the lane went by a deep cut in the earth that dropped to the glen below. I left the horse there, with a ringing slap on the rump to keep him running. Then I ducked down into the cleft.

Sliding and jumping, I reached the bottom and went into a wooded hollow, crossed it to a stream, and walked into the cold fresh water.

The afternoon was late when I left the stream and went up to the moors above. Long into the night I walked, then seeing a vast wood before me, I went into it, deep within it, and lay down at last, covering myself with leaves, and there I slept.

Again I was adrift, homeless, alone and hungry. And now I was hunted as well.

If they found me, boy though I was, I would die.

CHAPTER 9

I AWOKE IN the cold dark and lay still, confused. I had fallen asleep with my mind filled with thoughts of my boyhood. Now I was a castaway, lying on leaves in a Carolina forest with a stranger for companion and naught but enemies about.

I sat up slowly, trying to make no sound. Turley lay still, resting quietly. He, too, was no doubt accustomed to sleeping in the worst of circumstances.

My sword was at hand, and my other weapons. One by one I checked them, all the while listening. It was with difficulty that I shook off the memories of that long-ago night and that wild flight to escape the British soldiers. Yet I had escaped. A week later, starving once more, I had come upon the old man whom I had seen at the inn, the one who had smiled pleasantly and left, driving his cart with its donkey.

But no more of the past. Now was a time for thinking; now was a time to plan. In my hidden boat lay treasure, far more than I had ever expected to possess. By all the laws of salvage, it was mine, yet it was not truly mine until I could get it safely abroad and in a secure place.

I was beginning to understand that the finding of treasure was the smallest of problems. The greatest problem was to keep it. To do that I must keep its location secret until I could find a way to transfer it to

England. All of which would take planning and foresight.

That I had possession of the prize both Don Manuel and the big man now his captor were seeking made it no easier. Once the *San Juan de Dios* was discovered, the vessel would be looted of its remaining treasure, and I had no doubt they would suspect me of having what was missing and come searching for me.

Moreover, they would not be long in finding the ship, so the time left to me was short, indeed. Nor did I wish to take Silliman Turley into my confidence. Many a man has been murdered for less than I possessed, and I had no idea how far Turley could be trusted.

Yet with all my thinking of the gold and the getting of it, my thoughts were shadowed by the memory of Guadalupe Romana.

She was in their hands, and she had no knight errant to come riding on a white horse to save her. That she was a clever girl I was prepared to admit; that she could deal with the big man I doubted very much. He had a quality of ruthlessness about him that showed no leavening of mercy, consideration, or kindness. He knew what he wanted and he intended to have it, and he was the type of man to whom no particular woman is important. To such a man, women are something to be taken and then cast aside. Feminine wiles would mean nothing to him.

Softly, bitterly, I swore. Turley awakened and lifted his head. "You are thinking of the girl?" he suggested.

He sat up, brushing leaves from his hair. "It is ever the way. Seven times out of ten, when a man curses there is a woman involved. What is it now?"

"She is their prisoner. I must think of some way to free her."

"And then what? You will only have her on your hands. No, my friend, let her bring trouble to them; they will rue it soon enough. Why, you could do them no more harm than to leave a woman amongst them!

"She will divide them, split them, create havoc among them! They will argue over her, because of her, and about her. Some will betray others because of her, some will die because of her. By all means, let her remain where she is. They will be destroyed by it."

"She's a fine girl."

"Ah? Would she be as fine, or you so anxious to aid, if she were ugly? I think not. Worry not about the lass, Captain, and you'll save yourself much and cost them more. And do not forget it. There is evil yon."

I felt so myself. Yet why did that big man seem so familiar? What was there about him, that teased my memory? And the other man also, the one who had been lying on the ground, his back to me?

"She hoped I would help her. She expects it of me."

"No doubt," he replied grimly. "Do not they always?" He shook his head. "What do they see in her, anyway? She is but a woman."

"A woman is sometimes enough. But there is more, or so they believe. They take her to Spain to win from her the knowledge of where some Inca gold is hidden."

"Ah? Now she begins to make sense! Gold, is it? And Inca gold, too? How comes the lass by such knowledge?"

"She is but Spanish in part, and the other part of royal Inca blood. As you know, the Spanish demanded a great ransom for the Inca, whom they had seized. Then when they had the gold, they killed him anyway. What they did not know was that much gold was still on the way, and when they killed him, that gold was hidden. She, they believe, knows where.

"Also, it is believed that in the mountains there are strongholds where the old Incas still carry on, where the old gods are worshiped and the old ways continue. And there should be much gold there, too, for it is a metal born of the sun, which is their god."

"The girl then is a prize. I can see . . . yes, of course. And you, Captain, have an interest in her also? Well, well, Captain, keep your eye upon the gold. It never fades in beauty. Women? They do fade, and they also grow crusty with age, and shapeless. No, the gold is the thing. Women are forever young when you have gold enough."

He was silent. I thought of what I might do. To get Guadalupe Romana away from her captors would be no easy thing, but what to do after that was even more of a problem, for there would be no use in freeing her only to condemn her to a life in the forest. Somehow I had to contrive not only to free her but to see that she found her way home.

Worried as I was about my hidden boat and its treasure, there was nothing I could do about it for the moment, so I led the way down through the trees toward the pirate camp . . . if pirates they were.

It was quiet in the woods. Along the sunny side of the trees near a small creek the birds were singing, and I heard a loon call across the sound somewhere.

Turley put a hand on my shoulder from behind. "They'll be a-watchin', Cap'n. They surely will. You fall into that fat man's hands and you'll live long enough to regret it."

We waited, listening. Hearing nothing, we moved along. Suddenly we stopped, for there lay the camp. Don Diego and Don Manuel sat in close conversation. Conchita was at the fire, preparing something...coffee, if my nose was true.

My eyes searched for the Basque, for I thought him a true man, but he was nowhere to be seen, nor Felipe. Several of the pirate crew stood about, all armed but negligent. They probably had no experience of Indians yet.

What were we to do? The fact that I could not see the fat man worried me, for he was the one I wished most to keep under observation.

Guadalupe was seated near a tree, close to the trunk of it, almost indiscernible from where we stood. She held a mug in her hand, and from time to time would sip from it. I doubted she was woolgathering; I believed her attention was probably upon escape... or something of the kind.

She was sitting half-faced toward me and most of the others were facing away. The impulse came upon me suddenly, for if we were to help her she must know it. Deliberately, I stepped out from the brush where we were concealed.

Her mug was lifted toward her mouth, but stopped an instant, then continued. Yet I was sure she had seen me, and I stepped back under cover. A moment later she stood up and stretched, yet in such a way that both hands extended before her, palms out and toward me.

It might have been coincidence, but I was sure she was warning me back with her pushing gesture. She stretched again, then sat down again where she had been.

"Now what was all that about?" Turley asked.

"She knows I am here, and she was warning me to stay back. So, at least, it appeared."

He was skeptical. "Mayhap. If that was what she did she was most shrewd about it, and I doubt a woman would think so cunningly."

"She would," I said.

"We'd best lay low, then." He peered around. "The less we move the less likely we'll be seen." He peered about. "We've a good spot here, and should lie ready until they are all within sight, yonder."

"It may be a long time," I said.

"Aye," he agreed. "Do you sleep. I'll wake you an hour or so from now, or if there's movement yonder. Then I will sleep."

In the brush where we had sheltered there were several deadfalls and a place where the brush parted overhead and sunlight came through. There was grass there and the logs allowed for concealment behind them, yet their camp was still within view.

Down behind one of the logs I settled, and drawing my cloak about me, I slept.

––––––

AGAIN IN MY sleep I went back to my boyhood. What was happening now that inspired these dreams? Or the half awake pondering on the past? Why now, after all this time, should my thoughts be going back to the days of my first flight?

After my escape on Vypont's horse there followed days of running, hiding, begging for food, working a bit when I could, my clothes going to rags once more, and still no way before me except to keep moving. Then I came upon the kindly faced old man whom I had seen so long ago in the tavern before meeting the Vyponts.

The cart stood beside a lane. His donkey was feeding upon grass at the roadside. The old man had a fire going and I walked across the field toward him. He saw me coming, but went on with his business, and I suspected he had been troubled many times along the lanes and byroads by those who would rob or annoy him.

It was only when I stopped beside the cart that I could be sure. He looked up and smiled. "You have come a long way."

"I have. And you also."

"It is my way. Once I was . . . no matter. For these fourteen years past, this has been my life."

"You are a peddler?"

"Of cloth and trinkets, needles and pins. I am also a tinsmith, and I collect herbs from along the lanes and sell them in the villages or cities."

"You do well at this?"

"It is a living. It is enough. I am free. The nights are long and quiet, the mornings cool and bright, I live with the sun, the moon, and the stars. The air is fresh where I am, and there is no one to hurry me or to demand this or that of me."

"It seems a good life."

He looked at me. "You are hungry?"

I shrugged. "I ate yesterday, and once the day before that."

"Join me. I eat what the way provides, and a little that I buy. Sit you down . . . or if you will, gather a bit of wood for the fire."

Coming down the slope, I had seen a fallen tree, so I returned to it and gathered broken sticks, some bark, and whatever would add to the fuel.

He dished up a bowl of stew and handed it to me. "Try that," he suggested.

On the tailgate of his wagon there was a large book opened for reading. "What is the book?" I asked.

"Maimonides."

"You are a Jew?"

"I am English, but one finds wisdom in all languages. I read him often, for he has much to tell." He looked at me. "How do you know of Maimonides?"

"My father read him also. We had many, many books, and my father would often read to me. Sometimes we talked of them."

"I have few books now, but they are old friends." He looked at me sharply. "Where do you go?"

"To London, I think. I look for employment and to make a place for myself. I have much to learn."

"What is it you wish for yourself?"

"To become skilled with weaponry. The wars offer a young man his best chance, and I would have wealth."

"Wealth? Well... perhaps. It has its benefits, but is an empty thing in itself."

"We once had a home. It is now in other hands and I would have it back. The walls have memories of my father's voice and the pools there mirrored the features of my mother. My happiest days were spent walking the cliffs with my father and hearing him tell the tales of Achilles, Hector, and Ulysses."

"Ah, yes. It is good to have roots. I had them once... long ago." He paused. "Now I grow old. I am slower than I once was, and loneliness sits hard upon me. I go now to Yorkshire, but after that, perhaps to the edges of London."

I said no word, waiting for what was on his mind. After awhile he said, "If you hurry not too much, you could come with me. You could learn my trade and more. Also, I shall meet soon with friends, and among them there is a gypsy."

"There were gypsies in Ireland, too."

"Aye, they are everywhere, but this gypsy...he is skilled at all the arts of fencing. With whatever weapon you choose, he is a master. He has studied and taught the art in Venice, in Milano, in Paris as well as in London. Now he travels the roads."

"Why? A man of such skill—?"

"There was a duel. He killed a man of noted family and fled. Even now if they came on him he would be set upon and killed, or thrown into prison on some trumped-up charge.

"They did not know he was a gypsy, so they look not in the places where he is. Now he sharpens blades, shoes horses, and does odd things with metal. I will speak to him and he will teach you. Believe me, there is none better."

"How do you come to be a peddler? You speak as an educated man."

"Someday we will speak of that. I have education and once I had position. Now I am nobody, but I am happy."

I wanted to ask him more, but something in me warned against it, and I did not. That night beside the fire changed me. From being a fugitive I had found a place.

The following day, six miles further along the way, I met the gypsy.

What his name was, I never knew. Nor why they called him Kory, which was not his name. He was a gypsy not of this land, but of Hungary, Rumania, or somewhere yonder.

His wagon was alone when we came upon it, and he was squatted by a fire, preparing food. He did not look around until the old man spoke, and then he got up in one smooth, fluid movement and stood facing us.

Kory was quite the darkest gypsy I had ever seen, yet his eyes were green, and all the more startling under the black brows and the dark skin. His cheeks were lean and cadaverous, his cheekbones high. He might have been thirty, to see him, yet from tales told by the campfire I knew he must be sixty or more. He moved with the grace and ease of a dancer, and when he saw the old man his face broke into a smile revealing gleaming white teeth, startling, as were his eyes, against the darkness of his skin.

"Ah! My friend! It is you! How long it has been!" He glanced quickly at me, seeming to take me in with a glance. "You have come to go with me along the roads?"

"We have." The old man put a hand on my shoulder. "Kory, I have no son. But if I had, I would wish him to be this lad."

The smile vanished. Kory looked straight into my eyes, and then he nodded. "You have come to me ... Why?"

"He brought me," I said, "for I would learn skill with weapons." I paused. "I wish to become the greatest swordsman in the world."

He stared at me, and he did not laugh. "It is a beginning," he said, "to want much. If one is to be, he should try to be the best." His expression changed. "To be the greatest, you must become better than I."

"Only you could teach me that," I said, "for cannot the teacher always teach more than he knows?"

"Ah? It is good, that." He turned his eyes to the old man. "You have eaten? No? Then join me. I have more than enough for I knew I would have guests at the fire."

He turned to me. "We will need wood."

I turned at once and went looking and he stood watching me, his strange eyes following my every movement. I went up to the fence to go through it to the other side.

"Jump!" he said suddenly, and I did. I leaped the fence, and sensing it was some kind of a test, I jumped it again.

Then I went through the fence and gathered wood and returned to the fire. Kory talked to the old man of other days and times. Finally, he said:

"Why do you wish to fight? Is it that you wish to kill someone?"

"No. But I saw my father die, and he was a fine swordsman. I would be better, and when they come to kill me, I would fight the best of all. Even if they kill me, I would wish to leave my mark upon them. There was one man among my father's killers who was best of all. I would be better."

After pausing I said, "A man's destiny is a man's destiny. I would not look for him, but I think he looks for me. And when he finds me I would not wish him disappointed in the way I hold a blade."

"Hah!" Kory ate, and then looked at me again. "Your father, then...he taught you something?"

"Much. But he was a man of peace. He taught me to fight as a gentleman fights, and so would I, against gentlemen, but there will be others."

"Aye! There are always the others," said the old man.

"Yes." Kory looked at the old man. "I will teach him." Again he turned to me. "It will not be easy. It will be work until your muscles cry out in pain, and work again until the pain is all gone from them. It cannot be done in a month, or even a year, but I will teach you all I know."

"And that is more than any other man knows," the old man said. "Good. You will find him a good lad."

"Yes," Kory said quietly, "I know him. He will walk a bloody trail in the years before him, but the blood that is spilled needs spilling. Today we eat, tonight we sleep, and tomorrow...we work!"

How swiftly passed the months! How soon came the end of the year! Up and down the lanes of England we traveled, and over the border and into Scotland. We camped beside Hadrian's Wall and later by the shores of Loch Lomond. We went down into Yorkshire and we camped in lonely places. We sharpened knives, scissors, and all manner of blades, we did tinsmithing. We shod horses and we peddled cloth, thread, and needles. And ever and always, we fenced.

By dawn light and campfire, in clearings in the forest or on the lonely moors, in deserted bars and wherever we might find a place, we fenced. Always we sought seclusion, for gypsies or vagabonds who had skill with weapons were ill-liked. Also, Kory must keep himself from sight. It would be a hanging for him, if he were caught.

I was in the hands of a master. My father had been skilled, but Kory was a marvel, no less.

At night we read by the campfire, or talked of what we had earlier read, or of our experiences during the day. Sometimes Kory would join in. Usually he simply listened, smiling infrequently.

The old man was called Thomas Bransbee. What his true name was, I do not know, yet as we traveled, I picked up a few things about him. He had gone to the best of schools, had held some official position at one time, and his family had suffered because of it. I guessed that he had been involved, or was suspected of being involved, with one of the numerous factions that had supported the claimants to the throne after the death of Henry VIII.

Sometimes we parted from Kory for the day, even for several days, but then he would appear again. As my skill sharpened, so did his, for the constant fencing was renewing his old talents.

"It is a wrong name we go by," he said one day. "They call us gypsies because they believed we came from Egypt. It is not so. We were a wandering tribe from India who left there long, long ago. Our words resemble those of the Hindu: some of our songs are the same, and customs."

He was a wise man and had traveled much. During the periods when we stopped for rest or when I sometimes rode with him on his cart, or walked beside him to save the horses, he talked of his wanderings all over Europe and Asia. He had known many men of importance, serving them in various capacities, or simply traveling with them. His own tribe of gypsies had been largely destroyed by war and plague, yet he was known to other bands, and welcome everywhere.

We collected herbs at the roadside. There were many, often thought of as weeds by the unknowing. It was possible to bundle these into small bales or collect the seeds and sell them at various shops in the villages or to doctors who made their own medicines from them.

I was gaining education in much else, too, for Kory told me of the tricks and artifices used by thieves and pickpockets, swindlers and cardsharps. It was an education in the ways of the streets. Little did I know then how much I was soon to need it.

Wanderers along the highroads were always in danger from local thugs who felt secure in attacking or robbing those of us who were considered vagabonds ourselves, having no protection from the law... when there was any.

Wayfarers usually banded together, that they might protect one another. At the time when trouble came to us, there were three carts traveling together— Bransbee, Kory, and two gypsy brothers who were pugilists, often boxing at the county fairs.

They were good boxers both, and better than average at wrestling as well. Frequently they arranged a match or two with strong boys from the country towns, sometimes winning, sometimes losing, whichever might be the most profitable at the time— or sometimes whichever might be the wiser.

The old man was alone at the time, for I'd been walking with Kory and his cart. But we were only a short distance behind, and the place for our meeting was in a hollow just ahead of us.

Bransbee had turned the corner and we heard a clatter of hooves and then a shouting and we heard Bransbee cry out in protest.

While walking, I carried always a stout stick. Grasping it now, I ran on ahead. As I turned the bend of the lane I saw that a half-dozen young men and boys, all upon horses, had surrounded the cart and were throwing its contents into the road.

Two of the boys had pinioned the old man's arms and were laughing at him. Of the others some remained in the saddle, and the rest had dropped down and were looting the cart.

My first glance told me these were no ordinary ruffians, for all were well clad and well mounted. I rushed upon them. One of them heard me coming and turned sharply, raising a stick he carried. Stick fighting was something I had known from childhood in Ireland, and I thrust hard with the end of mine, bending to avoid a counterblow. The end of my stick took him in the wind and he doubled with a grunt. I knocked his stick from his hand and fetched him a clout across the shins that set him yelling.

Two of the others turned on me, but by that time Kory was coming at a run. And suddenly the two pugilists burst from the wood where their cart had been drawn up, out of sight.

At once we were in a fierce set-to with fists, sticks, and clubs, and I found myself facing a brawny youth, a wide-faced young man with thick, black, curly hair and two hamlike fists. He had turned suddenly on me and caught me off guard, and his first blow sent my stick flying. He would have dealt me another blow then but I dove under his club and tackled him about the knees. It was like hitting a wall, for his thighs were powerfully muscled, his calves as well, and his feet were solidly placed. He grasped me in his two huge hands, pulled me away, and swung a blow at my face.

Jerking back, I tried to break free and did succeed in avoiding the blow, but never had I felt a grasp so filled with sheer power. I was off my feet but I kicked out, catching him on the kneecap. He winced, his grip relaxed, and I broke free.

He lunged at me but suddenly Kory was there, the handle of an axe in his hands. "Do it," he said, "and I will smash your skull."

Powerful as he was, the young man was no fool. He stepped back and looked at Kory. "Oh yes," he said, "I shall stop for now, but we'll have the lot of you up to prison for this."

"You attacked us!" I protested.

He smiled smugly. "That won't be so when I tell it," he said, "and my father is a power here. I will see all of you hang. There's a highwayman about here, and I will swear," he pointed a thick finger at Kory, "that you are he, and that the rest are your confederates.

"I shall see you hang," he said grimly, "and when you do, I shall smile."

Two of the others were getting to their feet. One lad, scarcely older than I, was still on his horse.

"If you have attacked us in this manner," Bransbee said, "you will have abused others. It is in your nature. We will find those others. We will get our own witnesses."

The young man smiled. He was perhaps eighteen in years, four years older than I now was. "None will speak against me," he replied cheerfully. "All about are my friends—or they'll live in fear of what may follow. Oh, I shall see you hang, all right! I shall have the witnesses, and my family owns all about here. You will see."

"What a beast you are!" I said coolly. "You are a bully, and no doubt a coward as well."

He looked at me tauntingly. "A bully? Oh, yes! I like being a bully to all you riffraff, you vagabonds. But a coward? That I do not know, and I never shall, for I am larger, stronger, and a better swordsman than any about. I can defeat them all. As for you, had they not fallen around me, I should have beaten you blind.

"That was what I intended, you know, to blind you. I shall do so yet, and these others also, if they live."

He turned, gathered up the fallen reins of his horse, and swung to its saddle. "Come!" he said to the others. "I must arrange for these to be taken."

Abruptly he rode off and the others followed—all but the lad who had not dismounted. He lingered a bit.

"I am sorry," he said. "I am just lately come home and did not know what he has become. Be off with you, for he will do as he says. His father is a lord here, and will hear no evil of him. He is a tremendous fighter and a bad one, evil in all ways. He can do everything he says."

He looked at me. "You," he said, "he will hate. I know. Get away, if you can."

He rode off and over the rise.

Kory moved swiftly. He turned to Porter Bill, the nearest of the two pugilists. "Get your cart and follow me! There is a lane yonder!"

We fled. Yet our carts could move but slowly, and I wondered what it was Kory had in mind: yet there was some plan, for he was a gypsy as were Porter Bob and Porter Bill, the twin fighters.

We ran our donkeys and ponies until, a short distance along, he turned sharply into a lane past a haycock. Behind him he replaced the bars of a gate and brushed out the tracks of our turning.

We ran our animals a mile, then another half until we came upon some old haycocks and he turned from the hidden lane down which we had traveled. In the field he pulled aside some hay. There was an opening there, for the haycocks were old and were like hives. There was room under them for three carts, four if need be. Swiftly, we came out, rearranged the hay, and mounted upon the animals. We were one shy, and I shook my head at them.

"Go!" I said. "I shall meet you later. I can run and hide afoot: I have done it most of my life, it seems. Do you try to escape."

They hesitated, then Kory tossed me one of the two sticks he carried. "See? It is a sword-cane. Use it if you need."

And they were gone.

They were gone, and I was alone. Alone once more.

Quickly, I looked about. There was little time. Nor did I need any warning when it came to that big youth. I had seen the look in his eye. He was one who thrived on cruelty.

Turning swiftly, I went down the hill.

CHAPTER 10

THERE WAS NO time to think, no time to plan; distance was what I needed. I guessed that my mounted friends would head south and try to lose themselves among the lanes. They would scatter out, too, taking their loss as they would, or sending gypsy friends back for their hidden carts.

I ran down the slope to a stream, then along it under the trees to a lane. I knew not how much estate was claimed by the father of the large young man, nor which direction would find me safest, but I fled.

My condition was good. Well over a year of traveling along the lanes and byroads, walking much of the time, always active, fencing, boxing, wrestling, had left me in fine shape.

It angered me to be treated so shamefully by the leader of those rascals. There were many of their kind about, young ruffians albeit of good family, taking advantage of their position to raid and bully and steal. No man was safe from them, and no girl, either. They were thoroughly vicious.

We had lately crossed a wild and broken moor not too far from the sea. It was there that I directed my steps. Once, when I had begun to climb, I looked back.

Parties of riders could be seen sweeping along the lanes. I kept from sight and plodded on. Soon they would come this way, and I must find a place to hide.

Wandering the lanes as we did, we usually paid small mind to where we were, and I only knew that somewhere off to the west lay the sea. We were in the Lake Country or near it, and as once I had fled to the sea and escaped, it was in my mind to do so again. Soon I reached the cover of an oak wood and then a deep ravine where I climbed carefully over some mossy rocks, using my cane to good effect. Clambering out of the ravine, I crossed over a grassy place and entered a clump of yew that covered a knoll. There, under shelter of the woods, I paused to consider my course.

Undoubtedly when the lads who attacked us had set the countryside upon us, they had told some tale of violence or theft. Many parties of horsemen and others would be scouring the country in search of us, and were we found it would go hard. For no explanation would suffice against the accusation of one of their own.

The place I had now reached was on a steep mountainside and the yew was thick. No horseman would ride down this slope, and I doubted that any of the ruffians who attacked us would. Such folk were not apt to go where the traveling was hard. So it might be best to remain where I was for the time and not chance the moors or grassland above until darkness fell. What I feared most was dogs. If they brought dogs to search for us, we would be found. At least, I would be.

It was late afternoon and if the next hour or two were passed in safety, I might yet go free.

Below me the land lay wide under the mouth of the ravine. Here and there were clumps of yew, then patches of oak, and below a checkerboard of fields and pastures. A lovely, peaceful land, but not for me. I was again in flight... Would there never be a place to rest? Never a place where I could stop and serve? Where I could do something of worth without forever living in fear?

It came to me then that I must be away from England if I wished to be free. And yet I had grown to love this land and many of its people.

Why must London forever hold out a beckoning finger? What awaited me there, if anything? Had not many warned me against the hazards of that city?

Slowly the shadows gathered behind me while the valley below still lay bathed in sunlight. Here and there I could see distant troops of horsemen wending their homeward way. Had they found my friends?

The haycocks now...how had Kory known of them? Were there many such, scattered about in unused fields or ancient pastures, places of which the gypsies knew, and to which they could resort in time of need? No doubt, I decided, there were.

At last I arose. If I were to choose my way, I must be going now, before all was darkness. Slowly, I walked through the yew and emerged upon the hillside. My muscles were stiff from sitting on the damp earth and I was tired from the running and climbing, but I knew I must get on.

Over the rim of the hill I mounted, and out into the angry red of a vanished sun. Streaks of scarlet and gold-laced clouds lay in the west and the heather moor lay about me. I stood alone upon it as if in a world newly born from the primeval darkness, or sinking again into that from which it came.

And then they were coming at me.

There were four of them, walking their horses toward me, led by the same big young man who had led them below. "See?" he was saying. "Did I not know where to come? Did I not tell you?"

The others divided, and slowly they surrounded me. My sword-cane was in my hand. They knew it only as a stick, so let them learn if they would. At least one of them would die before I was killed.

No use for me to run. On their fleet horses, on this almost level mountain top, I would be an easy prey. Could I kill all four?

"We have him now, and we shall have some sport of him."

"Why not take him below," one asked, "and let the law have him?"

"Don't be a child!" the big one scoffed. "We will have him. The law can have what we leave of him."

The youngest might have been no older than my fourteen years, but the others were two to four years older. At least two of them were larger than I, and at least one was stronger. All were armed with sticks, at least two had daggers, and the large one a sword. If I escaped the circle and ducked back over the edge where they were not likely to try and bring the horses, I might evade them for a time or until those came who would take me to prison. For vagabonds had no rights that anyone recognized.

To allow them to have their way and torture me was unthinkable, and during the more than two years I had been dodging, evading, and hiding from the law, my mind had grown quick with stratagems.

Their method was obvious. They would move in upon me, ringing me with their horses and themselves, and at any move I should make to escape, a horse would be put before me. I was trapped, and they knew it. Deliberately, I put my sword-cane in my belt and spread my arms as if surrendering.

The big one laughed. "See? He is a coward as well! He will not fight! Well, we will see."

He thrust at me with his stick and I dodged. He was too strong, much too strong. The others began to do likewise, and there was one who was astride a splendid sorrel gelding, a handsome horse, long-bodied and long-legged.

He thrust at me, almost got me, then thrust again. A stick caught my ribs and ripped my shirt, tearing a thin scratch along my ribs. I felt the sting of it, but dodged again, caught a short but ringing blow on my skull, and then the lad on the sorrel leaned far forward, thrusting at me.

It was the moment for which I had waited. Instantly, I grasped the stick and jerked...hard.

He was too far forward and off balance, and my jerk took him from the saddle. He fell, crying out, and as he hit the earth I ducked under a blow, grasped the pommel, and swung myself to the empty saddle.

Once again my horsemanship stood me in good stead, and the horse beneath me was quite the best of the lot. The big lad rode as good a horse, perhaps, but outweighed me by fifty or sixty pounds. I hit the saddle, clapped my heels to the horse's ribs, and took the sorrel away on a dead run.

I had the start of them. Knowing what I planned to do gave me that start and my mount had three good jumps before they realized, and another before they straightened out to run. And I fled into the open land beyond, toward the still-distant sea.

They came after me. Their angry shouts rang in my

ears and I heard the pound of hooves behind me, but the sorrel was a fine horse and it loved to run. A glance back showed me I now led them by at least five lengths and was gaining. They rode wildly, heedlessly, thoughtless of their mounts. I eased my speed a little for I knew not how far I must go and I chose the better ground. Hence despite easing the speed I held my lead, and darkness was close upon us. Once the dark came, I should have a chance.

Glancing back again, I saw that one of them had fallen out of the race, for what reason I knew not. Lack of will, perhaps, for it had been easily seen that he who led them drove them as well. Two only pursued me now, and one of those was falling back.

On into the gathering dark I raced, straight toward the place where the sun had set, and now only one horse was pursuing. Suddenly, I know not what devil possessed me, I slowed my pace and swung my horse around to face him. He came thundering on, realizing too late that I had stopped, and as he pulled up hastily, I slapped heels to my sorrel and charged him. My mount hit his at the shoulder as he was reining in and his horse staggered and went down.

He was quick, oh, so very quick! He leaped from the saddle as his horse fell, and sprang at me. I reined my horse away and thrust at him with the sword-cane, the blade still sheathed. It grazed the side of his head and staggered him and I pivoted the horse and came at him again. He lunged at me but I swung the horse away and drove my heel into the big lad's shoulder.

It was a wrong move, for his hand grasped my leg and the next I knew I was sprawling on the earth and he was standing over me.

"Hah!" he said. "Now we shall see!"

Having wrestled much, I did not try to escape but threw my weight against his legs. It might as well have been against the side of a barn, for he gave not an inch but stooped to grab me. Catching his sleeve, I jerked hard and he fell forward. I was the more agile and was out from under him and on my feet.

He came up swiftly but I struck him hard in the face as he rose. It slowed him not at all, yet I hit him again before he was up, then leaped for my sword-cane.

He saw me pick it up and drew his sword.

We faced each other on the moors in the half-light. Already the stars were out, yet we had been in the darkness and each could see plainly enough.

From the sheath I drew my blade. It was a small blade, as such sword-cane blades are apt to be, shorter by inches than the usual sword. He had the reach of me, anyway, by several inches.

He whipped his blade this way and that as if to show me he knew what he was about. I simply waited, trusting to my new skill to equal the reach he had. That I was good with a blade I well knew. It had been obvious that in our last few weeks I had been forcing Kory to his limit, so I stepped forward willingly enough.

High on the western moors of England, then, we fought by starlight, and within a matter of minutes I knew I had met my master.

It was not to be believed. Kory was good. All had said he was the best, and I was now as good, yet no sooner had we begun than I realized that this tall youth had skill beyond belief. Nor could I claim it was the length of his blade or his superior reach, for he was simply better.

"Hah!" he exclaimed. "So you have fenced? What are you then? Who are you?"

"It does not matter," I said.

"No," he agreed, "for when I have had my exercise I shall kill you. I shall spit you like a goose."

He handled himself with consummate skill. He was casual with me, not careless, for he could see I was better than most. He handled my best with indifference, and I knew that unless I could think of some trick, some means of subtlety, I would be dead within minutes.

He was toying with me. Once he merely pricked my chest when he might have killed me with a thrust. He simply smiled tauntingly and said, "Next time!"

Back, back...I fought carefully, sweat pouring down my cheeks, a cold sweat, for death was very near. How could he be so great when I had learned so much? It was unreal. Yet even though death was near and I hated the man, I marveled at his skill. Despite his great strength he had the delicate touch of the master, and a strength in his wrist and fingers I could scarcely believe.

Suddenly I sensed a change in his blade, that most sensitive antenna reaching out to touch me. I sensed a change and *knew*. Now he would kill me. Now I would die.

Was my life all for nothing, then? My hopes gone? My dreams blasted? All my struggles for nothing? All the hopes of my father that I might found a family and let our blood march on down the centuries to come? Was this to be the end, here on this dark moor by starlight?

The ground slanted downward behind me. I found myself on a slight slope, which gave him the greater height, the greater advantage. What was happening?

Where was I? There was no chance to look to right or left now, it was parry and thrust, and then suddenly I felt rather than saw a vast gulf opening behind me. His blade was up, poised for a thrust, and I threw myself back and down, falling backward, hoping to strike the turf and roll, to get away, to escape by any means.

I fell, an impossible distance. My shoulders hit the ground with a thump, and I lost my grip on the sword-cane and it fell from me. I rolled over and tumbled, head over heels into a black, misty void. I tried to catch myself but there was nothing on which to lay hold and the slope was impossibly steep. I was falling, into what awful depth I knew not, but over and over I tumbled until suddenly I was brought up with a sickening thud upon some rocks.

How far had I fallen? Perhaps not more than ten or a dozen feet in that first sheer fall, but I must have tumbled down the rest of the slope, sliding, falling, tumbling again for several hundred feet.

A moment I lay still, surrounded by darkness and fog. Then, slowly, I rolled over and tried to push myself up, only to gasp with shock at my torn hands.

I rolled to my knees and stood up. No bones were broken that I could feel. Yet I hurt in every part of my body and my hands were bloody, my face as well.

I must escape . . . I must somehow get away. There was bound to be a way down and they would come for me. Dumbly, hurt and shamed that I had been so thoroughly beaten, I stumbled away into the mist. I could see nothing but the fog. There was heather around; I knew that because I brushed against it. I was on a moorland or something like. On and on I plodded, stupid with pain and weariness, knowing only that help—

if any there was to be—lay far from here. I must get away before the morning light came again.

I tripped and sprawled my length. For a moment I lay, as I was wishing only to stay there, even to die there, but something within me urged me up and on.

Time and again I fell, time and again I got up. Often I lay still for minutes, but always something drove me on. Finally, as day was breaking I came upon a copse choked with brush. Crawling into it, I lay still, more dead than alive. Yet the last thought with me as I lay there was: *how could I have lost?* How could he have been so much superior?

A long time I slept, muttering in my half-sleep, crying out as some sore place touched the earth, until at last the cold dawn came and with it awakening.

Cold and wet. There had been the mist, and then the dew, perhaps. I shivered and tried to sit up. My muscles were stiff and heavy, my head was hard to hold up, my eyesight blurred as I stared about. Only the copse, the brush, the fallen leaves, a few broken branches. Groaning, I crawled out and stood cautiously up.

Nothing was about . . . I was alone. Alone on a vast, wide, unknown land. Yet there was a smell in it of the sea, a smell from the westward.

From among the broken branches I found one that would do for a staff, and I started on. All the morning through I walked. Clouds gathered. The sky was a sullen gray. Rain began to fall. On I went, staggering a little at times, but pushing on.

To where? To a destiny somewhere, a destiny I must fulfill. At last I came to a stream and on its banks I sat down. After resting, I bathed my face, and bathed my bloody, gravel-torn hands. They were a fearful sight, and my face, too, from what I could see of it. Yet gingerly, I washed that, too.

Then I drank, and I drank again.

Refreshed, I looked around. A few trees bordered the stream, nothing else. At last, fearfully hungry, I got to my feet. Stooping to pick up my staff, I almost fell again.

I started downstream. For some inexplicable reason I was heading for the sea. What awaited me there I did not know, except that to me it symbolized escape. At the sea began all things—and ended all things, perhaps. In which direction was I pointed? To another beginning, or to an end? I had no way of knowing. Nevertheless, I continued, because it was in me to go on, to persevere; so it was, and so my whole life long it would be.

The stream wound onward, sometimes through low hills, sometimes higher ones, occasionally on the flat, but steadily it ran down slope, and somewhere ahead was the sea.

Suddenly, a voice. "You, there! What's wrong? Are you hurt?"

It took my eyes a moment to focus, for I'd taken a bad rap on the skull and they functioned not at all well. It was a man, a man in a cart.

"It would seem so," I said. "I had a fall."

"Come along then," he said. "Climb in and I shall take you where we can look— My faith, but you're bloody! Was it only a fall, then?"

"Only a fall," I said. "And a little hunger."

CHAPTER 11

HE GAVE ME a long, careful look. "You are but a lad," he said gently. "Have you no home, then?"

"I have none. What I once had is gone and will not be again until I make it of myself."

"Where are you from?"

The question was not one I wished to answer, so I simply said I had been going toward the sea and had a bad fall in the darkness and the fog. When I described what I could of the place, he nodded and suggested, "Near Hardnose Pass, I have no doubt. There is a rough, wild country yon."

The pony plodded steadily on. "My cottage is but a little way along," the driver said, "and you can stay the night if you are so minded. We can have a look at those hands, for they are in fearful shape."

On and on we went, interminably, it seemed to me. I dozed, awoke, and dozed again. I was awakened by his pulling into the yard of a thatched cottage, a well-built place with stables about and some other animals.

A man came from the stable. "Ben? See to the pony. I will speak with you later."

Staggering with weariness as I was, I hesitated. To stop here might be to be trapped, although I had come a goodly distance. "I have far to go," I said, "and must be getting on, although I am obliged for the ride you have given me."

"What is it? Are you pursued, then?"

"It may be that I am," I said, "although they be scoundrels who would pursue me. Yet I have no friends, and they have many."

"You have a friend in me," he said. "Come in, lad."

It was warm and pleasant within, a fire on the hearth and a table set with trenchers for our eating. A woman stood looking at us. Her hair was fair with a tinge of red to it and her cheeks were flushed from the fire. "I heard your voices, and there's a-plenty for both."

Then she saw my face. "Why, the lad is hurt! Come here to the fire, so we can see!"

She looked carefully at my skinned face and the bruises, and then put warm water in a basin and with a bit of cloth began to sponge off my face and take away the encrusted blood and gravel. After a bit she desisted and cleaned my hands a bit more, although I had washed them in the Esk, for such was the name of the stream.

"Here! Sit up and have a bite, then we'll get on with it. You must be fairly starved."

"I am that," I agreed. "Where is it I am?"

"The village yon is Boot," the man said. "The hall yonder is empty now for the family is from home to London. Most of them," he said with a wry glance at his wife.

The gruel they served was good, and there was a bit of fish, fresh caught from the sea.

"When I have eaten," I told them, "I had best be off, for I'd not bring trouble upon you." Briefly as I might, I explained how we had been set upon and what manner of folk they were.

He filled a glass with ale. "Aye, there's sons of the gentry who raid and roust about with no care for anything but themselves. Worse than thieves they are, and brutal to all they can abuse. But do not worry, lad, you have come further than you think and they will not come down on this side of the mountain."

"Be careful of him," I said, "for bully that he is, he is also a rarely fine hand with a blade."

"From what you said he was both taller and stronger than you. A man grown, and you but a lad."

"Aye, brute he may be, but I'll not take from him his skill. Height and reach are important. I could have handled them, but not his skill. The man from whom I learned was considered among the best, yet I had no chance."

"Rafe Leckenbie," the woman said. "There is no other fits the description."

"Leckenbie? Aye . . . it could be. He's a bad enemy, lad, and a worse man. He comes not here, but stays there where his family is important, but he has killed a man or two and it is said he will be off to the wars soon. For they wish to be rid of him, I think."

There I spent the night and the weariness fled from my muscles. When the morning came I was refreshed, yet weary still, for I had been long in fleeing and long without food.

"Where will you go?" Andrew asked, for that was his name, and hers was Mary, but their other names I never heard, neither then nor after.

"I would go to London, but I am far from there. If

I could find some fisherman, some boat that plies to Scotland, I would go there and be free of this place."

"These are bad times and no highroad is safe. Men's goods are seized, and often as not by gentry. And there is no appeal. The times are bitter, and he is at his wit's end who must live upon the roads, for there are none there but peddlers, herbalists, mountebanks, and jugglers mingling with thieves and outlaws. No man is safe upon the road unless with a large company and all armed."

"But it grows better," Mary protested. "I have heard you say as much yourself."

"Aye...better, but not better enough. There is much to be done before the roads are safe for travel."

Andrew glanced at me. "How old are you?"

"Fourteen years."

"Fourteen! And you have seen so much! And already a swordsman!"

"But not good enough. I must go where I can learn more."

"Italy, then. Or Spain. Although they do say the French are excellent swordsmen." He studied me. "Are you then so anxious to fight?"

"That I am not, but my father warned me I would have enemies, and to survive I must be prepared. I hope never to fight," I added, in all sincerity, "but experience has taught me that wishing to avoid a fight will not always be enough.

"It is all very well to wish for peace, but while there are such people as this Rafe Leckenbie there will always be wars. A man can convince himself that others want peace as much as he, but he will only be fooling himself, for it is the last thing many men want...unless they can take all they covet without having to fight."

We talked long. He was a man keenly aware of conditions in his country, although I could not place his role. He had a goodly farm here, but did not seem a farmer, albeit most of the farmers were of the gentry and some owned vast estates. That he was curious about me I knew, yet the long months upon the highroads had taken much of my accent and I had picked up words or phrases here and there. Kory, especially, had taught me a lot other than what I had learned of the blade.

"You have read much," Andrew said, finally, putting down his glass. "Your father was your teacher, you said?"

"He was a fine classical scholar," I said, "but he taught me much else, besides. Along the roads," I added, "I have learned much of herbs and their uses."

"Aye, learn what you can. There is naught that will not but be useful."

He was a friendly man, a gentleman obviously, and if I was not mistaken, of the nobility. There were many such who had a living but little else, younger sons or those who inherited impoverished estates or none at all. Even the King of Scotland had to borrow a coat from a friend to wear before a visiting ambassador. The possession of a great name did not always mean great wealth, and indeed, the visit of a king and his entourage might be sufficient to impoverish even a well-off man.

From the way he referred to "the hall" I suspected he was a younger son or a cousin, perhaps. The house was a good one and old, of squared gray stone and stout oak timbers. The cobbled passage down which we had come opened into the living room where we now were. The kitchen was beyond the passage and I had only a glimpse of the huge fireplace as we entered. There was little furniture and that quite heavy.

We talked of Greene and Philip Sidney, of Chaucer, and of Tacitus and Livy. Yet I listened more than I talked, for much as it reminded me of home, weariness lay heavy upon me, and it was his good wife who called Andrew's attention to my worn-out state, and soon I was off to bed, in a small chamber of my own. Worried as I was, I fell soon asleep.

M Y EYES OPENED suddenly and for a time I lay still, trying to recall all that had transpired. At last I arose. There was water in the room, hot water. Evidently whoever brought it had awakened me, yet had left before my eyes opened or I became aware. I bathed, combed my hair, and made myself as presentable as might be.

As I bathed and prepared myself, I thought over my fight with Leckenbie, if such indeed was his name. My memory for such things had always been good, and now I reviewed that fight in detail. His reach had helped him, and his longer, stronger blade, yet he had skill of a rare kind, and a genius, I thought, for the sword. Yet such genius breeds confidence, and confidence may well become overconfidence, if fed by continual success.

Mentally, I reviewed his moves, trying to discern a pattern that might be circumvented. I began to see that he had been surprised by my skill. Again and again I had warded off his most serious attacks, even though most of the time he was simply enjoying his command of me. He had won, and he would surely have killed me, but still I had come off not badly.

"All right," I said aloud, "he beat me once but he will not beat me a second time."

Very well to say such a thing, but before I could meet him I needed to learn much more.

There was a shout from outside. Opening my door, I went down the stair. The front door stood open, and Andrew was before it.

In the yard were at least twenty horsemen, led by Rafe Leckenbie. "We want him," Leckenbie was saying, "and we will have him."

"I think not," Andrew said quietly. "Think what you do, Leckenbie. I know your father well and he would not permit such a scene as this."

"Give him up," Leckenbie replied, "or we will take him."

Mary went around me and pressed something into her husband's hand. It was a pistol.

"I will go with Leckenbie," I said to my host. "I will not be the cause of trouble for you who have been so kind."

Andrew glanced at me. "This is no longer your affair," he replied. "They have come *here*, onto our land, to use force and make demands. I would not permit you to leave now."

"You have heard me," Leckenbie said. "I will have your house down around your ears, but I will have him!"

Coolly, Andrew brought his pistol from behind his back, and at the same time there was a rustle of feet.

Glancing to my right, I saw a half-dozen men armed with pikes, scythes, and halberds. Two men suddenly appeared on the stable roof, both with bows and arrows ready.

"You may try," Andrew said quietly, "but you will die. Also," he smiled a little, "you have yet to get yourselves home. I am considered a mild man. My brother is not, and he will be here this day. I think you will be fortunate if you get home at all."

There was a murmur from behind him. Already some of those who followed Leckenbie were backing off. I believe most of them followed him only from fear of what he might do if they did not, although undoubtedly some were as much the rogue as he himself.

"Rafe...?" It was the same one who had advised letting up on me. "There's always another time."

Leckenbie hesitated, but he liked not the pistol nor the firm resolution of Andrew. He turned his mount. "We will come again," he threatened. Then he looked at me. "And you...I will slit your gullet in my own good time."

"You will not have to come looking, Leckenbie," I said, "for I shall be back to find you. I have thought over our bout of yesterday, and now I know I can beat you!"

"Hah!" he laughed unpleasantly. "The man does not live who can best me, least of all you!"

Of course, I had boasted when I said I had thought over his actions and knew I could now best him. I knew certainly I could do nothing of the kind, but I also knew that in time I should. I would study, learn, work much with the blade, and then I would seek him out.

They rode away, and two dozen of Andrew's men mounted and followed at a short distance to see them gone. Several of them looked to be stout fighting men who had served in the Queen's forces by land or sea. I doubted not they could take care of themselves against the rabble who followed Leckenbie.

"I must get on my way now," I said. "You have been kind, but I have far to go."

"Indeed you have, lad," Andrew put a hand on my shoulder, "but I'd forget your promise to come and find Rafe Leckenbie. He's an evil one, and time will take care of his kind."

"We shall see." I paused. "I wish to make for Scotland now. Which is the best way?"

"There are fishing boats at the Esk that go north up the coast, but if I mistake not, Leckenbie will expect you there, so I would suggest you go north on land. I will see you on your way. I have friends at Workington Hall."

"I know the name."

"Aye, a few years back Mary, Queen of Scots, took refuge there. Perhaps we can find a letter for you that will open a way for you among the Scots."

"You are too kind."

"If you wished to stay, we could make a place for you here. You are a good lad, and should not be wandering about the country like any gypsy or vagabond."

"I have a way to go," I said.

"Aye," he replied gloomily, "one I might have taken myself at your age, but then I met Mary."

"You did well," I said, "as did she."

He smiled. "Aye. Now we will have up some horses and ride north."

"You do not fear to leave after all this?"

He chuckled grimly. "If they wish to return, let them do so! My lads will be about, and they are a rough lot. My father had a ship and was often at sea. Many of these men here sailed with him. They have endured many a hard-fought battle. You'll not find their like this side of the Highland clans!"

He was a careful man, and north we rode by starlight that we might not be observed from afar. At dawn we rested and ate at a drover's cot, a cozy, hidden place among the gray rocks and green rolling hills where a burn came down from the rocky hills, chuckling and babbling through the green hummocks and among wildflowers; a pleasant land, but a waiting land, too, for often had fierce Highland raiders come this way.

At Workington Andrew found a fisherman he knew, a Scot, by the name of Jamie, and fresh down from the west Highlands. "Aye, I will take him awa', and gladly." Jamie looked at my face and hands. "You've had a rough go of it, lad. What is it you wish for now?"

"To be well again and to find a fine swordsman who can teach me."

"And then?"

"Then I shall return."

"There speaks a true man. Well, he used you hardly, but not with a sword, I'll mind?"

"A sword it was. This is but from a fall I had, although thankful I was to fall, for it saved my life. A moment more and he would have had me."

"Was he so good, then?"

"The best."

"Aye? Wait until you've met MacAskill, lad. He's one of a fighting lot. Lead the MacLeods in battle, they do, and a brawny, fearsome lot they are, but the one to whom I'll take you...he's another matter, for he has served in armies abroad, and is a terrible man in a fight."

"If he can teach me, I will go to him."

"*If* he will teach you! I doubt he will. He's a man of independent mind and thought. He teaches no one... but he could. You are a brawny lad, surely, and we'll take you along to him. He can do no more than say no."

"And who is the man?"

"Fergus MacAskill. He's fought in the clan wars in the Highlands, but upon the Continent as well. 'Tis not only the claymore for which he's known, but every kind of a weapon."

"The MacAskills are to be found on the Isle of Lewis in the Hebrides, and some perhaps on Skye. I've not been there m'self, but they are allied to the MacLeods and have the name of strong fighters, always." Andrew added that comment and then arose. "I'll leave him to you, Jamie, and do you see him well ashore, for he seems a good lad and I'd like as much done for me was I left as he is."

"I am obliged," I told him. "You shall see me again one day."

Jamie led the way down to his boat. "Have you been upon the sea, then?"

"A time or two, and far from here, but upon water not unlike this."

"Good! You can help me then, for it looks to be a braw, bad night upon the water."

And a braw bad night it was, to be sure. The wind howled down the firth as if to bury us by its sheer force, and a driving rain with it. When I came ashore at last there was not a dry stitch to me, but I was in Scotland and free of my enemies.

And there was a man for me to find, the great fighting man, Fergus MacAskill.

Tomorrow, with dry clothes, a night's sleep, and a meal under my belt, I would begin.

CHAPTER 12

ALONE UPON THE shore I watched the fisher's boat turn to take the wind, and lifted a hand to bid farewell. I did not know if he saw me, but I stood and watched him go, then turned to walk up the path. I was in Galloway, with nothing in my hands and no place to go.

Yet a man must move, and I have discovered it is always best to keep putting one foot before the other, and so I did now.

A gloomy, foggy, mysterious place it was, and a fit one for the seeing of ghosties and ghoulies in the night. Boylike, I was wary of such creatures, wanting none of them.

After walking a bit I saw a light, but when I knocked upon the door no answer came and the light went out. Although I waited and knocked again there was no opening of the door nor any welcome.

A mile or more beyond I saw a cluster of lights. One belonged to a place that passed for a tavern, for as I came near a man emerged, weaving somewhat from the cargo he carried, which was shifting him about like a heavy sea. I hailed him and asked if there might be shelter for the night and a bite of something.

"Aye," the man swayed like a willow in the wind, "and good food it is, too, if you're of a mind to eat, but his ale's the better bargain. Sure, and I think the man is heir to that Pict who is said to have jumped from the cliffs yonder o' the Mull, holding the formula for heather ale."

"I'll speak to him then," I said, and went to the door and opened it.

The room was low of ceiling, heavily timbered, and there was a huge old fireplace with copper kettles and such, and a few benches about and a long table at which some men sat, boatmen, fishermen, and the like, each with his mug of ale before him.

"Why, it's a lad! And a sorry wet one, too! Come in, now! Up to the fire wi' y'!" The speaker was a wide man and deep, with reddish whiskers at his jowls and a queer sort of flat cap to his head. "John! A bit of something for the lad, now!"

"What'll you have boy?" The innkeeper was a fat, pleasant-looking man.

"Whatever," I said. "I've little enough money."

"Do y' not be thinkin' o' that! I've a son m'sel'!" The man with the red whiskers clapped me on the shoulder. "Sit close to the fire, lad, and drink up. A drop will do y' no harm this e'en."

When I had the glass in my hand and a plate of bread and gruel before me I said, "Can you be tellin' me now where I'm likely to find Fergus MacAskill?"

They stared at me, and my friend put his glass down hard upon the table. "Fergus, is it? Aye, there be a plenty would like to see Fergus, but there's many more would wish for no sight of him." He drank and wiped the back of his hand across his mouth. "Why would a lad like you be wanting to find Fergus?"

"I do not know him, nor him me. Yet it has been

said that he is a great fighting man, and I would learn."

"To fight? A man can fight or he cannot. 'Tis all!"

"Na, John! Y' know that isn't true, what y' say! A man may have the heart but no' the skill. Cannot y' see? The lad wants the skill! He wishes to learn!"

"Why, then?"

So I told it simply, how I fancied myself a swordsman, although I was only a boy, and how those who set upon me proved my skill was nothing like enough.

"And when you've the skill, what then?"

"I shall go back. I shall find Rafe Leckenbie again. I shall make him show me his best and then I shall beat him."

"Hah? Well, I'll be thinkin' y'll have to talk y' best to get aught from Fergus. He's no' the one to teach any who come, only those who seek him out for a fight—and they pay dear for what they get."

"Where to look, that's the question," I said.

The men exchanged glances. "Go north and ask for him. If he wishes to see you he'll find you soon enough, and if he doesn't y' will be whistlin' to the wind for all y'll see of him."

My gruel was hearty enough, and warmed my insides. The ale was good, and soon the chill began to go from me.

"Do y' have the Gaelic then?" He who was my friend put the question.

"Aye, although a different sound than yours, no doubt. But I have it, never fear."

"Y' will need it. There's some say he takes notions time to time and will speak only that."

One man got up. "It be late. I've a fair piece to go."

He went out, shutting the door behind him. My lids were heavy and I nodded above the last of the ale.

"John? The lad's dyin' for sleep. Can y' not put him down before the fire? He's not the pailing kind, I'll warrant."

"I am not," I said. "I would steal from no man."

"There's a bit of rug b' the fire, lad, if y' can make do wi' it."

"I could sleep on a stone," I said, "and think it soft, that tired I am. I crossed the Solway this night from England and traveled some before that."

"And hurt, too." John indicated my face. "But it heals."

The man who spoke for me helped to move back the table and they unrolled their bit of rug before the fire. He made do upon a bench, but I trusted no such place for fear of falling off in the night. John added a chunk or two to the fire, driftwood brought up from the sea it was, looking like a bit of some great spar from a lost ship. I said as much.

"Aye, a few have been lost yonder off the Mull. Some fine vessels, too, and some fine folks."

John left us then for his own bed. The candle was snuffed and only the firelight lit the room, and all was still enough except for a drop now and again as rain fell into the fire. It hissed at each drop, and sometimes a spark flew. The room was warm, but tired though I was, I could scarcely sleep.

Suddenly the man upon the bench spoke with a whisper. "Lad? Be you awake still?"

"Aye," I said, not trusting him, although friendly enough he had been.

"Lad, if you'll come along wi' me when morning

comes, I'll show you on your way and more. I'll pay you a bit. I need a sturdy lad who's not afeared to fight."

"Fight? I have no wish for it. Only in my own good time, and wi' those I choose."

"Lad, lad! D'y' think I ken not your Gaelic? You're Irish as Paddy's pig, and so am I, but there's those who would have my heart if the chance offered."

"Here? In Scotland?"

"Aye, even here. I need other eyes to watch, and you've a smart way about you." He paused. "Who are you, then?"

"I did not ask you," I said.

"That you did not. So be it. My way is your way, lad. I've a man to see in the Highlands, a man who is friendly to the Irish, but there's English spies about. Mind you, I find no harm in the Englishmen. I've friends among them, but they're Queen's men ... ah, that's another thing!"

"I go to the Highlands, and I seek Fergus MacAskill. If my way lies with yours, so be it."

"Good, then! They look for a man alone. Together we've a chance, and we can take turns sleeping."

"And tonight?"

"No ... I think tonight is safe, but if you hear a sound outside, touch my foot. I'll come awake soon enough."

The wind was rising, and the rain increasing. I liked it not and wished to travel alone, yet a fellow Irishman? A man seeking help for Ireland no doubt.... Well, I would see what the next day offered, and take each day as it came. I wanted no fight with any man except Leckenbie, and that only in its time.

I slept, awakening only to stir the fire and to listen to the hard rain fall, and the wind. It was an angry sea yon, and I knew why he who brought me turned so quick from the shore, for he smelled it on the wind. He knew the storm was coming. What was it the old wives said? "God have pity on the poor sailors on such a night as this!" Aye, and all who had no shelter, as I might not have had.

Gray was scarcely in the sky before my companion was up and outside, looking about at the weather.

John handed me a bowl of hot soup. "Drink it, lad. You travel a great distance, and I wish you luck." A movement of his head indicated the man outside. "You walk with him?"

I shrugged. "It was spoken of. For a distance, perhaps."

"He is a good man, make no mistake, but he walks a dangerous path. All who are with him are in danger, for what he does is close upon treason. If anybody could find Fergus MacAskill for you, he could . . . but do not become involved with what he does, and if danger comes, think of yourself and get away. He would wish that, too."

He paused; breaking a chunk of bread from a loaf, he handed it to me. "My mother was from Ireland so I've a sympathy for them there. Be careful, lad."

We walked away in the morning upon a winding road across the moors, and in all the wide land we saw no others but ourselves, save here or there some sheep, and once, a cow.

"Ahead lies Glen Trool," my companion said. "It is a dark and bitter land, yet with rare beauty, and stories! Ah, the stories it could tell! Murder and mystery and old things found! Spearheads pushing up from the soil after a rain, and once I came upon a length of ancient sword while hiding in the trees there.

"It is a place to lose a man, if he wishes to be lost, or a body if the killer wishes to make no explanation. There are thieves and outlaws hiding there, too, and not afar was where Robert the Bruce won a victory over his pursuers. A small victory, but a victory."

He looked at me. "What do they call you, lad?"

"They call me Tatt. It is enough."

"What they call me is another thing, but for the time I am a Scotsman, Angus Fair. I am a seafaring man returning from a long time at sea." He paused, turning to look back the way we had come. "You know nothing of me, lad, if questioned. Simply say honestly enough that we just met, and you understood I was returning home after twenty years at sea." He smiled. "That allows for me having no connection, no land, and only a destination.

"My family have all passed on, but I've a wish in me to see the place where I was a boy before going back to the seas again. And I have a wish to get on with it, for I have a feeling the Spanish will be mounting an attack upon us.

"Now you know my story, and as for you, I am helping you to go to relatives in the Highlands. Does it please you, this story?"

"Aye, and why not? It answers questions simply enough."

"One thing more, lad. There are those about who are no lovers of the Irish, so if I were you I'd be the son of a Scottish soldier who was killed in Ireland, fighting for the Queen, and you were raised there. Now you are returning to your own."

We walked on into the morning, and Angus Fair talked of Ireland, repeating some of the tales I'd had first from my father. "Ah, lad, the trouble with the Irish is that they fight best when fighting for others, and among themselves there is no common cause, no unity. In all the lands of Europe you will find Irishmen, often in command, and always fighting well while their own poor country is occupied by the British.

"Mind you, lad, I am not a hater as some are, but a patriot, a lover of his own land. I wish for its freedom, but do not blind myself to its faults. If the British would stay in their own land we'd love them well, for we've much in common, but freedom we must have. How we will use it ... ah, 'tis another question, lad, another question!"

As we walked he rambled on, talking of many things, and I listened, having much to learn. He was a man who had traveled, had known many kinds of men under all sorts of conditions.

The clouds were low and gray, heavy with rain. About us the grass was a deep, deep green and the distant mountains were somber. We walked steadily on, each with a stout staff for easier walking. Twice we passed farmsteads not far off the road, houses of gray stone walls and thatched roofs. Once a big dog stood watching us until we were safely by, but it did not bark.

Soon we saw no more people, no dogs, no distant houses, but only the stark and empty grassland and then the forest. It was a lonely land, and we talked not at all, each alert for we knew not what. Out here a man seemed to stand out, and there seemed no place to hide.

"Yet there is," Angus replied, "you have simply always to be alert. You and me, we must never forget that. So look about you . . . there are low places in the ground, rocks and sometimes clumps of heather. The thing to remember is to lie still . . . movement draws the eye."

And I did look, and from time to time did see places where a man might hide, if he lay still.

Now the land took on a wilder aspect and there was almost continual rain. It was with relief that we saw a cluster of houses before us, and smoke rising from several of them.

"There's a bit of an inn," Angus Fair said. "If the weather were not so gloomy I'd say to pass on, but we'll stop. A warm meal will do us well."

He lifted the latch and swung open the door, and we stepped in. As we shook off the rain and looked up, we knew we had done the wrong thing.

There were five men in the room, three of them armed like soldiers.

It was too late to draw back. To return to the night in such weather was enough to arouse suspicion of us.

" 'Tis a heavy dew," Angus commented. "A good night for a draught of ale and a warm fire."

They did not smile, but simply stared at us, nothing friendly in their eyes.

CHAPTER 13

THERE WAS NO place by the fire so we went to a rough board table and sat down on benches that faced it on either side. Angus pulled his bench around so he could sit with his back toward the wall and his face to the door. I sat around the corner of the table from him, facing the fire and the men who sat before it.

It was a good blaze, but there was chill at our backs, and not from the cold only.

This was a wild land where we now were, and few were the travelers who ventured to cross it. There were outlaws in the forest or lurking in the glens for unwary travelers, but these were not such.

Mine host brought us a slab of meat, good venison, too. Along with it he brought a loaf and then he drew two mugs of ale.

The inn, if such it might be called, was ancient. The stone-flagged floor underfoot was worn and polished by much use and a corner of the wall was old, too. Someone at a much later date had added the rest.

Angus stamped a foot on the floor. "Old!" he said.

"Aye," the innkeeper said. "Roman, they say. Not many came this far. They found the Scots too hard for them. Too hard by far."

We ate, straining our ears to make out the muttered conversation between the others. From time to time they looked at us, but in no friendly or curious fashion. Rather, it was suspicion. We could make out nothing of what they were saying, but when the chance came I eased my staff across my knees, ready to hand.

One whom we took to be a soldier stared hard at us and then said suddenly, " 'Tis not many come this way."

Angus wiped his mouth with the back of his hand. "Aye! Nor would I, but the lad returns home, and I am showing him the way. It was a promise made in an ill-thought moment," he added, smiling. "His father did me a kindness more than once, and now he is gone."

"Dead?"

"Aye! Killed in the Irish wars. He was a Scot whom they settled there, and there the lad was born and raised until his family were killed. We escaped together, and now when he is safely among his own folk, I shall off to the sea again."

"You be a sailorman?"

"Sailed with Hawkins. Two voyages to the Indies, trading and fighting, and the last time a prisoner in Spain. But Sir John looks after his own and ransomed me out, and now when I've taken the lad north I shall be off to join him again." He paused, gulping down a swallow of ale. "There's talk that the Spanish are readying a great fleet of ships to go against England, so the fighting may be here, along our own coasts."

This was news indeed, and for a while we were forgotten in the talk bandied back and forth. Many in Scotland were not at all friendly to England but most of them liked the Spanish even less. Yet the comment had done what Angus intended and taken their minds from us.

They argued the effects of such an attack. Some thought Spain was too mighty for England to stand against, but others mentioned Hawkins, Martin Frobisher, and mariners noted for their skill at sea fighting.

"There's another, too," Angus Fair suggested. "The name is Drake, Francis Drake. He sailed with Hawkins and made a name for himself among Hawkins's men. He is a man to be reckoned with."

"Ah," the innkeeper said gloomily, "England is but a small nation, and Spain is the greatest upon the world's seas. England will have no chance, none at all!"

We finished our meal, and I listened to the fury of the wind outside and the rain lashing against the shutters. It was a bitter bad night without, and the walls and fire were a comfort.

We finished our meal and I looked longingly at the floor near the fire, but knew it was not for me. Others had come first. Yet I drew my coat about me and huddled closer, fighting the chill at my back.

From outside there suddenly came a clatter and a banging and then the door was thrown open in a gust of howling wind that set the flames a-roaring on the hearth. In the wide open door stood a huge man wrapped in a sheepskin cloak, the leather side outside, and a great fur cap now sodden with rain. He had a red beard and bushy brows of red, and there was a great scar on his cheekbone partly hidden by the beard.

He stepped into the room, and even against that mighty wind he slammed the door so it shook the house. Without a word he strode to the fire. The men pulled back abruptly, although he said no word. He swept off his sheepskin and dropped it over a cask in the corner.

"Ale!" he said, and his voice boomed harshly in the small room.

Then he sat down with his back to the room and extended his big hands to the fire.

I stared at those huge hands. A finger was missing from one, two nails were gone from another. There were scars upon both hands, yet their power was obvious. The soldiers, who had appeared so threatening a few moments before, huddled back from him, eyes averted.

He carried a claymore, which was a huge two-handed sword, and a dagger as well. Seeing some apples on the table, he reached over and took one of them, turning it in his fingers. Then he drew the blade, lay the apple upon the back of his left hand and with a single deft stroke, hacked it in two without scratching his hand. That blade was obviously razor-sharp. But it was not the sharpness that drew my eyes but the serrated back edge of the blade. The blade itself was wide and strong, but that serrated edge made the knife what was known as a sword-breaker, for a blade caught in the notches could with a deft twist of the wrist be broken, snapped right off. I had heard of such knives, but never seen their like. My father had told me of fighting men skilled in their use.

The big man—and he would have made two of Angus—ate his apple, the crunching loud in a room where, but for the fire, a silence had fallen.

The innkeeper came with a great mug of ale, and

the big man took it and drank it half-empty at a draught. He glanced around the room then, impaling each of us with a glance that told him all he wished to know. His eyes lingered longest upon me as if for some reason I struck a discordant note. It frightened me, for it was as if he saw all that I was and who I was with that single glance. He said nothing, finishing his ale and calling for food.

He looked around suddenly at the innkeeper. "What distance to Ayr? I have gone that way but it has been long since."

"By the track . . . belike thirty mile. I have not gone so far, m'self."

Angus spoke quietly, almost as if to himself. "It is our road, too."

The big man stared at him.

"We seek a boat there," he said, "to the high coast of Scotland, or to the Isle of Lewis."

"We shall go together, then," the big man said, and thrust his mug out for more ale. "Before the break of day, if you walk with me."

———

SWEET WAS THE walking in the gray time of dawning, sweet the smell of rain-fresh grass and the dark loom of gray granite above the green, with here and there a darker shrub. It was the land I loved where no people were, only us walking and no talk among us for a long time.

The rain had gone but the clouds hung low, heavy with promise and warning. We walked on, matching our strides to his as well as we could, leaving the inn behind us and pleased that it be behind. A dark bird flashed across flying low, and a moor stallion lifted his heavy-maned head and stared at us from a quarter of a mile off, then tossed his head and walked a few steps toward us as if in challenge. I had no trouble for him; he was a noble beast and understood the sweet wine of freedom, which he drank deep on these lonely moors with the Highlands rising up nearby.

When we had walked a good hour into the morning the big man looked over at me and said, "You seek Fergus MacAskill?"

Surprised, I looked at him. "I do."

"And for what reason?"

"I have trained with the sword. I wish to be the best swordsman in the world, and I once thought I had been well taught by my father and a gypsy named Kory. Then I fought a lad but four years older than myself, and he beat me badly. He bested me at every turn. I would learn more, and they have said that Fergus MacAskill comes of a long line of fighting men, and that he is the greatest of swordsmen."

"You wish to go back and beat that one who bested you?"

"Yesterday I did. Today it is less important. What I wish is that it not happen again, with another than he, or even with himself, if we should meet again. And I think we shall."

"He had a name?"

"Leckenbie, Rafe Leckenbie."

"Ah!"

"You know him?"

"I do not. But Tuesday he killed a man at Kirkcudbright. I saw him there, and he was good, he was very good, and he was fighting a man whom I knew."

He looked at me. "You are alive; therefore you are no novice." We walked on. "It was said that he had killed four men before this, one of them a soldier at Carlisle, another a Danish swordsman at Berwick-upon-Tweed."

We walked along. "You are very young, but you are strong for a lad. I will see what we can do."

"You will teach me?"

"Is it not what you want? I am Fergus MacAskill."

CHAPTER 14

WE SET OUT for Ayr with the sun not yet up, and I doubt not there would have been trouble had it not been for Fergus MacAskill, for there had been those about the inn who liked us not.

Now he strode out upon the path and we walked beside or followed, as the way permitted. The man had massive shoulders, not only broad but thick with muscle, yet I hesitated over his swordsmanship. A claymore is a cut-and-slash blade, and a man with such power in him would be mighty indeed with such a blade. Yet it was the art of fence in which I was interested, as it was taught in the Italian towns or France, and somewhat in Spain. Could such a man have the delicacy to handle a rapier or a thrusting sword?

Ayr was a bustling place when we arrived, and it was nightfall when we came into the streets. Sore tired we were, and hungered, too, for it had been little enough we'd had in the dawning and naught throughout the day.

Angus Fair was a careful man, and in this town I saw him more so. He came to a halt inside the town. "Best I leave you here," he said. "There may be those about who seek me, and I would not involve you in my troubles."

"Aye," MacAskill agreed. "I would not have the lad embroiled in troubles not of his seeking, and I think he does not need questions now. The inn to which we go will ask no questions, but do you come along, after we enter. Do you speak quietly to Murray, who is host there. Speak for the room at the back. He will know at once what you wish, and it will cost you a bit more. But if those come who seek you there is a window over the back and an easy way down. Beyond that there is a narrow place between the stable and the brewing room and you may go through into a lane. Hold to it. Below lies the Doon, and not far off, is the Brig o' Doon, but if you wish there are boats. Take one, but do you leave it at Dunure. Yon's a fishing village, a small place with the harbor silting now. There'll be an old place by the waterside with two lanterns, one high, one low. Do you tie the boat below the high lantern and go your way."

"It seems," I said, "you have been this way before."

"Aye, lad, and not even a mouse trusts himself to one hole only. The inn is a safe place, with a half-dozen ways for a man to escape without being seen. There are smugglers an' such come there, and many who would not be seen too well, and I among them."

"But you are a man who could not be unseen!" I protested. "There are not two like you in the world!"

" 'Tis a broad place, the world. I doubt not there's a double for every man, somewhere about. But 'tis true. Not many have my size, and I am a known man. All I can do is keep myself from sight, for there be those who hunt me down."

He put a hand on my shoulder. "We've enemies, you and me, and not a few that seek us. I've a place yon on Lews ... the Isle of Lewis some do call it, but

Lews to me. I've a place there, and we will go there and listen to the gulls of a morning, and perhaps a lark in the afternoon, and we'll work a bit wi' the blades, you an' me."

He looked at me suddenly. "You've a face not to be forgotten, lad, so we must do something about showing you how to make it different. Although you'll find few enemies in Scotland, I'm thinking."

TATTON CHANTRY! WHAT a name it is! Someday you must tell me how you came by it, but there's no need now. Although," he added, "I'd have believed you had enemies enough without adding to them."

What he meant by that I did not know, but we'd come to the door of the inn, so I asked no question then.

We went down four steps and then took a turn to the right. Down three more he opened a heavy door and we entered.

It was a wide room, long and low-beamed. All was dark except for the fire upon the wide hearth and a low candle burning here and there. A dozen folk were in the place, men mostly but a woman or two also, and they looked around as the wind guttered their candlelight and the fire.

There was an empty table near the fire and I wondered if they had known he was coming, but he crossed and seated himself on the bench by it. A man brought ale for each of us, and then came again with slices of thick meat and bread which we broke in our hands.

Nobody spoke to us although all looked, and then

they went on with their eating, drinking, and gambling. It was not a place where men wished to be remembered.

As we ate I looked about. The floor was of stone flags, the walls were of stone also, and there were several doors, all closed but that to the kitchen and taproom. Some pots were on the fire, and there was a good smell of broiling meat, too, as a chunk of beef turned on a spit.

He who brought the bread leaned over and whispered, and I dimly heard. "Tammy is by the boat this hour, Fergus," he whispered. "He stands ready."

"We will be there."

The man put the bread over a bit toward me and took a quick glance at me. "Remember the lad well," Fergus said. "He is my friend."

"Aye . . . there have been some about not your friends, too."

The door opened again and I looked around, as did the others. It was Angus Fair. He looked not our way but went to a corner away from the fire.

We ate, and I had not known how hungry I was. Fergus looked at my hands. "You've good hands, lad. I think we will make a swordsman of you."

"MacAskill?" I said. "Are you not allied to the MacLeod?"

"That we be! And when the clan goes to battle there's ever a MacAskill in the forefront. Do you know the clans then?"

"Only a bit. My father knew of them and had some connection . . . I know not what."

"Y' know then the story o' the Fairy Flag? Many a way has it been told but the one I like the best is that the fourth Lady MacLeod, hearing a sound in her baby son's room, went in to find a lovely lady in filmy green who was lulling the baby to sleep. The lady in green vanished but left behind the flag. It was said to be a gift from Titania, queen of the fairies, and to be flown but three times, when the MacLeods were in dire need. By flying it they can call the fairies and all the powers of sky and forest to their aid."

"And have they ever?"

"Twice... at the battle of Glendale in 1490 and Waternish in 1580... just a few years back, that one. Each time the MacLeods needed a victory and each time they won. Some say they have one more time, then the flag will vanish as it came."

"My father told me the tale, only he said it was to be used when victory was needed in battle, when the heir was in danger, or when the clan faced extinction. But no matter, 'tis a fine tale."

"Aye... and a true one I am thinking. But it has other attributes, too, for they say that thrown on the marriage bed it brings children, and flown from the tower it will bring the fish up the loch."

Glancing around, I saw that Angus Fair had vanished. His empty glass was upon his table, but he was nowhere about.

Fergus MacAskill noticed my glance. "Gone," he said, "and well may he be, for there be spies here sometimes, too." He studied me, swallowed a gulp of ale, and put his glass down. "You're tall, lad, and strong. I'd have judged you two years older. We'll go to the shore soon and have a word with Tammy. If it is safe to go to Lews, we'll go, and if not, to Skye... there are MacAskills in both places, and on the Isle of Man they be some.

"We be Vikings long since... hundreds of years ago when Leod the son of Olav the Black came down and made a home in the Western Isles. Since then there's been much of marriage with the Celts, and with the Picts, too, if all be told."

The door opened and three men came in. I saw them come and felt something within me turn icy cold. For one of them I knew.

"Fergus...?" I whispered.

"I see them, lad. D' you know them, then?"

"The tall one...the one with the white-blond hair... he was among them who killed my father."

"Did he see you then?"

"A glimpse only, I think. I'm a good inch taller now, maybe two, and thicker and stronger, and a good deal more brown from walking the highroads."

They were coming toward us, weaving a way past the others. Fergus MacAskill held up his glass in his left hand. "Ale!" he said loudly.

Several men who sat about lifted their glasses, each with his glass in his left hand. Each called out, "Ale!"

The man with the blond hair almost missed a step. He looked about quickly as if he sensed something awry, something amiss. Then he came on.

"Fergus MacAskill?" he asked, but he looked at me.

"Aye, that be the name."

"Are you coming or going?"

MacAskill smiled. "Why, now. That depends on where a man stands, does it not? If a man is here I might be going, and if a man be on Lews, he might say I am coming."

"Is this your son?"

"My son? Ah, I wish he were! A fine lad. They raise

them well in Scotland these days, and they keep the Scotch well to them even when schooled abroad as is the lad here. I be taking him home to the clan."

"He's a MacLeod?"

"A MacLeod? Ah, no! Ken y' not the face of him? 'Tis no MacLeod. He's a MacCrimmon! He's come back to learn the pipe, for are not the greatest pipers of all the MacCrimmons?"

"The lad does look familiar." The blond man stared at me. "I have seen him before."

"Why not? Y've seen MacCrimmons before, and he has the look of them. Aye, if y've seen one MacCrimmon y've seen them all ... all, I say! But he's a good lad."

"I am not yet sure, but I think—"

"A MacCrimmon, I say! The favorite pipers o' the MacLeods, and right now there be a hundred MacLeods i' the town, and a dozen i' the place, and never a one but would shed blood to protect a MacCrimmon!"

———

Y OU!" THE BLOND man pointed a finger at me. "I have questions for you. Come!"

"Too bad it is," MacAskill spoke cheerfully, "y' didna come sooner, but we've no' the time." He arose to his full height, and I got up, too. The blond man was tall and strong but not so much as Fergus MacAskill. "We've just been having a bite while waiting, and now's the time."

"Stay!" The blond man put up a hand. "I am an officer of the Queen. I do not believe this lad is a MacCrimmon."

Fergus dropped a hand to his sword. "Do y' doubt what I say, then?"

The blond man stood very still. I had no doubt he was a brave man, but to fight Fergus MacAskill was certain death. He knew it, and he hesitated. MacAskill was of no mind to push the matter.

"Very well, then." Fergus took a step back. "Let us not make much of a small thing."

The blond man looked around him, suddenly aware that a dozen men were on their feet, staring at him, each with a hand on a blade.

He looked hard at me. "We shall see each other again," he said, bowing slightly. "I look forward to the meeting!"

"And I," I replied, bowing also. I jerked my thumb to indicate MacAskill. "When my guardian is not here to protect you!"

He had taken a step away; now he turned sharply around, his hand on his sword. I made as if to draw mine from its sheath, but Fergus MacAskill put up a hand. "No, lad, he must wait his turn. You have others to deal with first!"

With that he put a firm hand on my shoulder and thrust me toward the door, and I went. As we left, several men closed in behind us, not as if doing anything but talking or holding their glasses for drinks; nonetheless, the way was effectually blocked. Not one could be said to have offered resistance; they simply got in the way.

Outside in the dark, MacAskill spoke quietly but firmly. "That was a foolish thing to do! We were safely out of it, and then you had to challenge the man. You must learn, lad, that while such a man can evade some issues he will never avoid a direct challenge.

"That man was Dett Kober, and as he said, he is an officer of the Queen. He is also, I might add, a superb swordsman."

"But he was afraid of you!" I said.

"No, lad, not afraid. Simply wise. He saw the number of those who stood about him, and the issue was not great enough. Had he been absolutely sure you were whom he believed you to be, he would have fought. Now he will simply wait ... and watch. As he said, there will be another time."

We walked along through dark lanes to the shore. The boat lay waiting. When we were aboard, the sail was unloosed and soon we were well out upon the water.

"He saw you," Fergus commented, thoughtfully, "but he was not in search of you. It was some other he searched for."

Angus, I thought. He was looking for Angus Fair, but Angus had gone before he entered. Or at least I believed he had. And well away, I hoped.

Wrapped in a cloak Fergus handed me, I was soon asleep, liking the smell and taste of the wind, and the salt water that occasionally spattered over the bow. Where was it we were going? To Lews or to Skye?

When next I opened my eyes the sea was rolling heavily and it had grown colder. The wind blew strong, and MacAskill huddled near me, wrapped in his sheepskin. After a while I fell again to sleep, tired from my long walking and much worry.

When I opened my eyes at last the dawn was in the sky. Dark and shadowed were the waters where we lay, silent but for the lap of waves against the hull, and against the rocks not far off. The shore was only a little way over there, but the water between us was cold . . . cold.

I looked toward the shore, and could see only the darkness and the bold outline of a cliff.

How could I guess that it would be a year before I left this place?

CHAPTER 15

THE DWELLING TO which we came was a crofter's hut on Loch Langaig, and a comfortable place it was, seeming as old as the Isle of Skye itself. I had believed it was Lews we were bound for, but MacAskill made a change of direction. We arrived in the cold gray of a rain-filled morning.

Weary from our voyage, we slept until the sun was high. Then no longer to be denied the sense of where I was, I went outside to look around.

It was a place of foxglove and bracken where black rushes lined the water of the loch and birds flew low over the rocky shores.

A good place it was, a quiet place and a hidden place, for no other crofts were near, only wild lands, unbroken by the plow. The cottage itself was built in a hollow of the land so that only the thatch of the roof could be seen from a short distance off.

"D' you like it, lad?" Fergus MacAskill had come from the hut behind me.

"Aye, a lovely place it is. This is your home, then?"

"From time to time. A man with enemies should not abide too long in one place."

"Are the MacAskills of Skye?"

"Some live over on Lews, as well. It is said that long ago we lived on Man, and were of Viking blood, coming from the north to raid this coast, then settling here. We are restless folk, born to the sea and wild lands. Often of a night, lying awake, I think I shall go off to America and find a home there."

"There are savages in America, they say."

"Aye, and no doubt they are no worse than we, lad. In my time I have seen a sight of fighting and killing, and not a little of murder, although I've fought no man unfairly, m'self. No part of the world, I'm thinking, has a sole claim on savagery. There's a bit of it in us all, given the time and place and circumstance."

"It is said some of our people did go, long since."

"Aye ... Brendan from your island and Sinclair from ours."

An old woman appeared from the bracken as though rising from it, and I saw for the first time a path there. She spoke to Fergus and her Gaelic held a wild, strange sound unlike any I'd heard, but pleasant to the ear. It set me to thinking of the bagpipes sounding across the moors.

She went within and I stood watching the gray-lag geese flying low across the marshes. It was a wild place, a lonely place but marvelously green and secret.

"We will have some'at to eat soon, Tatt, and then we will get to it."

"Why do you trouble yourself with me?" I asked. "Grateful it is that I am, but why?"

He stared out across the loch, then kicked a small pebble at his feet. "You can ask, lad, and well you should, but the reasons are more than one and I'll not trouble you with them all.

"I like a fighter, let it be that at first. I have fought beside the Irish and found them strong men and willing, and once, too, a man took time with me when I knew nothing and was but a lonely lad, not unlike you. There's another reason, stronger than all else, but I'll not tell you now—only this.

"I know who you are, Tatton Chantry, and know that is none of your name. What your true name is I shall not say but that I know it, and there's a blood link between us, long ago though it be.

"There's still another thing. I am a lonely man with neither chick nor child, and no wife to my bed, nor proper home. I am a man feared and respected, yet a man with nothing. Once I wished I might have a son like you, with your fine shoulders and fine way of standing, with your clear eyes and the decency in you . . . but that was in another land, and the one who might have been . . . well, I'll say no more."

"My father is dead. I would be honored to be your son, Fergus MacAskill."

He put a rough hand on my shoulder. "Lad, lad, I've tears in my eyes! You'll make a woman of Fergus MacAskill, with tears and all. My adopted son then, Tatt. Let us get our blades now and have at it."

With his great hands and the strength of him I'd not have believed he could handle a foil as he did, but it took me but a moment to sense that here was a master. My skill, which I had thought great, and which Kory had thought great as well, was as nothing here. He had the reach of me, and the height, too, but it was the skill that made the difference.

For an hour we fenced, and he tried me in all ways, saying little at first, feeling me out, testing my responses, leading me into attack and defense with consummate skill. Then we put up our blades and went inside for a draught of ale and the gruel and meat the old woman had put on for us. There was thick cream, too, from those wild Highland cattle, all red they were, and maned like lions, with a fine breadth of horn upon them.

"You do well," Fergus said, "and you have been well taught...to a point. You have a strong wrist for your size and you are cool. We'll work with the rapier for a bit, and then with the claymore.

"For that we'll need stronger hands than you have. Although you've fine shoulders, we can make them better." He took a bite of the coarse black bread and looked up from under his brows. "Can you use a longbow? A weapon of bygone times now, but a good one still, and one easily provided for yourself."

"A little, I've used them," I said, "and a sling and quarterstaff as well."

"Good! We shall have a time, we two."

And so it was.

A month passed, then two and three. We fenced, boxed, and walked upon the shores and the mountains. Together we climbed the Storr and walked the high ridges and went down into the black gorges. Sometimes we walked in sunlight and sometimes in the deepest fog. At times MacAskill would leave me to my own devices and be gone a day or two, then he'd come back.

One morning when we drank our ale, he indicated the glass. "Be sparing with that, lad. I drink, but unlike many of those about, I am never drunken. When I have my wits about me I feel I can handle any man, or any circumstance, but when a man's wits are foggy he will do foolish things. I saw one of the greatest swordsmen killed by a mere lad because he had indulged too much, drinking wine until the small hours. He was unsteady, unsure, and his skill was off, although he'd not believe it when we warned him. He died when he need not."

There were days when we stayed quiet about the cottage, for there was a feud raging between the MacDonalds and the MacLeods, and much blood was lost. "When the time comes, Tatt," he said, "I shall fight. Until then let them be at it and leave me alone. There has been enough of killing.

"All about us, in this place called Trotternish, which is a northern arm of Skye, the MacLeods once held the land, then the MacDonalds took it from them by force of arms.

"It has ever been so. The strong move in and occupy land as they will. All across the world it has been thus. It is the way of the world, Tatt. When I was a lad I thought little of such things, but as I grew older the why of things worried my thoughts like a dog worries a bone.

"We MacAskills are the descendants of Vikings, who raided down from the north, as I have said, and we wedded women of the isles: the Gaels they were. Much did I talk in the dark hours with men of wisdom and warriors met from other lands, and everywhere it was the same.

"The men of the north wanted warmer, richer lands, the men of poor cities wanted the wealth of the rich, and so they came raiding and looting, then finally settling down to be raided in their turn. So it will be in the new lands beyond the sea, and so it has been in those lands long before any white man came upon them.

"Long ago when I was but a lad we took a Spanish vessel on the high seas, and brought her a prize to Skye. Aboard that vessel was a great Spanish lord and my father held him for ransom, as is the custom.

"We waited months for the ransom to come, and I spent many hours with the prisoner, for he lived as one of our own family. He told me of Cortez and his conquering of the Aztec peoples. He said Cortez could never have done it had it not been for Indian allies, tribes recently conquered by the Aztecs, who hated them.

"The Aztecs lived in great cities of stone, but those cities were built or begun by other peoples who came before. The Toltecs, for example, and others even before them.

"So you see, Tatt, we hold this land only for a time. Whether we win it in peace or war, we hold it only in trust for other peoples, and other generations.

"When I was a wild lad I thought only of the sword and of fighting. I loved the wild raids, the fierce attacks, the crossing of blades. It mattered little who it was I fought; the fight itself was the thing.

"Yet with time I have grown wiser. I still like the battle—it is in my blood—but I also question myself, and try to learn from others. A soldier in a lifetime meets many kinds of people, and so it has been with me."

I had listened in silence, but now I had a question for him.

"But if the MacDonalds hold Trotternish, how does it happen that you can be here, when you are of the MacLeods?"

"Oh, they let me be! Perhaps they think me not worth the trouble, for I am seldom here. They know when I am here, and they know when I come and go, but they walk a wide circle.

"Afraid? Not the MacDonalds. I know them too well to think they fear. I have shed MacDonald blood, and this they know, yet I believe they like me a little and think perhaps I am better left alone.

"Someday . . . ah, someday one of them may come seeking me. One or many. It is to be expected."

We fenced and fought with this weapon and that, and I could feel my skill growing, and my confidence. He was a great master. Whenever I seemed ready to equal him he uncovered a new trick, a new stratagem, a new device. His eyes would twinkle a little, and he would look at me slyly, enjoying the moment.

There came a night when we sat by the fire. Food was eaten, the dishes put aside, and there was rain upon the roof. Occasionally a gust of wind whined under the eaves. Firelight played on MacAskill's cheekbones, his shaggy brows, and the old scar.

"Aye," he said, "there have been bloody times. D'you ken the Isle of Eigg? 'Tis yonder." He gestured toward the south. "A few years back some MacLeod lads, denied the hospitality of the MacDonalds, butchered a beef upon the shore, but before they could flee they were come upon by the MacDonalds, who whipped them brutally.

"Norman, he who was the eleventh chief of the MacLeods, sent out his fleet. The MacDonalds, seeing themselves outnumbered, took their whole population into a cave and hid themselves. This was in 1577, if I recall. The MacLeods searched but could not find them and were sailing away when one of the MacDonalds, impatient to see had they gone, came from the cave and was seen.

"They tracked him by new-fallen snow, and when the MacDonalds would not come out, the MacLeods gathered brush and seaweed from shore and hill and placed it before the opening and set fire to it. All inside were smothered and killed. Not a one of the nearly four hundred survived."

"Was that an end to it then?"

"Is it ever? Ah, Tatt, we are a vengeful people, we Scots! The MacDonalds waited and they watched and they lurked about, wanting a chance for vengeance. It came on a Sunday morning. They slipped into the bay under the cover of a fog and they barred the door of the church which was filled with MacLeods and then they put a fire to the church and burned them alive, all but one woman who somehow escaped.

"Word had reached Dunvegan Castle where the MacLeods had gathered. Ah, how I remember that day! I was there, mind. I saw it with my own eyes, and did some of the killing that was done, too, for I lost a friend or two in that burning church, and a girl who . . . well, no mind to that. I was there.

"Our galleys were swift, and the church took long to burn, and they stood about so that none might escape, beyond the one woman who did.

"Then when the church was down, and in embers and blackened stones, they took their loot and returned to their own boats. But they had reckoned without the tides, for their craft were beached high and dry by the ebb tide. And here were the MacLeods coming, and their Fairy Flag flying, too.

"I was the first man ashore, leaping from the bow

of our galley and rushing forward. An instant and I was alone, surrounded by MacDonalds, and my claymore was out and swinging as I charged into them!

"Then all the MacLeods were ashore and the MacDonalds fell back to the stone dyke protecting the shore lands from the sea. They put their backs to the wall and they faced us! Ah, what a fight that was!

"The MacDonalds were *men!* Fight them I did, but I hated them not a whit! I loved them for their strength and their valor, and the grand fight they made!

"It was sword and sword. I had cut two down in that first rush, but they had nicked me a time or two, and we set to it.

"In my time I have seen fights, but never a better one than there against the sea wall in the light of a waning day. Again and again they charged us, again and again we drove them back! Yes, we outnumbered them. We surely did, but before it was over I was glad for our numbers, although we cut them down, every man."

Again and again during the weeks that followed did MacAskill regale me with stories of the fighting between the clans, for they were a hardy and ferocious lot willing to fight at the drop of a hat, and to drop it themselves.

Several times we sailed to Lews, once to Eigg and to Rhum. I became more skillful at handling a boat in a rough sea. It was on one of these days, as we tied the boat after such a voyage, that I suddenly realized I was fifteen years old.

For months I had fenced, boxed, wrestled, walked, climbed, and sailed. The food we ate was simple, indeed. The life we lived was along the shore of the loch or on the sea itself, and I had grown, both in height and in strength. Immeasurably had I grown in skill.

The sunlight had gone from the loch that day, and the wind was picking a few whitecaps from the crests of the small waves. The reeds were bending and ripples ran through the grassland as it bent before the wind. I had come up from the loch with several fish, fresh caught from the cold water.

For a moment, as I often did, I stepped up on a small hillock near the cottage and looked over the moorland. It was then I saw him . . . a rider on a gray horse, mane and tail streaming in the wind, the horse coming fast, weaving and turning to avoid obstructions of rocks or clumps of heather.

"Fergus!" I called it, not too loud, but above the wind.

He came to the door, book in hand.

"A rider," I said, "and he comes with grief and danger in his arms."

He came up beside me. "Aye," he said, "when they come that fast it is always trouble. Gather what you will take, lad, for we will be going now!"

CHAPTER 16

HUDDLED FOR WARMTH we were, a hard wind blowing and the shortened sail frozen stiff, with a strong sea running. The blown spray was like icy needles against exposed flesh. We had no means with which to war against wind and sea but could only ride them and keep what hope we had for living.

The waves were like walls of black ice rolling down upon us, their crests broken like bared teeth and spray driven before them like hail. It was no place I wished to be and I could only think of the snug cot we'd left beside the loch, and a peat fire burning on the hearth.

Three fishermen were with us, for the boat was theirs, a boat built for these strong northern seas they lived upon. Yet I knew from their faces that our condition was not one to seek, but to fear.

The Scots and the Norwegians of the Shetland, Orkney and Hebrides islands had galleys, sixteen to twenty-four oars, and in war-time, three men to the oar. They had birlinns also, a smaller craft with twelve to sixteen oars. Our craft was none of these but a simple fisher's boat fit for riding rough seas with a cargo of fish. Now she was empty but for us.

No voice was raised for none could be heard above the wind, and we huddled together, clutching our useless swords and losing our hearts each time the boat dipped into a trough between the waves.

Southward we drove, with the shores of Scotland far and away to the east and on the west all the wide width of the Atlantic. Our fishermen knew the strength of wind and wave, and how to handle their boat. We slid steeply down the slope of one wave only to rise abruptly on the cliff of the next.

Fergus MacAskill sat beside me, staring grimly into the storm, his beard streaming with blown water, his face like that of a graven image, hard cut against the wind, his eyes bleak as the stormclouds above.

Sharply he leaned forward, staring into the storm drift that obscured all before and around us. Something ominous and dark loomed there, low down on the horizon.

MacAskill grasped a fisherman's arm, pointing. "Jura!" he shouted, and I knew the name for an island.

The fisherman bobbed his gray head. Pointing to the westward, he shouted another name I could not make out. I saw him fighting to point our bow toward the black mass.

I clung to the boat. Suddenly she seemed to be making a hard time of it and I sensed that something was wrong. The fishermen began scooping water from the bottom and tossing it by the board, but I saw no sense to it for the next moment a great wave would leave us as full as before.

She felt soggy, and slower to rise, her buoyancy gone. We seemed to be tangled in something or caught in some underwater wreckage or mass of seaweed.

Then, through a break in the clouds we saw the island looming near, what must be the northwest coast of Jura. Fergus MacAskill grasped my arm. In his hand he held a small sack which he thrust at me. When I tried to push it away he would have none of it, so I hid the sack in my clothes to argue another time.

He put his mouth to my ear and shouted. "Don't wait for her to strike! When we are closer ... *swim!*"

Swim? In *that?* I could only ask the question of myself. How far to shore? A half-mile and closing. There were rocks along the shore so far as I could see, but the visibility was poor.

The boat was down now, well down. The gunwales were awash, but whatever was beneath her held us fast. Looking up, I beheld a snarl of raging white water, tremendous combers crashing upon a shore with a thunder beyond belief.

We rose upon a giant wave and I then saw the shore, only a short distance away now, the wind shrieking and howling like all the banshees in hell. Suddenly Fergus grasped my arm. *"Now!"* he roared and, leaping up, he dove into the waves as two of the fishermen went with him. Only the old man sat still, and I, who had leaped up, grasped his arm. "Come!" I shouted.

He looked up and smiled, then shook his head.

And then the moment was past. The backwash of a great wave carried us away. I started to jump, then realized we were even further out now. Wind and current, by some trickery of the sea, were carrying us further out and down the coast. I crouched beside the aged man, clutching his thin old arm.

Too late! The moment had come and they had seized it, and I like a fool had hesitated. Only the old man was calm, no doubt resigned to death. Either he could not swim or he lacked the strength, so chose to sink with the boat or ride with it, and now I had no choice but to accompany him.

Yet it was not in me to sit, to yield. I must see and do. Rising, I lunged toward the mast and linked an arm about it, staring into the storm. The wind ripped at my clothes and body with brutal fingers, yet I clung. Glancing down, I saw the old man's fingers move, so he was yet alive. We were afloat—at least we seemed to have ceased to sink—and being carried by the sea off to what seemed the southwest, yet now the waves were again sweeping us toward the shore.

A great gulf or bay opened to the southward and I saw enormous waves hurrying one after the other into that vast maw, as if the gulf were swallowing the sea in great gulps.

The old man was almost shoulder deep in the water. I clung; one arm wrapped around the mast, but squatting, I reached for him. He did not resist but came up beside me. He said something, shaping the sounds with his lips, but the wind robbed me of their meaning.

The shore was rushing upon us now, or we upon it, and I clung hard, both to the mast and to the old man. Suddenly the waves seemed to lift us and throw us bodily upon the shore. We landed with a crash, thrown clear of the boat and sprawled breathless on the gravelly shore.

Scrambling to my feet, I grasped the old man and lifted him to the grass above the reach of the sea, then I rushed back to what remained of our boat and its pile of weed.

The sea was rushing in again and there was but a moment. With a wild grab I caught up my sword and my bundle. I was searching for the bundle Fergus had brought but was too late. The sea tore it from my grasp and the wreckage of the boat was again carried back upon the waves.

I found the old man lying at the edge of the machair and helped him to his feet. Together we staggered back over the wildflowers and grass, our only thought to escape still further from the clutching fingers of the sea.

We paused then, gasping to catch our breath. The old man suddenly grasped my arm, pointing. Horsemen were riding toward us.

"Speak no word of MacAskill!" he warned hoarsely. "These be MacDonalds, and enemies to the clan! We are of Ireland, and cast away by the sea!"

We stood waiting, and I was glad that I carried a sword.

There were five of them, and they rode swiftly up. One was a fierce old man with flowing hair and a beard, the others younger, two scarcely more than boys.

"What land is this?" I asked.

"It is Islay," one of the younger boys said, pronouncing it "Ila."

"Ah? It is not Jura?"

"Jura is the next island, just yonder," he said. He was about my own age, but not so tall. He studied me curiously. "Where are you for?"

"Oban," I lied, yet not quite a lie, for eventually we would have reached there. "Then on across and to France."

"To school? Do you study there?"

"Aye," I said, for did I not study everywhere? "And mayhap to find a place in the army."

"Who are you then?" He was the old man with the beard, a strong, fine old man.

"Tatton Chantry, and I am of Ireland. This old man is a fisherman who was taking me yon when the storm took us. Our boat was wrecked, and all I have is about me."

"You saved your sword," the old man said. His eyes were sharp and I felt he missed nothing.

"Aye," I said dryly, "for a man without a sword on a strange shore ... or anywhere ... who is he?"

"Can you use it, then?"

"A bit," I said. "I wish to learn."

"Donal," the bearded man said, "do you take him behind you. And Charles, do you take the other. We'll see no man hunger upon our shore."

" 'Our'? You still call it that?" said Donal. " 'Tis no longer ours, and we've no' the right to be here, as you'll see if we come upon any of *them*."

"We'll not," the old man replied easily, "they be far from here—as we have been told. So we'll get what we came for and be off."

"And what of them?" Charles asked.

The old man looked at us again. "We'll take them wi' us. They'll not speak of what they see." He looked at me. "Will you now, Tatton Chantry?"

"I will see the way to Oban and your faces, and will remember how you found us upon the sea."

"Well spoken! We'll be off, then!"

We rode swiftly inland over the machair. I could see the blue of a lake, and then we circled and came back to where some gray stones lay.

One of the men swung down and made as if to dig. "Hold fast!" The bearded man spoke sharply. "Cut the turf in squares, and when we have what we want, put it carefully back so that no man may know what we find here."

He looked hastily around. "Scatter out and keep alert. We'll want no visitors now!"

With the others, I helped keep watch, yet from time to time I glanced around. The digging was done with care, the turf taken out in great blocks. I heard the shovel grate upon something metallic, and then a chest was lifted from the earth. Dirt was wiped from it and it was lifted to a horse's back. The horse was a powerful one, evidently brought for the purpose, yet he had no liking for the heavy burden. Then the turf was replaced and we started swiftly off. The others glanced back again and again.

"I had heard this was MacDonald earth," I said.

"Aye," the bearded old man replied grimly, "it was once so. Yet now the Campbells have it and I blame them not for taking what they could get, and making sure they kept it. Yet in my eyes it will be MacDonald land forever!"

We rounded a great pile of rock and came to a hidden cove. A boat lay there, and as we came into sight the men on board put down a gangway that led to the shore. Soon the horses were aboard, and ourselves with them.

Staggering with weariness, I found a corner away from the wind and lay down, and the old man with me. Not three hours had passed since we came ashore. The gale still raged out on the sea, yet we lay sheltered and waiting.

Donal came to me and squatted on his heels. "When it is dark we will sail. This is a hidden place and I think they will not come out whilst the storm blows." He gestured around him. "The wind blows fiercer up where you were, but the rain is less. Down where they are a storm blows hard."

"Where do you go?"

"We will take you to Oban, for it is our way, too." He lowered his voice. "Say naught of the chest. Only when my uncle died did we learn of it, left here long since by an ancestor of ours, and ours by right, too. Yet had it been known, they would have taken it also."

It seemed a long, long time that we waited and slowly the storm abated. I slept, awakened, and slept again, but the MacDonalds did not sleep. That they were worried was obvious, for to be trapped here could well mean their death. Among some of the clans there was friendship, among others only bitter enmity.

When I awakened we were at sea. The night was dark, the wind had died down, the sea was still making great waves, but our boatmen were skillful, and already the shore was only a dark line behind us. The clouds had broken and a few scattered stars could be seen.

Donal came to where I stood by the rail. "What of the others?" he asked. "You two were not alone?"

"There were three, I think. They were sailing to Oban and were willing to take me. I believe the old man was related to one of them. Orkneymen, I think."

"What will you do in Oban?"

"I shall go to France at once. Already I am over late

because of this. Perhaps I shall ride, but if there is a boat, I shall take it."

We stood together, watching the rise and fall of the seas. Morning was not far away. After a bit I walked back to the old man, who now sat up.

"I should have died there but for you," he said.

"I did nothing."

"You were strong when I had forgotten how good it was to live. You gave me the strength I needed." He paused. "You are truly Irish, are you not?"

"I am."

"It is a fair, green land. Long ago when the barbarians swept over the lands on the Continent, it was Ireland which preserved the torch of knowledge. They kept burning the lights."

"You do not speak like a fisherman."

"I am not. I am a pilgrim."

"To the shrines of God?"

"To the shrines of learning, of whatever kind. I seek for the old places, the forgotten places. The places where the great stones are."

"The standing stones? There are many in Ireland. My father often took me to where they are."

"Ah? And his name was Chantry?"

When I did not respond he said, "I see. And did he speak to you of those places? Had he knowledge of them?"

"That some of them were built long before the great pyramids of Egypt. Scholars had been born and died in Ireland long before the first pyramid was built. He told me that, and he showed me their tombs. Some were buried near the Boyne . . . I mean in the land it drains."

"Your father was a wise man. He studied much?"

"Always, and in the old books. He had many of them until our home was burned."

"Ah, yes. It is the way of fools to destroy that which could save them. That which they do not understand. And did your father teach you from these books?"

"He taught me . . . some things. He said there was much more to come, but that is true always. The well of learning is one that never ceases to flow and we have only to drink of its waters."

"It is well said. You will learn, Tatton Chantry, that all across the world there are men of learning, and they share common goals. No matter what the prejudices and prides of smaller men, these will go forward, learning, sharing, doing what they can.

"There are races and nations of men, but the land of learning has no boundaries, neither here nor in the heavens. We are guided by the lamp of curiosity, the light of desiring to know. Follow it, Tatton Chantry, for your destiny lies that way."

He paused. "Out there when I was near to dying I almost forgot the value of living, for I have not left anything of myself in the world; I have only learned. Each of us must leave a little behind to make easier the path of those who follow.

"Someday you will know, but there are in far corners of the world vast repositories of knowledge, places where books are stored and dreams are held waiting. Some have been destroyed . . . the libraries of Alexandria and Córdoba, the temples of Samothrace . . . these are gone. Others remain. Somewhere there is a niche for what I have learned."

"Come with me then," I said. "I go to London, then to France and Italy."

"What is it you want?"

"Knowledge...skill with a sword...and wealth enough to return and rebuild the home I lost. It was my father's wish. And it is mine, also."

He was quiet for a time, as if thinking. "Well, I will come with you to London. Perhaps we each can show the other a way to go."

A door had opened...a door that would never again be closed....

CHAPTER 17

B Y WHAT MEANS I should make a fortune I knew not, yet it was in my mind to do so. What I had told before was true, that I wished to buy again the land my father had owned and to rebuild his house, burned by our enemies.

To accomplish this would be no easy thing, for above all they must not guess I was my father's son, and one of that family they hated. But that was the least of my problems. The first was to obtain the wherewithal to even live, to exist.

Although I was but a lad, my travels had changed me more than a little. I had grown taller, stronger, and more agile. Also, I had grown wiser. I determined to pass myself off as older than I was, for in this way I might obtain preferment, or at least respectable attention.

Yet what was I to do? I had no trade, no skills but that of swordsman, and no means by which to earn my way. I was not minded to become a thief or a rogue, but to remain a gentleman, in action as well as in origin.

The small sack Fergus MacAskill had thrust upon me contained gold, sufficient to last me until I obtained some sort of employment, and longer. I had a few coins of my own, left from my trading days, and so I had no immediate fear of starvation.

Thinking upon it, I discovered yet some hope from my experience, for had I not followed the byways and lanes as a trader? Traveling with the old man, I had learned much, and now I might, discreetly, put the knowledge into practice. I suspected there was a deal of money to be made by buying and selling in a modest way. First, I must find a haven, a small harbor of security where I could take the time to look about, to avoid the press gangs which haunted the streets searching for men to man the Queen's navy. I must see into what niche I might fit myself.

This old man seemed to know the London streets. He led the way to a small tavern in a cul-de-sac off Chancery Lane, not far from Fleet Street. "It is a place little known," he explained, "and does not wish to be known. There are a few of us who frequent the place, and the custom we provide is sufficient."

"It is an odd keeper of an inn," I commented, "who does not wish to better himself."

"This man is well off, and those who provide his custom do not wish attention, but rather to remain unnoticed. In such a city there are men who come and go upon errands of their own."

There was a common room with a great fireplace and several tables and benches for those who came to drink and dine. There was a door that led to a hall where there were rooms, and a winding stair, very narrow, that led to rooms above.

The host was in the common room when we entered, otherwise the room was empty of people. He looked around but seemed in no wise surprised. I was sure he knew my companion but he made nothing of it.

"This one," my friend gestured to me, "is a friend. Make him welcome, whenever."

He sat upon a bench near the fire and I did likewise,

glad of the warmth for it was cold without. "I am Jacob Binns," he said, the first time I'd heard a name put to him that I could recall, "and this be Tatton Chantry, a young gentleman."

"They be calling me Tom," the host said, bowing slightly. "There be a room o'erlooking the street; would it please you?"

"It would, indeed, and now we'll have some'at to eat and drink."

Now I looked about me. Although small, the place had an air of comfort and well-being. Occasionally I noticed through the window that someone would go by outside, but it was not a busy place, hidden as it was by the taller buildings behind and around it.

"Long ago," Jacob Binns said, "this was a monastery. This floor and a part of the walls were of it, but additions were made and some of the old places walled up." He spoke softly that none might hear. "There are ways in and ways out, and much is hidden beneath the street."

"You are a puzzle," I said. "I believed you a honest fisherman."

"Honest, at any rate, and a fisherman when it suits me, but a pilgrim always."

"I do not wish to become involved," I said, "in any plots against the Queen. We in Ireland have been ill used, yet I wish for nothing so much as to be back, safe upon my native soil."

He shrugged a shoulder. "I am engaged in no plot. If what I do seems sometimes strange it is because what I am is beyond the ken. I travel much, but the shrines to which I make my pilgrimages are not those of God, nor of the devil. Someday, and in another time, you will know more of this, but for the now it is enough.

"You must waste no time, but choose a way for yourself, and it may be that I can help."

For three days then I roamed the city, learning a little of the streets and lanes, the taverns and the river front. Meanwhile I thought much upon what I might do. Surely there had never existed a more exciting town than London. Queen Bess, hard though she might be on my own people, was a good queen for her own and it was difficult not to be caught up in the contagion. The British had that spirit that comes to new nations or to those born anew, and all seemed possible, no dream seemed beyond realization.

Her ships were upon every sea, a challenge to the power of Spain. In all the streets and byways a new energy seemed alive in the people. But as always in such times, there was much crime. No man or woman was safe upon the streets, and all went armed and prepared. First, I had to know my way about, and to capture the language. Oh, yes! I spoke English and well, had spoken it all my life long, but I soon discovered there was a language of the streets that held words and expressions of which I had never heard. I went often to places where bards and actors went, to listen to their talk, and loitered along the lanes to pick up what I might. I haunted the bookstalls wherever they might be. Most of them were in Saint Paul's or close about it.

For all in London seemed to be learning, captured with a tremendous zest for knowledge that comes to growing, expanding countries. For a month I did little but wander the streets and read: cheap novels, plays, broadsides, and poetry.

I saw little of Jacob Binns, nor had I any idea what it was in London that engaged his time. He had recovered slowly from the exhaustion that attended our near-drowning and its aftermath, and then had begun disappearing for hours at a time. Nor did I concern myself with it. His business was his own, and if he wished he would tell me.

There came a day when I was seated in a tavern and a young man came over to my table. "Sit you alone from choice? If not, I'll join you."

"Do."

"You are a foreigner, and so am I. Although there's a-plenty of them about, the Londoners are not happy with foreigners these days."

He looked at me thoughtfully. "I am Tosti Padget, and I am of Yorkshire although I am told that my mother was Frisian."

"And I am Tatton Chantry."

He seated himself across the table and I ordered a glass for him. My guess was that he was two to three years older than the age I was using, and a shabby, attractive young man who seemed cheerful, perhaps because of the ale.

"You are a student?"

"Aren't we all?" he asked, smiling widely. "But yes...I was at Cambridge, and suddenly there was no more money and I had to make my own way.

"My father," he added, "was a yeoman who aspired to better things. He wanted education and preferment for me, and sent me on to Cambridge. He died suddenly and it was discovered that he had o'er-reached himself. After he was buried I had nothing."

"Your mother?"

He shrugged. "I never met her. She ran off, I hear, with some company of actors or something of the sort. My father never spoke of her except to say she was a good woman, that he was too dull for her."

He took a swallow of the ale. "That surprised me, for I never found him dull. Plodding, yes. He knew how to get forward and he worked at it, bettering himself and his business. Had he aspired for less for me he might have made it."

"And now?"

He shrugged again. "I am nothing. Occasionally an actor of small parts, a writer of ballads and broadsides, a cadger of meals or drinks, a seller of tips upon races, but never yet a thief...although I have known a few."

He had about him an extravagant manner with wide gestures and a conversation filled with exclamations. He seemed a decent fellow, although beneath his seeming confidence I detected an uncertainty, perhaps a doubt of himself or of his ability to cope with the times.

"To be an actor," he continued, "is to be a vagabond, admired on the stage, despised off it, always at the risk of the mob's displeasure, forever vulnerable. Fortunately, I have a landlady who lost a son, and is tolerant, a mistress who is without loyalty, and companions whose pockets are empty as my own."

We finished our glasses, and I saw in him a desire to linger. He struck me as lonely, as one without roots and destination. And I? My roots have been rudely torn up, and I had fled, so though without roots, I did have destination. Where I was going now I did not know, but eventually I would go home again.

"Do not be misled," I commented. "This is a new England today. It is not only those who were born to the nobility or the gentry who will rule in England tomorrow, it is also those of the yeomen who have ambition.

"Look you," I said, "they farm much land, they are the new merchants, and from them will come our new leaders. There is a place for us if we have ambition and will try for it."

"But how?" he said. "Words are easily spoken, deeds are another thing. I have no money, I have no position, I have not even the style of dress to attract a wealthy girl . . . I have nothing."

"You write ballads? Is there nothing in that?"

He laughed grimly. "Less than nothing. All copyrights are held by the Stationers' Company, and they pay a pittance. They control all and there is nowhere else to go. A man ekes out an existence only if he can do other things as well. A dramatist does scarcely better, for he must sell his copyright to the theatrical companies, and if he gets as much as six pounds he is fortunate. No, my friend, it is no way to earn a living."

He glanced at me again. "You have education, yet I cannot place you. Your voice has a curious inflection."

"I am only a fortnight from the Hebrides," I said.

"A Scot? Ah, that accounts for it."

"My father was a scholar of sorts," I said. "Not a teacher, except of me, but a scholar in the old way. He knew the old languages, and the old scripts, and could use a dozen alphabets, all from the Gaels or the Irish."

"I have heard of Ogam."

"Aye, and it was but one. Most of the old Irish books were lost, he told me, and there was much in them of which we now know nothing."

It struck me that perhaps he was not eating as often

as he would prefer, so I ordered a meat pie for each of us, and another glass.

True it was that due to Fergus MacAskill and my careful hoarding of the few coins that came my way I was for the moment secure, but already I had learned how slender is the thread that holds one from poverty and despair. Today a man may walk among his fellows esteemed by all, and having about him more than he needs of food and drink, but tomorrow all may be lost. To understand that lesson, I had only to remember my own father, and my own home. If for the moment I had something, I had always to remember how little it was, and must forever be looking about me to find some means of augmenting my fortunes.

We ate well. My guess that my new friend might be hungered proved true. During the silences I thought much on what he had said of playwrighting and ballads. My father had written a bit here and there, and sometimes as a child I had with him made up verses as we wandered over the hills, amusing ourselves with careless, casual rhymes.

Why not attempt this myself? At least, it would provide some small returns to hold off for a little longer the moment when I should again be without anything.

"How then do they live, these poets and playwrights? If their works offer so little, how can they exist?"

He broke a bit of bread from the loaf. "A patron. The secret is to find a wealthy patron who will, if you dedicate your works to him, provide you with a sum of money, or put you on a retainer. But a thankless thing it is to weave pretty rhymes for some empty-headed dolt who scarce realizes what it is you do.

"Yet I have tried. God knows, I have tried! None of them deigns to prefer my verses. They either did not reply to my offerings or they reply only with empty thanks and no money. And a poet cannot live on good wishes."

That night when I returned to the inn, Jacob Binns was there. With rest and proper food he had recovered his spirits as well as his appearance. He had gained weight and seemed stronger. Yet he was, as I could see, a very old man.

He listened as I explained my thoughts. "It be a good thing if it can be done," he said, "and I know of a printer, a young man from Stratford-on-Avon by the name of Richard Field. He was once apprenticed to a very old friend and I can bring you together."

"It would help," I agreed.

He studied me thoughtfully. "Is this what you wish to do? It is only a bit better than a beggar's life, and in the end you will have nothing. For you depend upon the whims of others, and whims change like a weathercock."

"Jacob? Have you heard aught of Fergus or the others? Did they make the shore?"

He shook his head. "Lad, you know there is little news of what takes place in the Hebrides, or even the Highlands, for the matter of that. I have talked with peddlers and traders and such like but have heard nothing. Yet he was a strong swimmer, lad, and if any could have made the shore it was he."

"He was like an older brother to me, or a father. He taught me much, and I wish—"

As we sat talking thus in the common room of the inn, of a sudden the door opened and a man entered. A man? A lad, rather, but a tall, well-made lad, only a bit older than myself.

He saw me and I saw him, and although each had changed we knew each other at once.

When Rafe Leckenbie and his men had attacked us, one young man had spoken a word for me and to me. This was that man!

"You!" he said. "You are here, and he is here, and you are the one thing that has rankled him most, that you escaped him. He meant to kill you."

"Rafe Leckenbie is here?"

"Yes. He's here. He was in much trouble there, and he ran off, and some of us with him. I, too was in trouble—and because of him."

"Leave him then. Be your own man."

" 'Tis easy said. He would kill me, as he will kill you. You have only one chance! Fly! Escape before he knows you are here!"

"Go to him," I said, "and tell him you saw me. Tell him I shall be glad of a meeting, whenever he wishes."

"Do not be a fool! He has one of the largest mobs of rascals in London! Thieves, cutpurses, and outlaws of all kinds!"

"Then perhaps I shall meet him," I replied, "for I am often about London and we have an old duel left incomplete."

"He is the greatest swordsman in England, perhaps in all Europe! Look you, I meant you no harm then, nor do I now, but Leckenbie is evil, totally evil."

"And you yourself? Why do you not leave him?"

Despite his drawn cheeks and tortured eyes he was

a handsome enough lad, I suppose, but he shook his head. "He would only follow and kill me, and I have no wish to die." He sighed. "Yet even that might be better than this. You do not know him. He lets no one escape him, neither friend nor foe."

When he had gone Jacob Binns studied me with his wise old eyes. "You have an enemy, lad, and I have word of him. Do not think you will face him alone."

Then he hesitated. "Tatt, do you go to this tavern," he wrote a name for me on a bit of paper, "and give it to Robin Greene."

"The playwright?"

"He is the one, a bold, handsome man, tall and with a red beard. A dissolute man much given to drink, a very gifted man who has wasted his gifts, but an able one, and shrewd enough. Tell him nothing about yourself before you met me in the Hebrides. It is well that he think the islands your home . . . but tell him about Leckenbie. Tell him first that you come from me or else he might not talk at all, or might even be rude. He is a very abrupt and sharp-tongued man."

He handed me a note on which was written: *If there is a fight let it be man to man. Speak to Ball.* The note was signed simply, *Binns.* But after the signature there was a figure set in a triangle.

"Waste no time," Binns advised, "and do not try to escape Leckenbie. You cannot."

Oddly, at the moment, I was not thinking of Rafe Leckenbie, nor of any danger for me, for my thoughts were upon this old man with whom I had escaped from the sea.

Who was Jacob Binns? What was he?

CHAPTER 18

WHEN I CAME upon Robin Greene it was in the Belle Savage on Ludgate Hill. He sat alone at a table with an empty glass before him and a half-empty bottle. He wore a green cloak, a flat hat of green velvet, and his face was somewhat flushed from drinking.

He looked up as I entered and his eyes fastened upon me. He started to speak, but I was already crossing the room toward him.

At a table a dozen feet away sat four roughs, one of them a lean, savage-looking man who was also watching me.

I walked directly to Greene's table and placed the note before him. There was an ugly look in his eyes as I walked up and he seemed in an aggressive, quarrelsome mood. "I come from Jacob Binns," I said.

His expression changed as if by magic. I had never seen such a complete transformation in a face. He put a hand over the note and gestured to the bench opposite him. "Sit you," he said.

He glanced at the paper, then looked up at me. Carefully, I explained my situation, as Jacob Binns had instructed me. He listened, and I would have wagered all I possessed that he could have repeated my story word for word when I was finished.

"Leckenbie, is it?" He lifted a finger and a man

from the nearby table joined us. Very concisely, Greene explained, "This be Cutting Ball. He is about when needed."

"You know Rafe Leckenbie?" Ball demanded. "You have actually met him?"

"Aye, but far from here. We fought then."

"Fought? And you live?"

"We fought, and I seemed to hold my own for a time, then he had all the better of it. I think he was about to kill me when I stepped back over a steep bank. I fell... very far. We were in the mountains, you see. To reach me was a long way around and I escaped him."

"It is said he never failed to kill a man once he began it."

"I was fortunate. Soon he will know I am here, and when he does he will come seeking me. We will fight again."

"What do you need from me? What can I do?"

"Keep the others away."

"But what of him? You confess he had you bested. What then?"

"I am older now, and I have learned much. Perhaps he cannot beat me now."

"Don't wager a penny on it," said Ball. "I have seen him fight. I think I have never seen better, although I hate the man and would gladly see him dead."

Greene smiled wryly. "Ball does not like him because he has usurped power that Ball once had, and such a lion leaves little for the jackals."

"Nonetheless," I insisted, "I will fight him if need be. I have learned much since last we met, and I am older and stronger."

"So has he, and so is he." Ball studied me cynically. "Who did you learn from?"

"Fergus MacAskill."

Cutting Ball whistled. "MacAskill, is it? A great fighting man, perhaps the greatest. I do not know how much he can teach, for some of the greatest cannot explain how it is done. You fenced with him?"

"For months."

"You must be good then, but that is not enough. It is not enough to be brave, and to have skill, for you must know what the other man might do. Such a man as I am, for example," he smiled, revealing broken teeth, "I would not fight as the gentry do. There are foul and evil tricks... I know them all."

"Teach me, then."

"I am no teacher, but there is another who is. He is skilled in the art of fence, but he knows the other things, too. He is Portuguese, and was twenty years in India, China, and the Indies."

My attention returned to Greene. "It is an honor," I said, "to speak with you. It is said you are the greatest writer in London."

He stared at me, his old truculence returning for a moment. "I? No." There was an edge of bitterness in his tone. "Perhaps once... I do not know. There are others now." He paused a moment. "Too many others. Writers come from under every rock, from behind every village wall! Bah! Most of them know nothing! Are nothing!"

I started again to speak, then thought the better of it. Let him have his say. The last thing I should mention was that I, too, thought of writing, although I did not think of myself as a writer.

He railed at English readers, at the playhouses, the managers, and at the Stationers' Company and their grip upon publishing.

Finally, I made my escape and Ball followed me outside. For a few minutes he talked, warning me of places to avoid, and suggesting I make myself small in London until I knew more. It was good advice, and I fully intended to take it.

The streets were crowded with people, sweaty, struggling people, open-faced innocents from the villages nearby, the wise and the tough from the city, the proud in their velvets and laces. Yet often the laces were not too clean, and the velvets were stained. Many carried burdens on their backs and shoulders. Occasionally a rider came through the streets, scattering the walkers, heedless of their safety. I kept close to the buildings as I went along the street, seeking my way back to the inn.

Yet even as I was aware of all that went on around me I was wondering about the odd effect of the name of Jacob Binns on Greene. Robin Greene was a bitter, scoffing man, yet the name of Binns had suddenly made him an attentive listener. I wondered why. There were secret societies in Europe, some of them very powerful, and I suspected Binns was a member of such a group.

Back at the inn all was quiet, yet I was uneasy. Was I afraid of Rafe Leckenbie? I considered that, and decided I was not. I was worried about his followers, men of whom I knew nothing, and the thought of that bitter night upon the mountain returned to taunt me. I had been beaten then, saved by an accident . . . There would be no cliff to fall over in London! Nor any to save me here. The fight was my own, and by the gods, I must win it myself. Yet if I had become a better swordsman, had not Leckenbie also? And he had fought... I had not. My training was from a master, yet it was training only. A sham fight remains a sham fight, no matter what. It is another thing when men draw the sword for blood.

Doubts would come. They thronged my mind despite orders I gave them to leave. I told myself I would win, yet I had not won before. And then, too, I had believed myself a skilled swordsman.

I held to my room. I slept, awakened, read and ate, then slept again. For not only was there thought of Leckenbie and all his dark crew, but of the need to find a place for myself in the world. I had money, but money idle is money soon departed, and I needs must find some way of rebuilding my fortunes.

When the hour was late I went below to the common room and Tosti Padget was there. He waved a hand and I crossed to his table.

"Ha! You are here! I was afraid Leckenbie had you spitted on his blade! Have you seen him then?"

"I have not. Nor do I wish to. I shall fight when the time comes. Until then I have much to do. Know you a printer named Richard Field?"

"Aye, he is new in the town but lately has set up for himself. He is a good man I think. What is it you plan?"

"I've the need to earn a penny or a pound. Even two. Money does not last forever and it is little enough that I have. I am no writer, no playwright or poet, but I know a few words and my father often wrote and inspired me to try. Perhaps there is a bit of something I could do until I can find a place, some-where."

"A place? Forget that. Unless you have friends who will speak for you there is no chance of preferment. There are too many seeking, and too few places for those who seek." He shrugged. "You might turn a penny with your pen, God knows there's little enough of talent in most of the ink spilled around now.

"Greene had it but wasted it with drinking, and Marlowe also, who has lately come from France. There is whispering that maybe he was a spy. Don't accuse him of anything, however, for he is quick with a blade, and handles himself well. They've lately had to put him under bond to keep the peace, for he has several times beaten a constable on his way home."

"I aspire to nothing but something with which to buy bread. I shall go into trade when I can. I have had a bit of that already."

"Why not? It was once only the ladies and gentle-men who wore the fine feathers, but now any trades-man's wife can preen herself about in silks and furs with the best of them. Times are changing, Tatt, but for the better or worse, who can tell?"

Across the room I saw a man with eyes upon me which he hastily averted when mine met his. He was a sorry, ratlike fellow with yellow cheeks and some lank strings for hair. He looked at me again, and I men-tioned it to Tosti.

"Aye, he is likely one of Leckenbie's runners! He has them sneaking about everywhere, listening for what he can use or to hear of something to steal."

When I looked again the man was gone. Inside me I felt a queer lightness, and an urge to get up and go, yet

I would not. Stubbornly I ordered another ale for each, and sat where I was.

It was not long, either. The door opened suddenly and there he stood. It was Rafe Leckenbie all right, and a broad, big man he was. Larger and stronger even than before, but with a set of expression on his face that had changed. There was no more of the boyishness that had somehow remained when I came upon him first. Now there was arrogance and a brutal power.

He looked quickly about and his eyes met mine. I stood at once, gesturing to the empty bench at our table.

He crossed, staring hard at me, to frighten me I think, but I was not frightened. I was a fool, maybe, but not a frightened fool. My toe nudged the chair toward him.

"Sit you!" I spoke more cheerfully than I felt, yet there was a lightness and a daring in me, too. "This is a far piece from the moors of Galloway! I hear you have become a greater scoundrel than ever, gone from attacking lonely wayfarers to raping and thieving. Is that it?"

He stared at me, but was not angered. He looked at me with contempt. "You talk too much," he said. "I may slit your tongue."

"You once tried that," I replied cheerfully, "but though I held back and gave you every chance for exercise, nothing came of it but a little dust and sweat."

"You held back?" He motioned for a waiter. "I should have killed you then."

"Aye," I agreed, "for you cannot do it now unless you set some of your thieves upon me."

"I'll not do that," he replied. "You I want for myself. It is a pleasure I have long promised myself."

The ale came and quickly. The waiter's eyes were round and frightened. He had no doubt with whom he dealt, I could see that.

Leckenbie drank, ignoring Tosti. "What do you here?" he asked.

"Like you," I said, "I came seeking my fortune. *My* fortune," I added, "not somebody else's."

It bothered him not at all, so I desisted. Taunts meant nothing to him, for as I was to learn, he simply did not care.

"A poor place to seek a fortune unless you have one," he said. "But they be recruiting men for the sea, if you've the stomach for it."

"Another time," I said. "Now I am for London. I shall find a bit to do around here and see what comes."

We talked then, quietly and easily as though we had not been enemies, although I had no doubt of what was in his mind, nor was he trying to ease my fears or entrap me. He was, I suddenly realized, hungry for talk of his own country, and so I spoke of it, and of Scotland.

He listened, his eyes wandering the room the while. "Will you have something?" he said suddenly.

"Of course," I agreed, "as I do not mind eating with a man I mean to kill."

He laughed, with genuine humor. "Ah, I like your nerve!" He looked at me closely. "Or is it bravado? Are you putting a face on it?" He looked again, and seemed surprised. "You know, I really believe you think you can do it. I really do! And after what happened back there." He motioned the lad over again and ordered for us three, and ordered well. "I was about to run you through," he said, "when you backed off the hill. I was sure it was an accident, but mayhap it was a trick, a device to escape me."

"Escape you?" I spoke lightly. "Rafe, I simply did not wish to kill you. I like a fine bout with the blades and you afforded me the best exercise I'd had in a long time. I had no wish to kill you then. I was saving you for another bout. Soon, I hope. I grow rusty."

He chuckled. "I almost like you, damn you," he said. "Well, eat up. It will not be tonight, and not here." He looked across the table at me, one thick hand resting on its edge. "Odd, that you should choose this one. The one place where even I dare not kill you."

I was puzzled. Why not in this place? I wondered. What was there about this special place that made him draw back? Yet I did not ask the question. If he was mystified I wanted him to remain so.

"It is comfortable," I replied cheerfully. "They do be most friendly here."

"Aye, they would be. There must be more to you than it seemed that day on the moors when I took you for a mere vagabond.

"Not many come here, you know, and fewer are allowed to stay. I wish I knew why!" His tone was petulant. "It is a mystery, yet the word is all about. No trouble here! None!"

"You could chance it," I suggested.

He shook his head. "No, I'll not. There is a power here, and I've a wish to command it. But first I must know from whence comes the power.

"Is it the Queen herself? I think not. Some secret

papist group? Again, I think not. Nor is it a place sponsored by some great noble. I've worked out that much, but every thief and cutpurse in London knows to leave this place untouched. I must find out why."

He looked quickly at me. "If you tell me, I will pay, and pay well." He grinned with thick lips. "I might even let you live."

"Perhaps," I said, and unwittingly hit upon it, "they do not want attention. Perhaps they wish to exist quietly and without notice, content to be as they are."

He glanced at me. "That might be it ... but why? That is what I must know ... why? And I must know, too, who comes here. And also how it is that you yourself are here.

"And you could tell me if you wished," he said, irritably. "How does it happen that you who are just come should be allowed here, and I who am known to all London am not?"

His doubts aroused my own. Why was I here? Who was Jacob Binns?

CHAPTER 19

ALONE IN MY room I took myself to my desk and began to think on what I might write to earn a penny. Sure, and it was no writer I was nor intended to be, yet many of those about me were no better, and I at least had command of language and some memory for tales heard.

In my grandfather's time there had lived an Irish thief and vagabond of whom many stories were told, yet I dare not raise questions by making him Irish. Nor was England in any mood for an Irish story when all was going badly for them there. So I made the man a gypsy and, using a little information learned from Kory and my own roadside experience, I put together a tale. And as the street name for a rascal was a *damber*, I called my story *The Merry Damber*.

It was written hastily but from stories long known, strung together by means of the road itself, and of that I knew a good bit. I wrote the night through and by the first light of dawn I had completed my story.

With a faint light already at the window, I lay upon the bed and slept, content that I was done, yet not knowing whether what I had written was good or ill.

There was unease in my mind that went beyond the writing, and when scarcely an hour had passed in sleep, I was awake, brushing my hair and considering where I might deliver my story in hope of payment.

The unease lay not in the story or the writing, but in the secret of this inn, and of the man Jacob Binns.

Where was he now? Was he sleeping? Or was he at large upon the town on some secret business, for he seemed to have no other?

Descending the stair to the common room, I found Tosti Padget there. He noticed at once the roll of manuscript.

"Ah? You have been at it." He looked at the roll again. "It is a lot."

"I worked all the night. Do you wish to read it?"

"No," he replied frankly, "and mind you show it to no one but he who might buy. The others do not matter. Most people are not fit to judge a thing until it is in print, and only a few of them then. If they want more, it is good, and if they talk about it among themselves, it is better. I had rather have one story talked about in an inn or over a campfire than a dozen on the dusty shelves of the academies.

"You may well ask, if I know so much, why I am not writing successfully ... well, I know what should be done, and I can talk well of it. But," and his tone was suddenly bitter, "I have not the will to persist. I tell myself I shall change, but I do not. I try to hold myself to a schedule, but I am diverted by the flights of fancy in my own mind. I dream of it, want it, talk of it, think of it, but I do not *do* it. Writing is a lonely business and must be forever so, and I am a social being. I want and need others about me and the loneliness of my room is a hateful thing."

"One can be alone anywhere," I suggested. "The quality of solitude is in the mind. If you wish people about you then write here, or in some other tavern, or in many of them, but sit among people only isolated by your mind."

"I have tried that," said Tosti Padget. "But my friends gather about me, they wish me to join them at games or walking after the girls, or they wish me to come along to another tavern where they gather with their friends." He paused, then shrugged. "They scoff. They say I should come along and write another time."

"They drink in taverns," I said, "and twenty years hence they will still be drinking in taverns, no longer so bright and cheerful, no longer so friendly, only grown morose and sour with years and disappointments. As for their scoffing, the Arabs have a saying: 'The dogs bark, but the caravan passes on.'"

Tosti stared gloomily into his glass, perhaps because it was empty. I ordered another round and wondered how long I should be able to do so. Yet I liked him. To me he was a window upon a world of which I knew too little.

We talked then of people about London, of those who came and went, of possible sponsors to whom a writer might dedicate a book with some hope of pension or remuneration.

"To whom," he asked me suddenly, "will you dedicate this? And what will you write next?"

Who, indeed? I knew nothing of those in London, and it went against the grain to curry the favor of some great man, yet all did it, and it seemed the only way to modest success. Nonetheless, my nature rebelled against it. At the same time an answer came to the second question.

Rafe Leckenbie!

To gather what was known about him and his

192 / Louis L'Amour

activities would be simple enough, and then to expose him for what he was. He had come into London and like a great leech had fastened himself upon it and now was sucking it dry. True, he was as yet only one of many others, but superior in intelligence and with connections in high places, he was rapidly advancing to a position of control.

But first I must sell what I had already written.

With morning I donned my best and went forth, to seek out Richard Field or some other printer, carrying with me the roll of foolscap on which I had written *The Merry Damber*.

Field was young. He had but lately married the widow of the man to whom he had been apprenticed and was ambitious as well as shrewd. If I failed with him, there were others. All belonged, as indeed they must, to the Stationers' Company, incorporated in 1557, and none was allowed to practice the art of printing unless he was of that organization. Each publication must be licensed by the government, and strict control was maintained over what was published.

Field's shop was in Blackfriar's and I made the best of my way there. He was opening the door when I arrived. Young though I knew he was, I was startled by the fact that he was scarce older than I. He looked quickly at me and then glanced at the roll of manuscript under my arm. "You are early about," he said, not unpleasantly.

"Some call upon heaven when they arise," I replied cheerfully, "I call upon Field."

"What is it then?"

"An account of cozenage and chicanery along the highroads," I said.

He opened the door and waved me inside. "And

have you knowledge of such things? You look the gentleman."

"I have some experience of swords," I said, "and one teacher was a gypsy. He told many a tale. Others come from people along the way."

"Sit you." He glanced at me. "Will you have a glass?" Then shrewdly he said, "You are Irish?"

"I am lately from the Hebrides," I said. "I am sometimes taken for Welsh."

"No matter," he said pleasantly. He picked up my manuscript and glanced at it. "Well, you waste no time. Into the story at once."

He read on, and I offered no comment, and did not interrupt. "Perhaps," he said, after a bit, "perhaps." He looked up at me, suddenly, sharply. "Who directed you to me?"

"I believe it was Robin Greene . . . or perhaps Tosti Padget."

"Ah, Tosti," he shook his head, "much talent but no perseverance, and that is the truth of it. He writes well but finishes very little. He chops and changes." He looked up at me. "My old master, George Bishop, used to say that writing was not only talent, but it was character, the character of the writer. Many are called, he would say, but few are chosen, and it is character that chooses them. In the last analysis it is persistence that matters."

He put down the manuscript. "There is something here we can use. It is light, gay, witty, and it smacks of the road." He looked at me sharply. "You say you know the road?"

"Somewhat."

"Ah? Yes, I suppose so. I am myself from Stratford.

I often watched the gypsies there, and the peddlers." He tapped my manuscript. "This rings true."

"You will buy it then?"

"A moment! Do not hasten too swiftly. You need money?"

I shrugged. "I do not need money, not at the moment. I do *want* money. Much money."

He smiled. "There is not much in this. Writers about London are a starveling lot. A good playwright such as Master Robert Greene, whom you mentioned, he will get but five or six pounds for a good play. And he, along with Kyd, is at the top of them."

"I was not thinking of continuing a writer, yet I have some other things. Do you know Rafe Leckenbie?"

He sat back and stared hard at me. "Aye, and who does not who knows aught of the streets? I know him not, but of him . . . yes."

"I know him. What would you say to a complete revelation of his activities? All the plots and machinations of the man."

"You know whom you deal with? Leckenbie is no catch-penny rogue but a thoroughgoing rascal. He's into river piracy and the lot."

"And a devil of a fine swordsman, too."

"Ah? I have heard of that, but doubted it. There is a rumor that he killed a gentleman in a duel shortly after he first appeared in London, and another one in Kent."

"I know nothing of that, but he is a superlative swordsman."

"You speak from experience?"

"I do."

"Yet you live?"

"That was long ago, and in another place than this. I was not as skillful then as I now am...yet I narrowly escaped."

"I see...yet you would dare this? He would set his men upon you. Not upon me, for I am of the company and no man would be such a fool. Yet I fear for you."

"Let that be my worry."

Field tapped his fingers on the manuscript. "Very well then. Two pounds for this, four pounds for the Leckenbie story—if it is true or nearly so. But do not think I shall pay so much again, for there are not many stories of the likes of Rafe Leckenbie."

"I understand."

He paid me two pounds and I took it gratefully. It was a goodly sum for the time, and evidence that he thought well of what I had written. Yet I was not misled, for the stories I had written down had been told and retold by generations of Irishmen and belonged to all who heard them. They had stood the test of time. Yet never had they been in print, for the Irish were not permitted to publish. They were tales told in taverns. I might do another as well, for there were many such stories, but that would probably be the end of it unless I could enrich my knowledge by talking to road people and gypsies.

Where was Kory? I wondered. I could use him now, and could pay him, too.

Tucking away the two pounds with my small store, I went back to the inn, loitering along the way. I saw nothing of anyone I knew, yet I did see a rogue or two who seemed to be following me.

Were they Cutting Ball's men? Those of Leckenbie? Or both?

For a week I loitered about the White Hart, the Red Lion, the Mermaid, the Three Tuns, the Golden Lion, King Harry Head, as well as the Bear and the Ragged Staff. I went from one tavern to the next, buying a glass here, or just sitting and watching, sharing a drink with some wandering rascal. But I was listening all the while.

Usually, I *just* listened. If the soil seemed fertile I might drop the seed of Leckenbie's name, and then sit back to hear what might be said. It was a way to learn, and I learned much.

Soon I learned that Leckenbie directed the affairs of three *stalling kens,* or places where stolen goods might be sold, each in a different quarter of London. He also had several stables where horses might be let to pads, as highwaymen were called. He had a fist into everything, and he was making enemies all over London. Cutting Ball was not alone in disliking Leckenbie or his ways. It was simple to see that he was a master scoundrel.

Swiftly then, I wrote. It was not the whole story, certainly, but it was enough. I entitled it *Rafe Leckenbie, Thieves' Master and Master Thief.* Then I hastened to Blackfriar's and put it into the hands of Master Field.

He looked at it, swore a little, and pressed on to read further. "I will take it," he said at last, "but do you look to yourself, Tatton Chantry. Once this is on the street your life will be worth next to nothing." He snapped his fingers. "Not that!"

"Four pounds," I said, "and I'll wear a loose blade."

"You will have it," he said, "but I fear for you."

And in truth, I feared for myself.

CHAPTER 20

NOW THAT I had come upon a means of earning a bit I did not neglect the pen, but my next two attempts failed of acceptance. These had neither the wit nor the novelty of my first successes. Yet it was about this time that the Leckenbie piece was published abroad.

In a day it became the talk of the town. When I went to the tavern below, the place was a-buzz with it, and not knowing who might be the author, they were of one mind: that he had but a short life left to him, once Leckenbie saw the piece.

Cutting Ball came hurriedly to the tavern. "What, Tatton Chantry! Is it you who had done this thing? You have destroyed him!"

"That was my purpose, but we do not know yet what may happen. We can but wait and see."

"All London will be about his ears," Ball insisted. "And to think that you have done this! A mere lad! And with a pen, too, and with no sword or mob or soldiers!"

Yet that day went slowly by and nothing happened, nor were any of Leckenbie's men seen about, nor on the second day. There was no move against him by the Queen's men: there was only talk. On the third day, well armed and with Ball's men about, I ventured into the street.

This time I was bound for Blackfriar's with another tale of the *Merry Damber,* which had proved successful. I sold the piece to Master Field for a pound, and turned about, planning to go at once to my own tavern.

Suddenly I found myself face to face with Leckenbie!

He stopped upon the street before me. My hand went to my sword. "If it is to be, let it be here," I said.

He laughed. "You mean then to fight me?" he roared, laughing the while. "Do not be a fool! You have done me only the greatest service! Why, had I ordered the piece written it could not have been better!"

He was chuckling and cheerful. I stared at him incredulously. "Take your hand from your sword!" he said. "I shall certainly kill you one day, be sure of that. But not today, when you have just done for me what I could not do for myself!"

"What do you mean?"

He chuckled again. "Come! I'll split a bottle with you, and a haunch of beef as well! Don't you see? You have made me sound so powerful, so evil, so revengeful that my enemies are trembling! A dozen thieves have come to my stalling kens whom I never laid eyes on before, although I knew them well by reputation. Suddenly I have gained respect in quarters where there was little before! At one fell swoop you have made me the strongest man in London! And to think that was all it needed! I am a fool, Chantry, a double-dyed fool! Now I have no need to destroy enemies who believed themselves o'ermatched and have come to me, pleading the wish to join me! What I could not have done in months, you have done in an instant! It is magic!"

We sat down across the table from each other. The

confusion in my thoughts cleared. In believing I was destroying a monster, I had created a worse one. In speaking of his strength, I had made him seem more fearful than he was, and frightened all who would oppose him.

He bought good wine and filled a glass for me, and the beef we had was the best, the tenderest cut of all. He served me from his own blade and laughed, his face flushed from wine and laughter.

"Oh, you have done it, Chantry! There's a string of bawdy houses that I've long wanted. Ill-kept places, but fat with profits. Now they have asked my protection, and they shall have it. Oh, they'll have it, all right, and a fat payment through the nose for it, too!

"Come! Drink up, Chantry! And be rid of those men of Cutting Ball's! You'll not need them more. And as for him, this will destroy him, too, or nearly so!"

As we ate he ticked off the things the unwonted publicity had brought to him. There were some men he had threatened who had not been convinced of his strength, yet before he needed to prove it, my piece had appeared and done the task even better.

"Much thanks, Chantry! By the Lord Harry, I am glad I did not kill you!" He reached into his sash and tossed a sack of gold upon the table. "There! Have that! It is little enough for what you have done!"

"Keep it," I replied shortly. "I'll have none of it, for I meant to destroy you."

He laughed again, his eyes bright with malice. "Of course you did! Think you I do not know that? But bother the reason! It is the effect that matters, and the payment there is small enough for what you have done."

There was nothing to do but put a good face on it

and think of what I should do next. Cheerful as he was, I could only doubt what he believed, for whatever effect this might have upon evildoers, it was sure to result in some sort of action by those in authority. Unless, of course, they were too occupied with Ireland and worried about Spain to bother with the evil at their doors?

"I have also read *The Merry Damber!*" Leckenbie said. "It is a good piece, too! You had some tricks there even I had not thought of! Stay about London, Chantry, do! For you will only make things the better."

He gnawed on a bone, then put it aside. "Look you, Chantry, I am no fool. I know this dodge will not last forever, but by the time it has worn itself out I shall be rich. Yes, rich! And I shall have those about who need me but who are themselves in power. I will buy an estate, I will hire some such a one as you to say that all your words are balderdash, and will show myself a respectable gentleman. I will keep a carriage—for such will soon be the fashion, believe me—and I shall ride to the hounds and be knighted. You will see! My poor father was a country squire, and a good man, most of the time, but he was never knighted or noticed by anyone.

"And two years hence, Tatton Chantry, I will no longer be heard of as such I now am. Two years I shall lie quiet while all this is managed by others. Then I shall reappear, hang a few of those who still oppose me, and within the third year I shall be received at court.

"I have plotted well the route I shall take, and a better one can't be found. I tell you this now so you can see it begin to happen. Unfortunately," he smiled, "you'll not be about to witness the climax. Although I shall miss you. I shall, indeed."

"You will never do it, Leckenbie," I said quietly. "Before then I will show you up for the villain you are."

He chuckled. "Do what you will, the result will not be changed. Not one whit. Besides, what can it get you? A few shillings here, a few shillings there. Trifling sums, and the poorest of livings. Whilst I shall be rolling in wealth."

He leaned over the table toward me. "Already I have friends! I have power! There are those who sit high in the land who will pull strings for me! Do you think I can be taken? That I shall ever end in Newgate or Tyburn? I am too much needed. When they need something done, I see that it is done, whether here or across the water.

"At this time I am a tool to them, to be used. But soon I shall change positions with them. Then they shall be the tools and I the user."

"You are ambitious," I said, "and ambition may destroy you."

"Aye. 'Tis a gamble, is it not?" The humor was gone from his eyes. "I know well the chance that I take, and the need they have of me. I must take each step with care. But you yourself have helped me, for they will read what you have written and measure my usefulness against what you have claimed for me. Now they will need more money when they come to me."

He pushed the gold toward me again. "Take it. Gold is a useful servant that never talks back. Had I hired you this could have gone no better, nor come at a better time."

He rested his powerful forearms on the table. His wrists were the thickest I had ever seen and his hands gave a sense of awful power. He was, in his own brutal way, a handsome man. His face suggested power and strength.

He motioned to the waiter. "A bottle of sack," he said. "Your best!

"Look you," he said suddenly. "I like you not, nor you me, but yet you could help me. You are shrewd, and you fight well. Not well enough," he added, "but well. Join me. I do not plan that you should become a thief, but rather an agent."

"A tool?" I suggested wryly.

"We are all tools in one way or another." He leaned toward me. "England is changing. Any man with his eyes and ears open knows it. We are coming to power. You shall see.

"Spain is all-powerful now, but Spain has come upon wealth in the wrong way—too much, too quickly. It will destroy her. Slow growth builds caution into a man or a nation, but sudden wealth is a spoiler. Now gold comes to her by every ship, and the living is easy. The great fighting men who graduated from the ranks of the army that fought the Moors will disappear. The politicians and the courtiers will take over—the gentle ones, the conniving ones! They will rook the fighters out of all they have won. Men like Cortez, Pizarro, Alvarado, and De Soto will disappear, and in their place the weak ones, the ones grown fat on easy wealth, will come to power.

"We are a young country, yet very old. We have the men and we have the ships and we will win. There are ships to be built, and equipment to be supplied to the ships. The press gangs will be after men and more men."

"What has all that to do with you?"

He shrugged, smiling. "I shall control it. The supplies will be bought from me or through me. As for the press gangs, I shall direct them."

"You?"

He laughed. "Who else? Who could do it better? Of course, if we should happen to press into service a few of the gentry who did not want to go...we can always make an arrangement."

"And I?" I asked. "What role have you planned for me?"

"To write when I need something written. You have made me out to be a king of thieves. Now I wish another broadside turned out. This one will deny that I am a thief, but will imply that I am a man of great but mysterious power. That I merely have a wide knowledge of what takes place and have been able to recover stolen goods from time to time. Protest that I am a good man but one who has great power in many quarters."

"I see. The thieves and the bawds have already had their message. Now you want to clean up the picture of yourself while implying you have still greater power."

"Exactly. And of course, when people come to me to recover their stolen goods, I shall recover them... for a price. I am sorry about the cost, but the man who reaches the thieves must be paid."

"And you will have it both ways. A friend to the thieves and a recoverer of stolen goods, and well paid by both."

He laughed with genuine amusement. "See how easy it is? In the end I shall be knighted and perhaps will stand for Parliament.

"For you see, I shall also be serving Her Majesty. Even now there is talk in Spain of a great fleet of ships, an armada to sail against England. My spies tell me this, and I pass it on to those close to Her Majesty so that she also knows."

"To Walsingham?"

He laughed again. "Perhaps!"

"And is he your protector?"

The laughter died. "Protector? I have no protector! I need none! I stand alone!"

Yet it seemed to me there was a false note in the statement, and when I finished my sack and parted from him he stared sullenly after me. I believe I had reminded him of something he wished to forget.

Cutting Ball's men fell in around me. That worried me a bit, for how far could I trust Ball? And why, even at Greene's behest, should he serve me in this manner? For that matter, who and what was I to Greene?

I would do well to keep a loose sword in my scabbard. I was thinking of that when suddenly a voice spoke from an alley. "Tatt? I must see you." It was Padget.

"At the Boar's Head." I spoke softly but hoped he heard me, continuing on without missing a step. There had been anxiety in his tone, and I knew he was my friend. What now, I wondered. What more could come?

Much, I realized well. I wished no association with Rafe Leckenbie or his kind. It might be true that what I had written had done him good rather than ill. Some might read it as an evidence of his power, but others would know better, for a thief exposed is a thief soon taken.

When Cutting Ball's men left me at my inn and vanished into the night, I took a side door into a dark alleyway and went on to the Boar's Head. There were few about, and Tosti sat alone toward the back of the room. I went to him.

"You keep late hours," I suggested.

"I am received of a message," Tosti said. "For you."

"Why not directly to me?"

He shrugged. "I do not know. The man came to me. I did not like him but he was not one to trifle with. You were to come to a certain place, and you were not to be followed."

"And for what?"

"There is one who wishes to speak to you of a private matter. He would give no name."

"I do not like it, Tosti."

"Nor I, my friend, but I think you have no choice. I think this man has power, for his messenger was a soldier—or had been. He carried himself well and knew what he was about. One who can command such a person is no ordinary man."

"All right." I made a decision suddenly. After all, I carried a sword and a dagger. "I shall see him."

I was directed to a street of quiet elegance. Entering the gate, which stood open, I went to the door and used the brass door knocker.

The door opened almost at once and a man stood facing me—no doubt the one who had delivered the message to Tosti. "You are . . . ?"

"Tatton Chantry. I was asked to come here."

"This way." He indicated a door at the end of a short hall. As I stepped inside, he looked past me. The street was empty, as I well knew. Then he led me down the hall, rapped lightly at a door, opened it, and stood aside.

The room I faced was rectangular and lined with shelves of books. There was a fire on the hearth.

A man of something over medium height stood near a table, an open book before him. As I entered he did not look up but turned a page, and read a bit more.

"Please be seated." He looked up then, but not at me. "John? A bit of malmsey for me." He glanced then at me. "And for you?"

"The same," I said. "It is a rare wine."

"Aye, so it is." He sat down opposite me and crossed his knees. "You know it?"

"We sometimes drank it at home," I said. "My father would have a butt of it from time to time."

"Ah? And your father was?"

"My father," I said.

I knew the man at first glimpse, but he did not know me. Something about me disturbed him, a hint of familiarity, perhaps? I must have changed much in the past few years, but he almost none at all. The same white hair, the identical features, as if carved from marble, and the same wide, intelligent eyes.

"Do I know you?" he asked suddenly.

"No," I replied.

The less of me he knew, or anyone else, the safer I would be. With a hint here, a hint there, a man might well be traced.

"You are younger than I expected," he ventured, frowning a little. "You're little more than a boy."

"Age is ever an indefinite thing," I said, "and perhaps the poorest way to estimate or judge . . . except in wine, and even there one finds exceptions."

He had done me a favor once, and I was disposed to do one now for him—if the situation permitted. I could not forget that moment at the inn when he had spoken for me and prevented my being cheated. Yet he would have no reason to remember a tired, lonely, and rather untidy boy.

"Yes," he mused, "much younger than I expected."

"I have never been older," I commented.

The barest hint of a smile touched his lips, a wry smile. He tasted the Madeira and I did likewise. It was excellent. My father would have approved.

"You have written some pieces," he said. "You seem to know much of cheating."

My expression did not change. "I observe," I replied. "I do not participate."

"I see. And where does one acquire such knowledge? Much of what you wrote in the *Damber* piece was strange to me."

"There is always something to be learned," I said, and waited. What did he want? Why was I here? The man was obviously a gentleman, a man of means.

"You have lately written a piece about a kind of ringleader of thieves."

"I have."

"How did you secure that information?"

"It is quite commonly known about London," I replied, "and I listen well."

He stared at me for a moment, not liking my reply. "Yet you seemed to have some personal knowledge of this . . . man."

"We had a brief encounter."

"And you are still alive . . ."

"It was an indecisive battle. However, as you suggest, I *am* alive."

He frowned and seemed to be wondering just how to

proceed. My obvious youth had surprised him, also the fact that I was of gentle birth. He had not yet succeeded in placing me and I had a feeling he was one who liked to put things—and people—into their proper niches.

"Having written such a piece, I am surprised you are alive, if this man has the power you suggest."

There seemed no appropriate comment for that, and I let it pass, yet I was puzzled. Who was this man? What did he want with me? Was he a friend of Leckenbie? An enemy? Or did he think my writing might be used in composing a broadside of some kind for him? Many such were written and passed out in the streets to advance one cause or another, for there was no other means of getting information about except by gossip.

He sipped his wine and after a bit, he said, "This is your means to a living?"

"It contributes," I replied.

"I do not seem to place you," he muttered. "You are not from London, nor Lancashire nor Yorkshire..."

"I am from the Hebrides," I replied, not wishing him to get around to thinking of Ireland.

"The Hebrides?" He spoke as if it were the end of the earth, which no doubt it seemed to him. "I did not think there were gentry there."

"The MacLeods and the MacDonalds would not like to hear you say so."

"Ah, yes, of course."

He finished his glass and put it down. I retained at least half of mine, for even Madeira can be heady, and I wished to be thinking clearly.

He was puzzled by me. A man accustomed to command, he was now uncertain of how to proceed. I was enjoying myself. The atmosphere was pleasant, the room warm, and I liked the candlelight on the backs of the books.

Suddenly he said, "You would like a bit of supper? It grows late and I have not dined."

"I should, indeed."

Some unseen signal brought John again, and when he departed, my host seemed to relax somewhat. He had not offered a name nor had anything been said of mine, although obviously he knew it.

"I would assume," he said after a moment, "that Leckenbie was irritated by your piece?"

Did he know that I had encountered Leckenbie since? I decided he did not, and merely shrugged.

"If I were you," he continued, "I would avoid him in the future. You seem an intelligent young man, obviously an able one. There is no reason to run such risks."

I sipped my wine, and made no reply. *What did he want?*

"Such stories could destroy the man."

"Or make him even larger."

He glanced at me sharply. "Did he pay you to write the piece? Was that his intention?"

"He did not pay me, and I do not know his intentions, except..."

"Except?"

"Does not every man wish to grow larger? To improve his lot? I have heard rumors that since the piece was published some of his enemies have yielded and come over to his side."

He changed the subject and began to talk casually about troubles with Spain. I listened, offering no comment. He seemed to be merely thinking aloud but I had a suspicion he was trying to lead me into some comment that would give him a hint or two about me. For some reason I disturbed him and offended his sense of order.

Why was he interested? How had I disturbed him?

And then, like a sudden shaft of light into a darkened room, it came to me.

He—this man here—must be Rafe Leckenbie's protector!

Many men in high places, or climbing to high places, had utilized the services of such. It would be very convenient to have thieves at one's beck and call, to steal papers, to frighten, to murder.

Now, at least, I had a theory, an inkling of what *might* be the truth. He needed Leckenbie, and I therefore represented a threat. Or perhaps he felt Leckenbie was growing too independent and he wished to know more....

John entered with a tray bearing two plates of cold meat, cheese, and bread, and two glasses of wine. One plate, one glass, were placed before me, the others before my host.

Suddenly of one thing I was sure. I was not going to drink that wine.

CHAPTER 21

M Y HOST LIFTED his glass. "Your health!" he said, cheerfully enough. I picked up the remnants of my malmsey and drank, then put the glass down. There was some irritation in his glance as he watched me but he said nothing. I made up my mind to leave as soon as chance offered.

This man I did not like, despite the fact that he had befriended me long since. What was on his mind I did not know but I suspected he wanted to see what might be among my clothes, and if I had any message that would tell him more of me or what I was about.

"I have come at your summons," I said at last. "I do not know what you wish. I thank you for the food, but I shall be going now."

"Sit," he spoke sharply, commanding me. "You have written a piece about Rafe Leckenbie. I believe that you conspire with him, but whatever you do, I wish no more of this."

At a stir behind me, I arose so that none could come at my back. "I have nothing to do with Leckenbie or any other. I am my own man," said I. Then I thought to warn him off. "Although I have friends enough who wish me well. I shall write what I please."

"He will see you dead!"

I laughed. "Once he has tried to kill me, and several

times he has promised it. Think you that another warning will matter?"

My hand rested on my sword. "I bear you no ill will, whoever you are, or whatever you do. I shall go now. Do not send for me again."

"You do not trust me?" he asked, smiling.

"I will trust you," I said, "if you will drink that wine."

His eyes were not pleasant to see. "That wine? I drank my wine. I want no more. What has wine to do with it?"

"Then let your man drink it."

"There is no need for that," my host protested.

"Very well then. I shall go." Then I spoke to John, who barred the door. "Do you stand aside."

John made no move. "He seems a good, trusting man, this John of yours." I spoke quietly. "If you wish not to lose him, have him stand aside."

"Bother him," said John. "Let him come at me."

"I do not wish to kill your man," I said, "but I fought more than half an hour with Leckenbie."

John looked at his master.

"Stand aside then, John," said the man. "This can be done another time."

John stood aside, and I walked past him, ready to turn upon them if need be, but neither moved. When I was outside upon the dark street I ran a dozen steps quickly and dodged into a lane. Within minutes I was far away, still puzzling over it all but sure of one thing. The man was somehow allied to Leckenbie, and probably his protector.

If I had enemies I wished to know them and from what corner they might strike. So it behooved me well that I find out this man, and know his name and strength.

Tosti Padget was nowhere about when I entered the inn, but Jacob Binns was. I went to him at once and recounted my experiences. Binns himself had changed. He had filled out somewhat, his eyes were clearer, and for all his years, he was much more agile. He was rested now, of course, and eating with more regularity.

He listened without question until my story was complete, then asked several questions. Finally he said, "I know the man."

"There is always," he began, "a struggle for power, for a place close to the center. In England Queen Elizabeth is the power, make no mistake about it. There are some who believe it is this minister or that, or some favorite or would-be favorite, but such is not the case. The good Queen Bess has things very much in hand. Any who wish to use her had best examine their position with care.

"There is much pulling and pushing for power. There are some who believe that no woman can be strong, that if close enough they could manage her. They delude themselves. She is an uncommonly shrewd woman.

"The man we speak of is one of those reaching for power. Leckenbie is a convenient tool. Four persons who would have blocked that man's reach for the throne have had accidents. One, a woman, was struck by a horse racing through a lane and killed. A man fell into the Thames and drowned. At least two others have been killed in duels."

"Duels?"

"Aye, this man of whom we speak has several swordsmen who are in his pay or who owe him service. One of these is a Captain Charles Tankard. He has killed five men in duels in England, another one or two in France and Italy. He is a skilled swordsman."

"Better than Leckenbie?"

"Who knows? They have not fought, nor met each other, I think, although they serve the same master."

He changed the subject suddenly. "You spoke once of wishing to make a small venture in trade. Are you still of such a mind?"

"I am."

"There is a vessel being prepared for a trading voyage to the north coast of America. They are not looking for gold but for something more simple. They seek to trade for furs and will bring back a few ship's timbers, also. The master is a solid man, the vessel a good one."

"I have only a few pounds."

"It is a start."

"Very well. Whom do I see?"

He wrote a name on a slip of paper. "This woman."

"Woman?"

"Aye, lad, and a shrewd one she is. Her husband was a ship's captain who set himself up in trade, and when he passed on, becoming ill after a surfeit of pickled herring and Rhenish wine, she took up the trade herself. Go to her. She has a number of small ventures and will take yours. I have spoken to her."

"Her name?"

"Delahay. Emma Delahay."

It was not until after I left that I realized I had not learned the name of the white-haired man.

Emma Delahay lived in Southwark and had a place

of business there. She was a handsome woman of perhaps forty years, with large dark eyes and a lovely skin.

At a desk near her sat a man whom she presented as Mr. Digby, who was her keeper of accounts, runner, and general helper. He was a small man with a dry, wrinkled skin and bright, birdlike eyes.

She gave me a receipt for my money, and when I commented that two pounds was very little, she shrugged. "I know some who are now rich who began with less." She looked at me thoughtfully. "You are young. Would you consider going upon a venture yourself?"

"Not at present, but I have given thought to it."

"Give more," she said. She was studying me as we talked. "You did the piece on Leckenbie, did you not?"

"And some others."

"It was good. We have had no trouble of him yet, but it will come."

"Delahay," I said. "It is an uncommon name."

Her features bore no expression, but her eyes were cool. "So is Chantry." She frowned suddenly. "I have heard the name but once . . . it was something told me by my husband." She continued to frown, trying to remember. "Ah, yes! I do recall! It was something about a man lost at sea, some inquiries about him. But," she gestured, "that was long ago."

When I returned to the inn, I learned that Jacob Binns had gone. In the months that followed I saw no more of him, nor of Rafe Leckenbie, although his name was spoken abroad now and again. All went quietly with me. I wrote several small pieces and attempted a play, which came to nothing.

Discreetly, I made inquiries of Fergus MacAskill, but could learn nothing. If he had been lost in the Hebrides I did not know, or killed in battle.

My first small venture at sea was a success and my money was tripled. Adding two pounds more I then divided my investment between two ventures to lessen the risk.

I was quite sure Emma Delahay was Irish, but she spoke not of that, nor did I, for to be Irish in England at the time was to be suspect. No good could come of it being bruited about.

Certainly, I was making my way, yet what I had put by was so little that life was ever from hand to mouth. My clothes were neat but not rich. I ate with some regularity and had a bit over for the theater from time to time. My second attempt at a play was also a failure. Nonetheless, I sold a ballad on the hanging of a highwayman, and another about a pirate.

In all this time I had altered much from the boy who left Ireland behind, for I had grown several inches and was close on to six feet high, tall for my time. My hair was dark, almost to black, and my eyes of a gray kind. But my skin was darker than many, for I was of the Black Irish on one side of the family.

I maintained my skill by fencing two or three times each week with any man I could find who wished to cross a blade. Often on the greens I would have at Tosti Padget with the quarterstaff, for I found him uncommonly good. And also with another man, a burly fellow who was an apprenticed bricklayer named Jonson. Many a good bout we had, and all to keep my skills sharpened, for I had no doubt the time would come when I would have need of them.

Knowing that someday I must test my strength against Rafe Leckenbie, I worked constantly to increase my skill and agility. Once after leaving the warehouse of Emma Delahay I was set upon by thieves and used them quite roughly, breaking the jaw of one with my fist and ripping up the second with a dagger.

Whether Leckenbie was warned by the white-haired man to have no dealings with me, I knew not, but I saw no more of him.

By lingering along the riverfront I soon became familiar with various mariners, men of the sea and those who dealt with them. And with some of the members of the Muscovie Company.

Of these I made inquiry to discover what manner of goods would fare best in trade with foreign lands, for it was here I hoped to make my fortune, if such I was to have. All talk was of piratical raids, the taking of treasure galleons and such-like, but it seemed to me too chancy to warrant the effort and the risk.

Trade with America, I learned, was best. Listening to the talk of the savages that lurked in the forests of America, I deemed it wise to acquire a stock of edged tools, needles, copper bells, and brightly colored cloth.

At that time I also chanced a small venture of my own, exclusive of Emma Delahay. It was a ship to the Baltic lands and I spent a little on gloves of knit and leather, linens, and spectacles of the common kind.

From these loiterings along the river and talk with mariners I obtained material for a short piece entitled *A True Relation of a Voyage Along the Shores of Muscovie, And What Took Place There*. It was only a few years since the return of Anthony Jenkinson from

Muscovie and there was much interest in those lands. A paper paid me a few shillings, and the trade after a few months returned fourfold. I had done well. Carefully, I put by such small sums garnered here and there.

I could never be sure of what would transpire in London. Being Irish, I might be at any time found out and forced to flee. Jacob Binns had vanished as mysteriously as he had come, and I was not surprised. I suspected he was a Freemason, although I knew naught of them, only that theirs was a secret society.

Unusual sightings, miracles and prodigies of all kinds were exciting to me and I listened avidly for news of them. There had been extraordinary appearances in October of 1580 and again in the spring of 1583. Strange apparitions were seen in the air and evil things appeared in storms. I thought much on these happenings, believing little yet willing to speculate.

Several times I turned these happenings into items that could be published, and from each made a few shillings. From a seafaring man in the White Hart I obtained a story which I soon published. *A True Relation of the Frightful Experience of Shipwreck by Hans Goderik, And the Results Thereof*. Then from a Spanish prisoner I obtained a hint of a story which I pursued for some time, resulting in two pamphlets, one after the other, entitled *A Recital of Events Following Cruel Murder of Inca King and Vast Treasures Then Buried*.

Only a day after this last publication I was leaving the house of Emma Delahay in company with Mr. Digby when a young girl ran past us, pursued by two rough-looking men. They caught her only a few yards on and commenced to beat her, but before they could strike more than a pair of blows, I was upon them. Seizing the first by the shoulder, I jerked him away and flung him against the side of the house. The other then dropped his hold of the girl and turned on me. He had a sword in his hand in an instant, and he had at me. In no mood to trifle, I parried his blade and ran him through the sword arm.

He dropped his blade, cursing me with vile words while the first man straightened up. "Ah, what a fool you are to interfere with *us!* We have those above us who brook no such trifling."

"Are you Leckenbie's men?"

They were suddenly wary. "And if we are?" said the second.

"Tell him he would be better attacking men than girls. As for you ... if you bother her again, I'll slit your gullets."

"Hah! It is your throat that will be slit. I know you now, and I will speak to those who will have a care for you."

"Get on with you!" I replied shortly.

They walked away, the one trying to bind up his arm, which was bleeding badly.

Mr. Digby shook his head. "Lad, you've but one choice. Be off from London within the hour. The girl was a bawd, one of those forced to pay monies to Leckenbie and his like. They will permit no interference."

"If they wish to find me, they know where I am," I replied quietly. "But what I meant to ask Emma Delahay I can ask you. What news of the *Good Catherine*?"

"She was sighted not long since, and should be coming up the Thames within the day."

Arriving back at the tavern, I ordered a slice or two of beef, a bit of cheese and bread with a glass of wine, and waited for Tosti Padget. He had scarcely come when another man entered. A tall man, lean and strong. He looked sharply around, then crossed to me.

"You are Chantry?" His tone was a challenge.

"I am."

"I have read your paltry tales of shipwreck and treasure. They are trash, and they are lies, and you yourself are a liar!"

Suddenly my initial surprise was gone. Strangely, I was cool. "And your name?"

"Tankard," he replied, "Captain Charles Tankard."

"Of course," I said, "I have been expecting you. What took you so long? Or were you afraid?"

"*I?* Afraid?" He was both astonished and angry. "I am Charles *Tankard!*"

"Indeed? If I were you I should be ashamed to speak the name. I know of you as a paid murderer, as a creature in the employ of Rafe Leckenbie . . . and perhaps of others.

"They tell me also," I stood up, "that you are a swordsman. Now I have no doubt that you came here to kill me, sent by the masters for whom you run your foul errands. Is not that true?"

He was angry—coldly, furiously angry. I wanted him so. He was reputed to be dangerous, and no doubt he was. His rage would do him no good, and might make him rash.

He started to reply, but I was before him. "Please!" I interrupted. "If we must fight, let us do so! Your breath is as foul as your manners, and the sooner we have done the better!"

I gestured. "There is an inn yard close by. It will be convenient. Be hasty now, for your masters will be awaiting the report from the dog they sent to do their bidding!"

Oh, it reached him! He rushed at the door. "Come then," he said. "This is one fight I shall enjoy!"

"Briefly, perhaps," I replied.

Tosti whispered, aghast, "That man is Charles Tankard! He's killed a dozen men!"

"Then perhaps thirteen will be unlucky for him," I said.

This was what I had trained for. This was the moment I had known would come. And now, would my hours of fence be enough? Or would I die by the blade that had bled so many others?

Now was the moment.

The light in the inn yard was ill. There was night upon us, with only the stars above and some light from windows close about. But enough, enough.

The footing would be bad. There were paving blocks about, roughly squared before being set, yet an easy means of tripping a man. I must be careful.

Charles Tankard walked past me and turned, sword in hand. He was a handsome man in a dissolute way, a hardy rogue no doubt, and experienced at this sort of thing.

No matter. I had chosen the moment.

CHAPTER 22

THE AIR WAS cool. The inn yard smelled of fresh hay and manure. There was a cart at one side loaded with several casks. A few of the people in the common room trooped out, drinks in hand, to stand as spectators.

Tankard slashed the air, whipping his blade this way and that, perhaps to overawe me. He was an inch or two taller than I, hence longer in the arm. There was no measuring of blades; we fought with what we had. At least three of those who came from the common room to watch were henchmen of Leckenbie's, a thought I knew I must keep in mind so as not to present my back to them.

Yet Tosti, too, was there, and suddenly possessed of a stout staff. "I will stand at your back," he suggested, "but have a care!"

Surprisingly, I was not nervous. Several times I had fought in actual combat, but never in such a duel as this was to be. Yet it was for skill at such moments that I had trained. Tankard knew naught of me, or little enough. My one strategy should be to lead him to believe me less than I was, hence to make him grow careless.

We crossed blades and he looked at me, sneering slightly. "What a pity! To die so young!"

"Young? I did not consider you so young, Tankard,

but it is certainly a pity. Still, better the sword than the gibbet!"

He moved in, feinting a thrust. I made as if to parry, deliberately clumsy, then retreated a step as if puzzled by him. He moved in with confidence, and in an instant I knew I was facing a strong fencer with exceptional skill. His point circled and he stepped in with a quick thrust low down and for the groin. That I parried—and almost too late. He came on swiftly and I was hard put to keep his point away.

He drew back after one swift exchange, his point high. "I shall kill you," he said coolly. "It is almost too easy!"

There was little sound from those who watched. They stood about in a loose circle, stepping back occasionally to remove themselves from our way.

Then Tankard lunged suddenly. But his boot slipped on a bit of mud or some such and for a moment he was exposed. My point could easily have had his throat but I stepped back swiftly, permitting him to recover.

"You are gallant," he said, surprised.

"I am a gentleman, Captain. I will kill you, but I do not indulge in murder."

"Hah! You make me almost regret what I must do!"

"If you wish to withdraw, Captain, the choice is yours!"

He laughed. "And leave London? I'll not do it. I respect you, Chantry, but I also respect the dead!"

He came at me swiftly again, thinking to end it so, but I parried his best attacks. I was learning the true man now, studying him as Fergus MacAskill had taught me to do. His style of fence was English, with some touches picked up on the Continent, but I felt he had grown careless from easy victories. He was sure of himself, a little arrogant.

He intended to kill me, and quickly. He moved in skillfully and attempted a classic cut at the chest, sometimes called a *banderole,* a flowing, slicing movement. It was a pretty move, spectacular to see. But it held a risk, for it exposed the forearm.

In a duel with anyone taught by Kory or MacAskill, it was a wrong move. My reply was instantaneous, needing no thought—a reply rehearsed so often as to be automatic. My point pierced his arm, slicing through the tendons and driving into his chest.

He staggered back and I quickly withdrew to an on-guard position. Blood streamed from his arm and there was a darkening stain on his chest. My point had not penetrated deeply, but enough for a serious wound.

He caught himself by grasping the cart wheel with his left hand. He clung there, his sword down— although still gripped tightly. Blood ran down his arm and over the blade.

I lowered my point, a part of my attention on his followers. Tosti stood hard by, and ready.

"Damn it!" Tankard said, "I was a fool to try that with you!"

"A lovely move, Captain, but a foolish one. Shall we call it quits?"

"I meant to kill you."

"Of course." I wiped my blade. "Another time, perhaps?"

Turning, I started toward the inn door. A movement took my eye. It was John, the servant of the white-haired man. His eyes met mine and he smiled a little, not a friendly smile, but an acknowledging one. "I was well warned," he said quietly. "You are very good."

"Have you a message for me?" I asked, wondering at his presence.

He did not smile this time. "I came to carry the report of your death," he said.

"I will stand you a drink," I said, "for you'll have a dry welcome on your return."

"I'm obliged," he said, "but another time."

He turned away, then paused. "You fought well," he said, "but be warned. This was thought to end it. Now it will be murder. You must flee, or die."

He walked away and I went inside with Padget. It had been hot work, and the ale tasted good to a thirsty man, yet I liked none of it. My skill had been proven to me, but I had not wished it so.

My thoughts went to the *Good Catherine*. Had she come in? How had my venture fared?

I thought back to my victory. My blade had gone through the forearm, the force of the lunge driving it back against Tankard's body. The point had gone in, but not far. He should recover.

Alone in my room I wiped my blade yet again and dropped into a chair. In a severe test of skill, I had won, yet I liked it not. My room seemed suddenly to be an empty place—only a place to sleep and keep those few small belongings I had.

What had I accomplished since coming to London? I had lived. I had earned a few pounds, I had acquired a little knowledge. But aside from Tosti, I had no friends. Emma Delahay and Mr. Digby were merely business associates, and neither cared for me nor had any personal interest in me. I was alone as I had ever been since my father died.

My life was empty. The warmth of a home, the love of a girl, these I had not—nor any chance of them, it seemed. Fergus had been a strong, easy-going friend, but where was he? I could go back, but to what? There was nothing for me in Ireland, nor was there here in London.

I wanted my own Irish home. I wanted that coast again, and I wanted a love. I was lonely. Now I must go out with a ship, accompany my venture, do my own trading. If I could return with some small wealth I would go back to my own country and find an Irish girl.

So I thought, and so I planned.

London had given me time in which to grow. It had enabled me to learn. Now there was nothing for me here any longer. Fear did not drive me, for my victory over Tankard gave me added confidence, yet why remain where there would be endless attempts to kill me? And I knew they feared me for I had written of them once, and might do so again. I was not their creature, and what next I might do they could not know. But suddenly I knew one last thing I could accomplish.

I would write a piece that would destroy Rafe Leckenbie, and then I would go.

Yet, I asked myself, why did I wish him destroyed? Was it because he had bested me in our long-ago duel? Was it because the man was my announced enemy, and had warned me that he intended to kill me?

Reason enough, I told myself, but mine was not

that. The man was evil, wholly committed to evil, and although I doubted that he would achieve what he had set out to do . . . he might.

So far as I knew, I alone knew his plans. So far as I was aware, I alone could stop him—or could at least make an attempt. I had the necessary information, I possessed the weapon. Oddly enough, I did not believe that it was he who had set Charles Tankard upon me. Rather I believed it was that white-haired man, the master of John. Rafe Leckenbie would wish to have the pleasure of killing me himself.

Yet I recalled the girl I had helped just a few hours past. How many such girls were brutalized, beaten and held in virtual bondage by him or those he protected?

If men of goodwill would not step forward to war against evil, then who would? The spotlight I had put upon Leckenbie had aided him, he said. Indeed, it had. Yet it must have left disquiet in many minds, some of them official. From such a man, who was safe? Where was security when thieves and outlaws could run at large, doing their will of the populace?

For a long time I lay on my back upon the bed, my hands clasped behind my head, thinking of what I might do, and how the last piece must be written.

To indict Leckenbie was not enough. I must support my claims with arguments, with facts, with names, dates, and places. I knew this sort of thing was little done, but it must be done in this case. I doubted I would have more than one chance, so all must be done at once.

Also, I must be about my business. Already I had been over long in London, my progress only adequate.

Many men of my age were already captains of ships, commanders of regiments, and active in political life. Charles Danvers, at eighteen, had been elected to Parliament, and many another had done as well. I had no preferment, so must make my own way. But this was a time of change, when many yeomen and less were coming to high place through their energies alone.

Mentally, I began to calculate. My little ventures had all but one returned me a small profit. The major investment was aboard the *Good Catherine,* now due into port. Item by item I calculated what I possessed, and it came to a tidy sum. I had succeeded in saving something in excess of twenty-five pounds, and this at a time when a hard-working playwright might earn thirty pounds in a year. And this counted nothing of my current venture on the *Good Catherine.*

Carefully, I studied my situation and decided what I must buy. Now I knew the sources of the stuff of trade. I knew where to buy the brightly colored cloths, the copper bells and the edged tools, and where to obtain them at the least cost.

At last I slept, restless with thoughts of all that must be done, but eager for the morrow. Awakening suddenly, with the first light, it was in my thoughts that I must no longer live so solitary, but must make friends. For if trouble came I had none to speak for me, while Rafe Leckenbie could call his friends by the dozen.

No sooner did I come on the street than Padget was there. "You are famous," he said, "the talk of London."

"I?"

"Your victory over Captain Tankard. He was a man much feared, and one with many enemies. There is much talk of your gallant conduct against him."

"I fought to save my life."

"That may be, but you are much spoken of, and there is a man about, waiting for you."

He was a servant in livery, at a glass of ale in the common room. He came to his feet when I entered.

"I am from Sir George Clifford, the Earl of Cumberland," he announced. "I am asked to accompany you to him. He would speak with you."

Yet it was to no great castle that I was taken, but to a place upon the riverbank where Clifford was seeing to the outfitting of his ship, the *Elizabeth Bonaventure*. He gave me a quick glance. "You are the man who defeated Tankard?"

"I am."

"Know you aught of the sea?"

"Of small craft only. I am from the Hebrides."

"Ah? Fine sailormen those. Well, wish you to serve with me? There is word of a great armada the Spanish are sending against us."

"I know of it."

He threw me a quick glance. "What do you know?"

"That Spain is preparing more than a hundred ships. Some have gathered in Cádiz, even now. Thousands of men are recruited, and more than two thousand brass cannon with much else."

"How does it come that you know all this? There has been talk, of course, but—"

"I have ventured some small sums in trade. Thus I try to be aware of what is happening at sea. I have myself been contemplating a voyage to America, and to that end have spent much time talking with sailors and fishermen along the shore. There are no secrets there."

"Would you serve with me then? England will need every man." He paused. "And I want bold ones, for when the Armada is defeated—and we shall defeat them—I wish to sail for the Indies, for the Spanish waters."

"I would be honored to serve with you in any capacity that befits a gentleman," I replied.

"Could you command a prize vessel if need be?"

"I could."

"Good! Provide yourself with what you need and report to me here. And," he added sharply, "no more dueling. Her Majesty does not look with favor upon such things." He smiled then, friendly enough. "Although I should like to have seen that duel!" He changed the subject. "You have written some booklets?"

"I have."

"Then keep your eyes and ears open. I should like this story well told when it is over. I want a report to the Queen, but I shall want more, a pamphlet to go out over the city, recounting the story of the *Elizabeth*."

"It would be a pleasure."

As, indeed, it would. I had never written of a battle, and this would be one, perhaps the first of many, that I should not only witness but partake of. Yet I knew little enough of what my duties would be, nor of command afloat. It behooved me to learn as much as I could.

I hurried back to my room at the inn to make my

plans. I should need pistols, some clothes fit for the sea, books for reading, and most of all the help of an old salt, if such there was about, who could talk to me of battles at sea and their conduct.

When I came down from my room, Tosti arose to meet me. "Do you have a patron?" he asked.

"A patron?" I laughed. "No, not I. Patrons are for poets or playwrights, not for mere scribblers. No, I am recruited to war against the Spanish dons." I explained to Tosti what lay before me and he went with me while I purchased two excellent pistols and the equipment and materials for charging them.

For several days I was busy, yet I took the time needed to write the final piece on Rafe Leckenbie.

Being no literary craftsman, I did my best with what came to mind. I wrote it as a story from some ancient land, yet kept the subject so close that none could miss what I intended. I entitled it: *A True Relation of How a Master Thief Became a Great Lord*. Writing in words that implied a long-ago story in a distant land, I yet painted so close a picture that none could fail to recognize Rafe Leckenbie. I told of his plotting to become the thief-master and controller of bawds. Then, almost using Rafe's own words, I told how he would become a knight and then a lord of the realm. At last I pictured him fat and gloating, so strong that not even the ruler could displace him.

During those last days I threw myself into the task of preparing for sea with all my energies. The problems were new for me, but I quickly perceived what must be done. And by discreet questions and observation, I learned much. I directed the loading of supplies, food, extra canvas, and I watched the storage of powder and shot. In every way I attempted to make myself useful. Clifford might wish for bold men, but useful men were just as necessary.

We put to sea in company with a number of other vessels, many of whose names I never knew or heard but in passing. My life aboard ship was brief and hectic. The Spanish were coming, this much we knew. My informants along the Thames had known much from the gossip of fishermen and sailors of coastwise or across-channel boats, many of whom operated regardless of war or threat of war. Lying low in the water, their fast-sailing craft swept back and forth across the channel, many of them engaged in smuggling or other clandestine activities, but the servants of Elizabeth would have done well to have listening posts among them. Drake, I believed, did just that.

The *Bonaventure* was a good sailer, as for weeks she proved as we beat back and forth across the channel and sometimes off the coast of Brittany. But never a Spanish sail did we see.

We put back into port to renew our stores. There were stories that Sir John Hawkins was now to command the vessel.

As soon as we dropped anchor I made it ashore to see Emma Delahay.

"Ah!" She looked up from her table as I entered. "It is you! Have you not heard then?"

"Heard? What?"

"There is an order for your arrest. It seems you have offended someone."

An order for my arrest? For a moment I seemed to turn cold. It was what I had feared. Once they had me in prison they would somehow, some way, discover who I was, and I would be killed.

If not by the Queen's men then by those of Leckenbie or his protector.

How much could I trust Emma Delahay? No matter, I had no choice. Only a moment passed, but I knew what I must do.

"What of the *Good Catherine*?"

"She lies yonder. She has discharged her cargo and is reloading."

"My venture?"

"You may see the accounts. You have fifty-five pounds due you."

"Your captain did well. When does he sail again?"

"Within the week." She shuffled some papers upon her table. "There is a place aboard her if you wish." She paused then. "It would be safer, Tatton."

It was the first time she had called me by my given name.

"If you wish to make a venture," she said, "you could go with it and learn the trade for yourself."

He is a wise man who does not overstay his time. "I shall go," I said.

"Be aboard by the Sunday coming, and be careful."

I would, indeed.

CHAPTER 23

WHAT, THEN, TO do? The Queen's men wished to arrest me, something contrived no doubt by Leckenbie's protector. Or had they discovered my true identity? There was always that danger, a danger I would never be without.

With honor I could not simply leave Sir George Clifford, yet to remain about when the order for my arrest was made out was to ask for trouble. I went straightaway to him.

He received me at once and sat back in his chair. "If you have asked to see me at this time," he said, "it cannot but be serious. What is it?"

Risking arrest there and by him, if my crime, whatever it was, proved serious, I told him simply what had been done. I spoke of the broadsides and pamphlets I had written and now of the order for my arrest. Of course, I said nothing of my Irish ancestry, trusting not even him so much.

I knew somewhat of the man. The Queen's champion he was, but he had also lived a wild, reckless life himself and at present had his own troubles.

He listened patiently. "They will not arrest you while you serve me," he said, after a bit, "and no doubt you are safer here. Yet if you wish to go, then go you may.

"However, I would suggest you serve me yet

awhile. You have spoken of your wish to make money with your ventures. It is my wish also, but believe me, Chantry, one good prize and we should all be rich. I need money as much as any man. And I mean to have that prize."

Little I knew how much my life depended on the decision I was then to make, yet what might have happened if I had chosen otherwise? I only know my entire life was changed when I decided.

How often it is that a whim may alter the course of our existences! How often the simple decision whether to go right or left when one leaves a doorway can change so much! A man may turn to the right and walk straightaway into all manner of evil, and to the left, all manner of good.

It was ever my way to push forward, and ever my way to hold to a bargain. My word once given was precious to me, and I had promised to serve with him.

"Sir George," I said, "I dare not be arrested. I do wish to serve you, and to serve England in this hour, yet to be arrested would be fatal." I paused, not wishing to explain why it might be fatal. I trumped up a reason, and logical enough it was, too. "I am convinced that I am to be arrested only to be murdered, that once in prison I would be set upon, when unarmed, by Leckenbie's felons."

"Have no fear. You shall go aboard my ship, and no officer will reach you there, if I have to go to Elizabeth herself to protect you.

"Look you...I have many men, but most serve in hope of prize money, of gaining my attention and hence preferment. Some are mere loiterers, putting in their time. Some are lusty fighters who have often proved their courage and strength. But none has taken hold as you have done.

"Within the short time you have served me you have laid hold of problems and solved them. You know much of the ship's care and husbandry. Any task I set for you I need never think of again, for it is done. You have proved yourself my strong right hand, and already I have mentioned you to Sir John Hawkins, if he should take command."

"And he may?"

"It is possible. The Queen wants me nearby, although I should prefer to be at sea. Well, one more voyage, perhaps. At least one more." He looked up at me suddenly, then glanced about to see if others were near. "Chantry, I shall give you this word and no other, because I wish you to remain with me. I have word . . . very secret word . . . of the sailing of a great Spanish vessel, loaded with treasure. I hope to seize that vessel."

He took up a bottle and filled two wineglasses, putting one of them before me. "Chantry, I will tell you this much. I have an Irish friend . . . oh, do not look surprised! I have an Irish friend who now serves Spain. The information comes from him.

"We have much trouble with Ireland. Most of the Irish would gladly burn England to the dust. But—a very important but—they do not wish anyone else to do it. As one of them once said to me, 'The English are our enemies, but they are *our* enemies. We do not wish to share them with others.' Amusing, is it not? Yet I trust this man, and he has told me of this great vessel coming."

"When?"

He shrugged. "I know not. Only that she will come and we must be out there, waiting."

"Will you have further word?"

"Perhaps. I doubt it. Word is not so easy to receive. Possibly you, with your river-front friends, might learn something. But the less it is talked of the better. Look what I have to contend with—not only the Spanish but so many of our own people who would love to find such a juicy plum ready to fall from the tree.

"I have a fine ship, but I am not Drake, nor Frobisher, nor—"

"But you may be Hawkins?"

He smiled. "That I may be, but even he does not know of this yet."

"I will stay with you, Sir George."

"Good!" He held out his hand. "I thought you might. Now go and finish up whatever it is you have to do and return swiftly, for I think we shall wait but little longer and then return to sea."

Leaving my plumed hat aboard, I chose a dark cloak and a flat cap to wear ashore. Then, armed with my sword, a dagger, and two charged pistols, I went ashore again and made my way to the place of Emma Delahay.

Swiftly as could be I arranged my business with her. Sixty pounds in goods I trusted to her. "Do the best you can. When this is over, I shall be back. If I come not back immediately, do you administer my funds to my best interest and hold the profits for me, for eventually I shall come."

I wonder what strange hint of disaster caused me so to phrase it? Surely, I knew nothing. To my thinking I was but being cautious, having no knowledge of all that would transpire before I came across this threshold again.

The *Bonaventure* went again to sea, and I with her.

Fair blew the winds, and the sails filled as we breasted the seas for the French coast. Some Spanish ships were reported there and beating their way north for England. But we found them not, so Sir George changed course and stood away to the south for the Azores, casting about for prey.

Owner of vast estates, he was encumbered with debts, and a rich prize might make up for all he had wasted in wild living. As he grew older he had also grown wiser, and wished to establish himself once more. Vessels laden with treasure from the Indies or the coast of America might be along soon, and it was one of these we sought.

We had been but ten days at sea when, just as dawn was breaking, I heard the cry from the masthead, "Sail ho!"

"Where away?"

"Three points abaft the beam!"

Our bows came around and we headed down toward her. She was a fair tall ship, a Spanish galleon fresh from the Indies by the look of her.

The decks were cleared for action and we rounded to. As we came alongside we let go with a broadside that toppled the foremast, and shot away a piece of the bowsprit. We closed in then and Sir George motioned me.

"You will lead the boarding party. Secure control of the vessel and make repairs at once, then keep in our company and prepare to assist."

As we came alongside I jumped to the rigging.

Followed by the members of the boarding party, I made ready for the attack. Men were swarming her deck, but much destruction had been done by our broadside and whoever stood upon the poopdeck seemed to have lost command.

As one man we swung in close and over the narrowing gap. There was a brief, fierce struggle as we landed. A man rushed at me, swinging a cutlass. I greeted him with a thrust, then fired a pistol at a second man. Two more closed in about me but one of them fell before the blade of one of our crewmen, a husky lad from Yorkshire. We drove them back, and I noticed a slackening of effort on a part of the crew, men who appeared to be Basques.

A dozen of these had grouped together. Suddenly, as one man, they dropped their swords and surrendered. One of them, a tall, blond lad with a splendid set of shoulders, merely handed me his sword. "Captain, we were forced to sea. None of us wished for this."

"Get forward then, and if it seems to you the mast can be restepped and made useful until it can be replaced, save it. If not, cut it away. Do you and your mates stay forward. Give us good service and you shall be freed."

They went quickly forward. Elsewhere the fighting had well nigh ceased. Here or there some hardened soul held to his blade. I disliked seeing good men die and persuaded some to surrender.

On the poop the young officer awaited me. Near him lay two bodies, of whom one must have been the sailing master—though I knew nothing of the command on a Spanish vessel. The other appeared to be the second in command.

The officer could be no more than sixteen—one of those given command, no doubt, due to family and prestige, with carefully chosen lieutenants who could carry the burden for him. Our fire had killed both, and now he was alone. A handsome lad, too, standing straight and pale with shock, but with no fear in him.

"You have taken my vessel," he said, staring at me in an incredulous manner. The shock was still on him, for our broadside had been remarkably effective. Fortunate for me, unfortunate for him. "It was my first command."

"And this is mine. If you give me your word to cause no trouble, I shall not imprison you."

"Of course, Captain, you have my word."

"Captain?" It was Wilsey, one of my own men. "Look!"

Four ships were bearing down upon us, although still some distance away. We had, in the short time since boarding the Spanish vessel, become separated from the *Bonaventure,* which was hull down over the horizon. The oncoming Spanish vessels looked to cut us off.

"Wilsey, get the prisoners below, all but those working on the forecastle, and make ready the guns."

Again I glanced at the oncoming ships and at our own vessel. "Tell Brooks I said to get some sail on her."

Of commanding such a vessel at sea, I knew little, scarcely more than the Spanish don from whom I had taken command. Nor had Sir George intended to leave me in command, I am sure. He had no doubt expected to come aboard and straighten matters out himself before we proceeded with our mission. Now I was alone.

Ordering the young Spanish officer below, I moved swiftly to get the decks cleared and to pull away from the oncoming Spanish vessels. To escape from them meant also to draw away from the *Bonaventure,* yet there was no other way.

I went below to the cabin, which was beautifully furnished. Disconsolate, the young officer sat slumped in a chair. "Do not despair," I told him. "You shall be treated as a gentleman."

"But I have failed!"

"One failure is not a lifetime, and this was no fault of yours. Remain here. I must go on deck."

With our foremast gone and much of our rigging damaged, I swiftly realized our chances of escape were few. Darkness was hours away.

As I emerged upon the deck, Brooks came to me. "Captain, we are in a bad way. With the fo'm'st gone and damage to the rigging, we can scarcely make steerage way without repairs." He glanced astern. "They'll be up with us long before we can get any sail on her to speak of."

"The guns?"

"Six of them out of action."

"Our men?"

"No losses. Twenty-two men aboard, Captain, only some minor cuts and scratches. Nothing serious." His face was stiff. "We've no chance, Captain. They'll come up to us within the hour . . . two at most."

My thoughts raced, seeking every possible solution. Capture for the crew meant a Spanish prison, with small chance of escape or ransom. Capture for me meant the same, but the crew were my responsibility.

The vessel moved easily upon the water. It was not a rough sea, and the wind was fair.

"Brooks? Would you rather chance capture, or an

open boat for England? It can't be more than two days' sail."

"An open boat?" His face changed as if by magic. The eagerness was apparent. "You mean now? They wouldn't be apt to pursue, and...We'd chance it, Captain. I can speak for them. We'd all chance it."

"All right then, food and water, Brooks. Get the longboat over the side, out of sight of the Spaniards. Arm yourselves, but if they pursue, don't resist and I will do what I can for you. But you've a good chance to get away."

He left on the run, and I turned to the Spanish captain. Of his language I knew a good bit, for Spanish smugglers were often off the Irish coast when I was a lad, and their officers had often visited us at my father's home. Those who would be career soldiers went elsewhere, a career with their own army or the British being out of the question.

"Your name, Captain?"

"Don Vicente Uvalde y Padilla."

"I am Tatton Chantry. Don Vicente, you have lost your ship. Do you wish to regain it?"

His eyes lit with hope. "Regain it? How?"

"It is a matter of honor, Don Vicente. I will surrender the vessel to you if you will give me your word not to pursue my crew, allowing them to put off in the longboat."

He looked at me for a long moment, thinking it out. "My ship is damaged," he said, "too badly damaged, perhaps. You foresee capture, yet you think of your men."

"We could stay and make a fight of it, Don Vicente. We might lose. Our other ships," the plural was only a slight shading of the truth, "may come up to our aid. And they may not. I wish to save my men."

"And you, Captain Chantry?"

"I would surrender myself to you ... to you personally, a Spanish gentleman."

He smiled. "Ah, Captain! You are shrewd! I am permitted to show myself the victor, your crew escapes, and you become my prisoner, trusting to my honor."

"Exactly."

"How close are our ships?" he asked.

"Close," I admitted.

He laughed, delighted. "Oh, this is beautiful! Beautiful! I must remember it, Captain!"

He looked thoughtful. "Your flag is flying, Captain? I think we had better lower it before our ships open fire."

"By all means," I agreed. "I have your word?"

"You do. You do, indeed."

On deck my first glance was off the starboard side. The longboat was there in the water, sail up, making good speed. She was even now a few hundred yards off. I glanced at the Spanish ships. Slower, heavier to handle, they would need another half-hour at least, probably more. By that time the longboat would be over the horizon and out of sight.

Turning, I looked at Don Vicente. Already he had opened the hatch and his men were emerging on deck.

He studied me a moment, his eyes cold and measuring. Yet whatever came, nothing could help me now. For better or worse, I was his prisoner.

CHAPTER 24

A PRISONER I truly was, yet surely no prisoner was ever treated better! Whatever Don Vicente's position, his influence must have been great, for his decisions in my case were not refused. He explained simply that his ship had been severely injured by our broadside, that we had taken the ship, and that he had negotiated its release and a surrender by me on the consideration that the crew be released.

His brother officers accepted me as an equal and from the first I was well treated. In the weeks at sea, constantly using Spanish, my command of the tongue improved. It is a beautiful language, and having ever a love for the music of words, I enjoyed speaking it.

We came at last to Cádiz. As our ship dropped anchor in the ancient harbor I felt a twinge of dismay. Aboard ship all had been well, but this was the Spain of our enemies, the Spain of the Inquisition. What would become of me now?

Not long was I kept waiting, for a vessel put out from shore and came alongside.

The officer who came up the ladder was a sharp-visaged man of perhaps forty, looking every inch the soldier.

"Don Vicente? I am Captain Enrique Martínez. I have come for the prisoner."

"*You* have come for him? The man is my prisoner,

Captain. *Mine*. I took him, I shall keep him. At least until such a time as ransom has been arranged for."

"But I did not think—"

"That is right, Captain. You did not think. Now you will have time for it. Let me repeat, the prisoner is mine. I might add he will also be my guest. If your superiors feel it necessary, they can find him where I am."

He started to turn away but the captain spoke again. "Don Vicente, I regret—"

"Please do not. Regret is a vain thing, my friend, and you no doubt have pressing duties elsewhere. I might add for your personal information that when I was briefly his prisoner I was treated as a gentleman, and while he is my prisoner he, too, will be so treated."

His poise and coolness were remarkable. I stood very quietly, as Don Vicente walked away upon other business.

"I am sorry, Captain Martínez," I said, "but this was the agreement we made."

He shrugged. "Of course. I understand, Captain, and might add that you are fortunate, indeed. I am sure no prisoner Spain has ever taken will be better treated. Don Vicente and his family are noble in every sense." He shrugged. "I was but doing my duty." He paused again. "You may have trouble with the forces of Inquisition, for they are less likely to honor Don Vicente."

The home of Don Vicente was more elegant than any I had ever seen. The apartment to which I was shown was furnished sparsely but well.

He was younger than I, Don Vicente, a handsome man and an only child. Once we were in his home, we talked much. We wandered throughout the world in our long conversations, but then one day he spoke to me of ransom.

It was a question I had dreaded, for who would pay ransom for me? I was alone. I had no one. Some captains and leaders of men, such as Sir John Hawkins, had been known to arrange ransom for prisoners, but I had scarcely been a month at sea when this had happened.

The Earl of Cumberland? But what was I to him? Nor was he a man of great wealth. Although he possessed vast estates, they were heavily encumbered. There was no one to come to my aid.

My own small investments would pay no ransom. Once this was understood my chances of release would be few—or even of staying where I was. The Spanish no doubt thought me a young man of great wealth, and I had nothing.

"I do not know, Don Vicente," I told him. "My family were Irish and they were destroyed in the wars."

He looked at me gravely. "To be without family is bad. How then did you live?"

"As best I could," I replied. "I had thought to be a soldier and win a way to command."

"But is it not your custom to buy your commands?"

"It is. But sometimes—"

"Ah," he exclaimed suddenly. "You are Irish! I know an Irishman! He is a general among us. General Hugo O'Connor!"

Startled, I looked up. "But I know him! And he knows me. Is it possible to see him then?"

"But of course! He is my very good friend, and a most able man. Come! We will go to him!"

On the way Don Vicente related several stories about the general. He had long lived in Spain, was much admired there, and was no longer thought of as other than Spanish. He had done well at the wars and lived in the finest style, and he was much trusted by the King.

The house itself was Moorish, undoubtedly one of those taken over from the Moors when they were driven out. The walls were stark and plain, with only a few high, barred windows, looking out upon the street.

The houses were largely square, with a central patio in which grew flowers and vines, usually around a fountain. The ground floor rooms opened upon the patio, and the upper story possessed a continuous balcony offering access to all the upper rooms. In summer, when the heat was great, the patio was cooled by water sprinkled on its pavement.

We pulled a cord that sounded a bell inside. After a short wait we were admitted to a dark, cool passage, the floor of tile in an interesting pattern, the walls covered with religious paintings. We were shown to a drawing room on the first floor, its walls adorned with tapestries. As the weather was cool, a fire burned on the hearth.

Several braziers were standing about also, containing olive stones which burned with very little odor.

We had scarcely entered when the door at the other side of the room opened and the general stepped in. He was a tall, powerfully made man thickening slightly about the waist, but a man of commanding presence. He was dark and swarthy, Black Irish, as I was in most of my ancestry. He wore a pointed beard, carefully trimmed, and mustaches. He was dressed now in black with a heavy gold chain around his neck and a gold-hilted sword.

He glanced first at me, then started to speak to Don Vicente. Then he paused, looking back at me. "Do I not know you?"

"Don Hugo," Don Vicente said, "I wish you to meet Captain Tatton Chantry. He was taken by me from a British ship. He has said that he knows you."

For a moment I was in a quandary. The name Tatton Chantry would mean nothing to this man, yet he had seemed to recognize me.

"Do not be surprised at the name," I spoke in Gaelic, "it is one I have chosen to wear. He who owned it is now dead. He died at our house, in fact, long ago."

Hugo O'Connor studied me carefully. "It cannot be that you are . . . ? No, no, they are all killed."

"My father was killed. I escaped. I was advised, General, to tell my name to no one, but I must assume that it is known to you. Do you remember Ballycarberry?"

"It was near there, was it?" He spoke in Gaelic and looked at me again. "Aye, you have the look of them, great fighters all, and strong men, but thoughtful men, too! Aye . . . but how did you escape?"

"The story is over long for the telling here," I said, also in Gaelic. "I am Don Vicente's prisoner, and he has spoken of ransom. I have no money, and no friends. I have lived by trade and a little by writing. I have some ventures now at sea, but unless I return to England—"

"To England? You are daft, lad. If they find you it is the headsman's axe or hanging."

"Nonetheless, I intend to buy back the land that was mine, or a part of it. I wish to live again where we did when you came to visit us, when you hunted upon the moors with my father. It is my home, and I long for the view of the sea there, the rocky shores and the high meadows. I will have it again, General."

"Aye," he said gloomily, "I miss it myself. But come! We cannot carry on in Gaelic and leave our friend standing."

He turned to Don Vicente. "I do know him, and I cannot thank you enough for behaving toward him as you have done. You have been gracious and considerate."

He paused. "It is a delicate matter, Don Vicente. This man is no ordinary seafaring man, nor even a soldier. He is of the blood royal, although a man without domains."

Don Vicente shrugged. "I guessed as much. He has the manner."

We seated ourselves and our talk was in Spanish, and pleasant enough it was. General O'Connor I found to be an urbane and charming gentleman, a skillful politician as well as a military man. To have survived and advanced himself to his present status in a foreign country was proof enough of that.

"We must talk again," he said finally. "Do you come when you can." To Don Vicente he said, "We can certainly reach some understanding."

Two days later we met again. "You must have a care," O'Connor warned me, "for there are spies about."

"Spies for the Inquisition?"

"Yes. You are Irish. If they suspect who you are,

you will be murdered. There are also those in Spain who are spies for England. They suspect all Irishmen of plotting against England, so all are suspect."

"I am not thought to be Irish, but from the Hebrides."

"Ah? A nice thought, that. It may help. In the meanwhile, what is it you wish to do?"

"To return to England. I have my ventures there."

"I am afraid that will be impossible. Ransom can be arranged, I think, and luckily for you, Don Vicente is your friend. However, even he is powerless against the Inquisition. And no matter what your beliefs, they will wish to question you if you should draw attention to yourself. There are those among them who do not take kindly to any foreigner in their land. Even we who fight for Spain are suspect."

"Where then should I go? What should I do?"

"I would suggest the Lowlands. I am taking a detachment of troops to join the Duke of Parma there. You will volunteer. That will take you away from their eyes to where much can be done."

"You are very kind."

"Kind? No, not kind. We Irish serving abroad have learned we must stand together. You are one of us, even though what your family was they will never be again—not in the lifetime of any who now live, at least."

We talked the hours away, and planned the steps that must be taken. If I were to volunteer to serve in the Spanish army no thought of ransom would remain, although a small indemnity might have to be paid. I knew naught of such matters and left negotiations in the hands of General O'Connor, who had much experience.

In the meanwhile, I fenced each day and rode with Don Vicente over his estates in the country. By night I read much in the admirable library Don Vicente possessed. I say possessed, but this was all he did with the books. For I discovered with some surprise that he could not read, disdaining the practice as not befitting a gentleman. The library had been in the home when it was taken by his grandfather from the Moors. Some of the books were in Arabic, of which I knew nothing, but most were in Latin, at which I was proficient.

Yet every day and every night I bethought me of ways by which I might escape once I had reached the Lowlands, for my only wish was to return to England and my ventures, such as they might be. And each day in Spain I must walk with care, for I was free only upon a whim of circumstance and might at any time be imprisoned.

Carefully, I had avoided women. In England those I met were not the sort who appealed to me. Those I was meeting in Spain were ladies of great houses and ladies of the court. To give attention to such women even if they wished for it was to incur trouble from some other less favored man. And true it was that with Don Vicente and General O'Connor I constantly met women, many of whom were lovely.

Although I was permitted to move about with seeming freedom I knew I was not free, that I was under observation most if not all the time. My movements, comments, and actions were subject to scrutiny.

Meanwhile I was learning a good deal about the Spanish army from General O'Connor. "Many Germans and Irish serve with us," he explained. "Young Spanish men of good family wish to avoid service, as do many of the others. A few years ago volunteers thronged to serve, but now they grow fewer. Yet it is a good army, and the men are well trained."

"How long," I asked him, "will it remain so if the citizens themselves do not wish to serve? In ancient Rome the mercenaries soon controlled the government, and I hear it has been so in other places as well."

The general shrugged. "I ask only to serve. When we lack for government or army of our own, some of us must needs find careers where we can. I am loyal to Spain because it is Spain that gave me opportunity to be so. But you are right. Those who do not wish to be bothered with service to their country soon find there are others only too willing to occupy the places they shun. Those who shunned service soon become the servants rather than the masters."

Suddenly I was restless. Too long had I remained inactive and I wished to be about my business. I was never one who could spend my days in social activity, no matter how pleasant. I said as much.

"Soon," O'Connor said. "We are preparing now to send men to the Lowlands. I shall see that you are among the first to go." He paused then, walking to the window that overlooked the narrow street. "You know," he suggested, "there are worse lives than this. You have started well. You have made a place for yourself here.

"Don Vicente likes you. You are important to him as evidence of his first success, but he obviously likes you personally, as does his family. They have great power here, and I am sure your every success would be considered a success of their own."

"That may be as you suggest," I replied, "but my future must be elsewhere. I must return to my own country."

"Sooner or later they would find you out."

"That may be, but there I must go. I will serve with you, and serve you well, but sooner or later I must return to Ireland."

"Very well." He buckled his sword. "It is time for me to go. You are meeting Don Vicente?"

"I am. We are going to some races. I—"

"A moment!" O'Connor lifted a hand. "I have been meaning to warn you. There are family feuds here in Spain as well as in Ireland, and Don Vicente and his family have enemies. Only last night one of my people informed me that Don Vicente is in grave danger.

"He is fiercely proud, as are all *hidalgos*. His enemies intend to destroy him, and with him the pride of his family. For as you know, he is an only child."

"Destroy him? How?"

"One of their number is Don Fernand Sarmiento. He is one of the finest swordsmen in Spain, and lately returned to Spain from France, where I understand he killed two men in duels. For one reason or another, he is desperate to establish a pretext for challenging Don Vicente."

"You are sure of this?"

"I am. One of the principal ways of remaining secure in a country not your own is to be aware, to know where the power lies, and what moves are being made. Long ago I established my own lines of communication. Believe me, my information is reliable."

I considered what General O'Connor had said and debated what best I might do.

Warn my friend? That would do no good, for his pride was such that he would not flee from danger, or even try to avoid it. In fact, to warn him might only precipitate the situation I would be trying to avoid.

I had fenced much with Don Vicente, and held my skill from sight, careful not to seem too proficient, but to let him have the better of me at times. After all, he was my friend, and what had I to gain by proving myself better than he? With a skillful swordsman for an enemy, Don Vicente would have no chance at all.

The place we had elected to start out for the races could scarcely have been worse. It was at the top of the Calle Mayor where stood the church of San Felipe el Real, where people of the arts—writers, painters, dramatists, and others of the theater—were wont to meet. Mingled with them were young gallants of the town, soldiers home from the wars—and many another who called himself soldier but who avoided any battle other than those found in taverns or boudoirs.

Standing there, awaiting Don Vicente's arrival, I listened to the talk and laughter, the witticisms and attempts at such with only a piece of my mind. Rather, I wondered what it was I should do.

Don Vicente's conduct toward me had been most courteous. Without his influence I should have been in prison or pulling an oar in a galley.

Suddenly I heard a strange voice behind me. "Luís? This is my friend Don Fernand Sarmiento."

"A pleasure, señor!" said the man named Luís. "You are to be in Madrid for long?"

"A few days only. I regret, but it is true. A small mission here, and then I shall return to Málaga."

Another voice broke in. "Quiet now! He comes."

And indeed I saw Don Vicente approaching. They must have known of his coming, and been awaiting him here. He must often come this way . . . that might be it. But there might also be a spy in his household, someone in Vicente's own establishment. Yet the servants whom I knew were fiercely loyal, or seemed to be.

Don Vicente came up the steps. "Tatt! You are here before me! I am sorry, for I would not have you wait."

"Think nothing of it," I said. "Down the street there is a place—"

Don Fernand had turned sharply, bumping into Don Vicente. Instantly, I stepped between them. "Señor!" I spoke sharply. "You are rude!"

For a moment he hesitated, his eyes going from Don Vicente to me. It was Vicente with whom he wanted to quarrel, not I.

He was a narrow-visaged man with piercing black eyes and a face somewhat pocked, a lean and savage man. "Out of my way!" he said. "I have no business with you!"

"But you do, señor. And you have a sword with which to conduct it."

Trapped, he glared at me. Dropping his hand to the hilt of his sword, he spoke in what he meant to be a menacing tone. "Once more, señor, I command you. *Step aside!* I do not wish to kill you!"

CHAPTER 25

AVE NO WORRIES, señor. It will be my pleasure to see that you do not."

He frowned, furious, yet hesitant. It was Don Vicente whom he intended to kill. Who in God's name was I, this interloper, this stranger?

"Who are you?" he said. "I know you not!"

"Captain Tatton Chantry, señor. At your service, *if you are not a coward?*"

"A *coward?* For that I'll—!"

"But not on the steps of a church, señor. There must be a secluded corner where we can enjoy the festivities."

"In the alleyway then, and I'll slit your gullet."

"What has come over you?" Don Vicente was astonished. "He sought to evade the quarrel!"

Another man, a slim and handsome fellow with red mustaches, had come to stand beside us. "It was you, señor," he said to Vicente, "it was you I believe he wanted. The man is a famous *matón,* a killer for hire."

Don Vicente's lips tightened. "If it was I he sought, then it is I who must fight him."

"I am sorry, my friend," I said gently. "It may have been you he intended to fight, but it is I who named him a coward. Therefore, I must give him satisfaction."

"That is the way of it," our new friend said, and then he added, "I am Tomás O'Crowley, an officer in His

Spanish Majesty's service." He bowed slightly. "I have heard your name spoken, Captain Chantry. We are to be brother officers in the Lowlands, I believe. If you please, I should like to be your second in this affair."

"I accept the offer. Shall we go? I have no wish to keep them waiting." Turning to Vicente, I said quietly, "Keep your back to the wall. It is you they wished to kill, and he may have others with him."

The alley was a cool and quiet place, and secluded. As I approached, Don Fernand Sarmiento had drawn his sword and was waiting.

"Come! Let us have done with this!" he exclaimed impatiently. "You, Señor Whoever-You-Are! On guard!"

I was young, and he who faced me older. It was his mistake that he coupled my youth with the assumption that I must also be inexperienced and therefore impetuous. He was cool, adept, and disdainful. My whole intent had one purpose: to catch him out of time, for timing is of the greatest importance.

My opponent was a killer, hired for the task, yet I was not his prey. Therefore he wished to be rid of me quickly. In several brief exchanges he seemed to have the better of me, yet I had learned to trust to my subconscious instinct for the proper moment of attack. When it came . . . he lunged. His recovery was a little slow, but my riposte was not. My cut was for the cheek but my point was a bit low—or perhaps he shifted his head at just the wrong instant. My point struck his jawbone and was deflected downward. He took four inches of my blade through his neck.

My withdrawal was instantaneous but already he was choking on his own blood. I stepped back, blade still on guard. And it was well that I kept it so, for in one wild, vicious effort he swung the edge of his sword at me with a wide cut, in a desperate effort to take me with him.

My blade caught his and deflected it, although the power of the cut was staggering.

He stumbled forward, his own point striking the pavement as he fell. Then he rolled over, face upward, his ruff stained red with blood, his eyes already glazing.

"I think," O'Crowley suggested, "we had best be away from here."

"Just one thing more," I said, my naked blade still in my hand. "You, who came with him. Tell your master there is to be no more of this. If other *matónes* are sent to do his bloody work, tell him that I shall seek him out, and *he* shall pay, not such as this." I gestured toward Sarmiento.

A few minutes later we sat in a small *bodegone* or tavern. "A glass of wine?" O'Crowley suggested. "Or would you prefer some chocolate?"

Chocolate was a drink newly arrived from the Indies and one very popular in Spain, where they drank it at all hours. The Spanish also drank wine, I had noted, but rarely to excess.

"Wine first," I said, "and then, perhaps, some chocolate." I felt the need of nothing, and was shaken. What I wished for most was simply to be still, to recover myself a bit. For swordsman though I was—and certainly no novice to fighting and bloodshed—I liked it not.

"How did you know what he was about?" Vicente asked me. "For know you did."

"I was forewarned, and so ready."

"You risked your life for me."

"You are my friend. You have been gracious. I knew that you would fight, but I also knew that the man was certain to be very dangerous."

"Yet you fought him."

"My training," I commented dryly, "has been good. We Irish are an embattled race, and I have almost as many enemies as you have."

"Nevertheless—"

"My friend," I said to Vicente, "you are of great courage. This I saw when first we met. You would have fought bravely, but Sarmiento was a professional assassin and it needs more than courage against such a one. Courage, without the fighting skills, can get a man killed—and quickly."

"I thank you, and my family will thank you also. Whatever you shall need, call upon us."

"I am obliged, but what I need I can find. Although I appreciate your consideration and want only the respect and affection of your family."

"This is all very well," O'Crowley said, "but to live a life well, discretion is needed as much as courage. And in this case I would suggest that discretion would be a fast horse to Málaga where a ship is being laden for the Lowlands, and it is there that I myself am bound.

"There will be an inquiry, and it might well be that you would lie in prison until the problem is resolved. And that might be this year, or next, or the year after."

I finished my chocolate. "Vicente, my thanks for your hospitality. . . . Take care to guard yourself. I am off."

The most-traveled road to Málaga was a busy one, so we took another, to be out of sight. The death of one *matón* in Madrid was not apt to attract notice, but that he had been killed by a foreigner was. Those who hired Sarmiento could ask questions.

Our mounts were good ones, for none are better than the Spanish horses. We rode swiftly, taking lonely trails through the mountains, places where a man must ever ride with a loose blade and a charged pistol. Yet we came at last to Málaga and reported to our ship.

Aboard, I saw at once what could be done, for I was just lately from doing the same on the ship I had sailed from England. Thus I went quietly about, making myself useful at familiar tasks.

The following day General Hugo O'Connor came aboard and we put to sea. And it was well we were away, for the general told me that an order had been issued for my arrest.

"Do not worry about it," he said. "I have spoken to the uncle of Vicente. Steps will be taken to clear your name. The charges against you will be dismissed within a fortnight. And should you ever return to Spain, all will be well."

How CAN I relate the passage of years? Now that I look back, the memories are confused. The fierceness of one battle is lost in the glory of the next, the splendor of the days between like a tapestry of joy, of sorrow.

I remember with pain a fine horse shot from under me at Ivry ... such a splendid animal! I regret him still, for we had served much together. But, strangely, he was wooed and won by battle, the sound of trumpets, of drums marching, the clash of arms; they were enough to fill him with excitement. He longed for the charge, the fray, the heat of battle.

How many times he carried me where I might else not have gone! How many times was I called a hero because of that steed and the melees into which he took me! Truly, we were one, but often it was his decision that took me into the hottest part of the battle.

Even a distant fight filled him with impatience. He would toss his noble head and tug at the bit, and his hooves would move restlessly, eager to be away.

A history of my life during those years might be written in the history of the horses I rode. At Arques I was wounded with a pike. At Ivry I sustained minor cuts, bruises, and a small wound in the muscle of my thigh from a musket ball that all but missed.

And was my side always the right side? I did not know, being but little versed in the politics of Europe. It was enough that it was the side I was on, the side that was paying me, for I had no country, no army, no government. Perhaps I was no better than Sarmiento, whom I had killed. I only know that war for many of us who had no country was a way of life.

We were roundly defeated at Arques. Henry of France, who commanded against us, was a shrewd as well as a brave man, and he tricked us into a defile on the Bethune River. It is futile now to say I saw it coming, for during our long talks Fergus MacAskill taught me much of the tactics and science of war. That defile smelled of blood, and I shied from it.

I spoke to O'Connor of it. "Aye!" he said grimly. "But our orders take us there." More than three thousand died there. That was September '89 and a bloody time it was.

At Dreux, besieged by Henry, he lifted the siege and slipped away because as at Arques his forces were less and he chose to fight on ground of his own selection. That proved to be Ivry and again Henry won.

My horse killed, I joined the Swiss contingent, and when all others fled the field the Swiss stood fast, and I with them. Obtaining honorable terms, the Swiss surrendered. Once again I was a prisoner.

It was to Henry IV himself that I was taken. Aside from the soldier who guarded me and two aides, we were alone. He looked up from the map he had been studying and eyed me coldly.

"You were with the Swiss, yet you are not Swiss. What are you then?"

"An Irishman, Your Majesty, taken at sea by the Spanish."

"Yet fighting on the side of my enemies."

"My only means to escape was the army, sire."

"You were on an English ship?"

"I was, sire."

"Yet you later fought valiantly against my men."

"I had no choice. It was fight or be killed. Besides," I admitted, "once the battle is joined I like to fight."

He smiled ever so slightly. "I know," he said dryly, "I fight with some Irishmen, too." He sat back in his chair and studied me. "There is an air about you," he said at last, "that puzzles me." He looked down at the paper before him. "Tatton Chantry . . . I do not know the name."

"I shall make it known, sire. A name is only what one makes it. In the years to come there will be other Henrys, as there have been in the past, but only one Henry of Navarre."

"Like all the Irish," he said, amused, "you talk easily, and always with the right words." He scowled. "Chantry. I know not the name. Should there not be a *Mac* or an *O* before it?"

"I had another name once," I said, "but put it aside long since. I discovered," I spoke wryly, "that those of my name did not live long. When a land is taken and the people remain unconquered it is considered wise to eliminate all those about whom an uprising might gather."

"Ah? And you are such a one?"

"I am descended," I replied, "from Nuada of the Silver Hand, chieftain and king of the *Tuatha De Danaan* when first they migrated from the east into Ireland."

"A son of kings, then?"

"We have no kings in Ireland," I said, "and the Hill of Tara is now grown over with grass. Where our halls and palaces once stood, the sheep now graze."

"The son of kings? Can I do less than treat you so? Yet how do I know this is not merely a clever story concocted by your Irish wit?"

"I have said so much," I replied, "only because you are a king, and I am young enough still to believe in the honor of kings. There is no one to attest to what I am, and few who care. The English wish me dead, as I might in their place."

"You seem to hold little enmity toward them," he mused. "I find this strange."

"Each of us does what he must do. I may kill the wolf who kills my sheep, but I understand him, too. If the wolf must die that my sheep may live, so be it. But I need not hate the wolf for what it is his nature to be."

"Hah! You are a philosopher, too? Well, what would you have me do?"

"As Your Majesty wishes. Had I my choice, I'd be freed to return to England to someday buy the land that was once my own."

"What was it like, your home?"

"It is a green place, sire, green among a chaos of granite, bold hills and great boulders leaning, moss growing at their feet. The forests that once covered Ireland are gone, but the land holds a memory of them, as all the rocks there have a memory of the sea that once washed upon them and hollowed and polished.

"The walls of my home were gray granite, and the beams and panels of oak. There was little furniture but what there was was also of oak. And at the door a stream ran past, swiftly it ran, hurrying down the steep rocks to fall over a cliff and into the sea.

"There is a cove there, almost landlocked, where a man can have a boat. And there is the sea beyond, with fish awaiting. And the sound of the sea snarling and growling among the worn rocks. Sheep graze there, and there is a garden sometimes, and paths by which to walk the hills in the morning mist or evening shadow.

"There are far moors to gallop over on our fine Irish horses or the wild ponies of the moors. It is a place to live and love in, sire, and I would go back there and abide, nor ever come away again."

He shook his head. "No man should be kept from such a dream. Does the house stand yet?"

"It was burned, sire. But what men built, men can build again. I shall go back."

"Aye! Do you go then!" He tossed a purse upon the

table. "Let a king share with a king. You have no sword?"

"It was taken from me when I surrendered."

"So?" He turned to an officer standing behind him. "Gabriel? Bring me the silver sword."

"The silver-handled one? But, sire—"

"Bring it. These are hard times, and this Irishman has brought me something of pleasure with his words and his ways. Perhaps he is a king, and certainly the sword should go to nothing less."

The sword was a fine one, with a thin blade, at least forty inches long, edged on both sides with razor sharpness. The hilt was of silver, beautifully turned, an emerald set in the top and on either end of the guard. The scabbard, too, was finely wrought.

"Take it, and go your way. Gabriel, see he has a horse—a fine one—and this, too."

Taking up a sheet of paper, he had written in a fine, flowing hand: *Let this man, Tatton Chantry, ride where he wills*. And then he signed it, *Henri*.

"Go now, and may luck ride with you!"

Just before I vanished from earshot, I heard Gabriel say: "Do you believe he is a son of kings?"

King Henry laughed. "It does not matter. He carries himself like one and has a certain style. He brightened my morning, and these days are dark, very dark."

My horse was a dappled gray with a black mane and tail, a splendid horse. As I mounted, I remembered the words overheard.

"You, too, Henry," I said aloud. "You also carry yourself like a king, and you, too, have a style!"

CHAPTER 26

ALONE I RODE along the byways of France. Alone I dined at wayside taverns, or pausing beside the road, ate of bread, cheese, and wine, while my good steed cropped the green grass of the roadside.

Dark and thick was the cloak I wore for strong blew the wind, and often cold the rain. Continual war had made the people sullen and remote, wanting no dealings with such as I, a wanderer returning from the wars, although some looked long at my horse and my sword of the silver handle.

Yet always I rode on, avoiding the main roads for fear of being stopped. And I was but once.

An imperious officer accompanied by six men waved me down. "Who are you, and from whence do you come?" he demanded.

"I ride to Rouen," I said, "and I come from Henry of Navarre."

Some of his truculence vanished at that, but he did not truly believe until I rode close and showed him my letter. He stared at it, astonished, and then at me. "I have never seen such a letter!" he said. "You must be a great man, indeed!"

"I am a wayfarer, wishing to go on. Now, if you have done?"

The sky was sullen and a light rain was falling.

Bundled in my cloak I rode the dim sun down and into the clouded night where the eyes gained only blackness and the faint shine of rain pools in the muddy road. I drew my horse to a walk, for the footing was slippery. "Walk gently," I said to him, "for you carry an Irish lad on his way home."

He twitched an ear at me. That I could see, but little else. What I dearly longed for was an inn, or any place at all to shelter my head. Suddenly before me the road took a branch off to the side and I drew up, peering into the night.

High above the road I saw a dim reflection of light. The light tempted, but a faint smell of broiling meat scored victory, and for better or worse I turned my horse into the side road and mounted steeply to what I soon saw was an ancient castle, long in ruins. A sensible man would have turned back, but I was Irish and hungry to boot.

Under a noble arch and into a courtyard I rode. At one side was an empty stable. I swung down and led my horse within. There was fresh hay there, and I tied him at a manger, bundled hay to him, and then loosened my sword in its sheath. I'd a brace of pistols with me, and I tucked them behind my belt and under the cloak. Then I mounted some ancient stairs, my nose following the aroma of the meat. I emerged in a room where there were five men and a girl, and the girl was bound.

The surprise was complete, for myself as well as for them. The door I used was obviously not the one by which they had entered, for had I been a ghost they could have been no more astonished.

The men drew their weapons. "Hold!" I said. The

eyes of the girl lighted with hope when she saw me. Yet I knew not what happened here, or was likely to happen—except that five more miserable cutthroats I had never seen.

"Attack," I said calmly, "and there will be bloodshed."

Truer word was never spoke. The trouble was that the blood might well be mine, a chance I viewed with some discomfort. If I bleed, I bleed better in the sunlight, not upon a dark and stormy night in such a ruin.

Yet it needed no seer to realize that I had stumbled upon some proper rogues—thieves or worse. Spread before them and beside the fire was a nice collection of rings, candlesticks, and chains, most made of gold.

"Who are you?" The speaker was a bold rascal with somewhat protruding eyes and a greasy, unwashed look about him. A pity to thrust a clean blade into such a dirty ruffian.

Who was I? A stupid question, for what did it matter? In a moment they would realize that I was one and they were five and that I had come upon them at an inopportune time from which I must not be allowed to escape.

The girl they held bound was of quality, a lady by appearance and dress, though somewhat bedraggled at the moment. With all of that, a decidedly pretty girl.

"I have come for her," I said, reaching with my left hand for the spit on which broiled the meat. I had not been a soldier these past many months for nothing.

I took a generous bite of the meat. "And," I continued, "if you be fleet of foot you may make it to the river and so 'scape hanging."

"Hanging?" One of them frowned sharply, a cowardly rascal if ever I saw one. *You I'll spit last,* I told myself, *for you'll hang back and let the others risk.*

"Who talks of hanging?" the bold dirty one said. He must be first, clean blade or no. "Who in this forsaken land is there to hang anyone? And where do you come from? If you toss us your sword we may let you go."

I smiled. Dirty though he was, I could almost like the man for his daring.

"A column of troops awaits me below," I said. "I came up looking for a bit of shelter"—here I took another bite of the meat—"and found you. There are the battlements here, and we have the ropes.

"Do you cut the lady free." I pointed the spit at the cowardly one. "The rest of you have one minute to decide whether to run or hang."

"He's lying!"

"Do you want to risk it?" I said cheerfully.

"If you have so many men, call them up," the bold one said. Ah, he was a worthy scoundrel!

"In due course," I said.

"He's lying!" the bold one said. "Take him!"

I had never thought to fool them, so when the nearest man raised suddenly up, coming off the ground, turning and drawing his blade, I thrust the end of the spit into his gaping mouth, taking a couple of his last remaining teeth with it.

With my sword in my right hand, swiftly drawn, I plucked a pistol from my belt. It was point-blank, scarce ten feet, and I fired. The ball took a man in the chest and he went down.

Still clutching the now-empty pistol, I crossed

blades with a third man as the others closed in. Stepping quickly around, I was beside the girl with the fire between myself and the others.

Two were down and I was faced by three, one of them a hulking brute missing one thumb.

"See? He has no men outside! That shot would have brought them!"

"Can't you hear their voices?" I suggested. I lowered my blade and flicked that razorlike edge through one of the ropes that bound the lady's ankles.

They began to circle the fire, coming from both sides. To face two I must turn my side to another. I faced the two, and went at them, moving swiftly toward them. The sudden attack made them back up. One lifted a heavy staff and struck down at my head. Avoiding it, I went in low, lifting the pistol in my left hand to ward off the blow. At the same time I thrust. He had lunged when he swung his stick and he spitted himself neatly on my sword. His mouth gaped at me and his eyes, a milky blue, stared owlishly. I drew back sharply at a howl of agony from behind me and glimpsed the third attacker scrambling from the flames. The girl, bless her heart, had somehow tripped him as he passed her, spilling him into the fire.

He scrambled out, screaming and beating at his flaming clothes.

Now it was just the bold one and myself. I looked across my blade at him, and smiled. There was no coward in him, and he came at me. Suddenly, and surprisingly, I knew this was no ordinary rogue. I faced a master.

We fought desperately, silently, our blades like dancing light. Time and again I thought I had him, but each time he had a counter, a swift riposte. Nor could he reach me.

Suddenly he drew back and stopped. "Who *are* you?" he demanded. "From whence do you come?"

Stepping back in my own time, I flipped my blade through those ropes that bound the girl's wrists. Quickly, she freed herself.

"Does it matter now?" I said carelessly.

"You handle a blade exceeding well," he replied. "There are not five men in Europe who can stand against me."

"I would think you could find a better trade," I commented, "and better company."

He shrugged. "It is the fortunes of war. I was a gentleman once and knighted. My name is Tankarville. I held vast estates from my father and mother. There was much intrigue about court and I supported the wrong side. We lost. Some of us were beheaded, some fled, some were imprisoned. My estates were taken by the crown and I was lucky to escape with my head and a sword. That was ten years and now I am a brigand, living as best I can."

"And what of the lady here?"

"Take her, and welcome. But guard yourself well, my friend, or she will have a knife in your ribs."

I laughed. "You asked my name. It is Tatton Chantry, and I ride to Rouen. If you wish another bout with the blades you have only to seek me out."

"And I may," he said cheerfully.

Tucking the empty pistol behind my belt, I touched the other to make sure it was still with me, and then, sword in hand, I backed from the room. The girl came with me.

When I had recovered my horse she said, "Their horses are down below, and mine, also."

"You were riding when they took you?"

"Oh, no! They raided the chateau where I live. They came when they knew that all were away, and looted it, stealing all they could find. When I discovered them, they took me as well, exchanging their horses for our better ones."

"Then let us get your horse."

Leading my own and walking beside her, we went down a steep path, and there in a clump of trees were the horses.

She went straight to her horse. At the base of the tree to which he was tied, she picked up a small bundle.

I helped her to the saddle, and together we rode down the slope and back to the high road which led toward Rouen. It led across a high, open plain with only rare clumps of trees. We rode briskly, and she seemed disinclined to talk.

She was a comely lass and I'd not have minded talking, but my few attempts to open a conversation came to nothing.

"Where lies your home?" I asked finally.

"Yonder," she pointed off to the south, "but I dare not go there now for fear they might come back."

"Were there no servants?"

"They were away when the brigands came and will not know what to make of my misfortune. I dare not go back. Take me with you to Rouen."

"Do you have friends there?"

"Of course! Although," she added, "it is a town to which I rarely go. Our market town was Dreux, although there were villages closer. My family is gone and I am afraid to go back alone."

It seemed a far way to take her from home, yet she must know best so I asked no further questions. The night was already well along and I, for one, was weary. All day I had been riding and my horse needed rest.

The road was dark, and there were no stars. "Know you a place where we might take shelter?" I suggested. "The night has far to go, and my horse and I have been long upon the road."

"There is an abbey further along, and also an inn, the Great Stag, I believe, or something of the kind. I have not often come this way."

The village was small, and built along the banks of the Seine. But the hostelry itself was large for the time. Half-timbered in structure, it was a post-house. And I did recall some story that this was the place where the father of Henry of Navarre had died after being wounded at the siege of Rouen. A single light showed from a lower window.

The door opened readily enough at my knock and a man in a leather jerkin held high a light. "Two wayfarers," I said, "seeking food and shelter."

"You be late, but come in nevertheless."

"We have horses," I suggested.

"Aye, aye! Cannot I see? They will be taken care of." He spoke in a mixture of French and English and with a strong English accent.

"You are an Englishman," I said.

"I am! Although I married a Frenchwoman and have lived much of my life here." He peered at me. "You be English?"

"From the Hebrides, if you call that English."

He showed us to a bench by the fire, and a fine fire it was with a goodly blaze on the hearth. I extended my hands to it, and saw the man's eyes go to the maid with me. Her clothing was soiled from the rough treatment she'd received.

Curiosity can be an ill thing and can lead to all manner of speculation, so I thought to quiet his doubts at once.

"The lady and I have had a rough night of it. An encounter with brigands," I explained.

"Well, well! 'Tis not uncommon! They be fond of this country hereabouts, but not of this place. Here you may rest secure."

He gestured. "All are asleep but me. Sit you, and when I have put up your horses I shall find what food I can."

He disappeared, and after a few minutes returned and brought a loaf, some cold meat, and cheese to the table, and with it a bottle of cider.

He looked again at me. "The dapple is your horse? I seem to know it."

"It was given me," I explained, "by the King."

"Aye," there was respect in his tone, "a fine animal! I knew I had seen it." He glanced at my companion. "And your horse also. I know it."

"We recovered it from the brigands," I said.

He looked at my companion again but offered no comment. Nor, to my surprise, did she. Although her home was some distance off, such a man as this would be likely to know any noble family thereabouts, know *of* them at least.

When he was gone I said, "You have not told me your name."

"Marie d'Harcourt," she replied.

It was a familiar name. There were several d'Harcourt families, I believed, though I knew little of French names.

Soon the man returned. When we had eaten, he showed us to our separate chambers. Marie clutched tight the strings of her bundle and refused help in carrying it, but once when it bumped her leg I heard a faint *clank,* a metallic sound.

No sooner had my body touched the bed than I was off into a sound sleep, and did not awaken until the sun was high. For a few minutes I lay still, then sat up, ordered some water brought, and bathed.

The maid lingered at the door, glancing at me with large eyes and what seemed an inviting expression, although I was but a poor judge of such things.

"Has the lady next door eaten?" I asked.

"She is gone."

"Gone?"

She smiled openly at my astonishment. "She left hours ago, before it was light."

I did not believe it, but a quick glance into her room proved the maid was right. Marie d'Harcourt was indeed gone.

When I reached the common room of the inn food was placed upon the table for me. He who served me was not the same who had served me the night before. He explained that the lady did not wish me disturbed. She had left at daylight on the road to Rouen.

"It is not safe for her to be on the highroad alone," I objected. "You should have awakened me."

"Do not worry," the innkeeper said dryly, "she will fare well. She has beauty but she also has wit."

"You know her then? You know Marie d'Harcourt?"

"I do not know her," he replied, "nor is she a d'Harcourt, for of them I know much, and a fine family they are. What her name might be I know not, but it is not d'Harcourt."

So...I had been fooled! But who was she then? And who did the brigands believe she was?

"You had trouble along the road?"

I explained my adventures of the night before and when I described my opponent he shook his head. "My friend, you are fortunate, indeed—or one of the finest swordsmen in Europe. The man whom you met is Andre de Tankarville, and it is said no man has stood against him."

He related the story then. It followed the one Tankarville had told. "The family had two branches, or so I have heard, the one intelligent, religious, devout. The other not religious, though nonetheless they were loyal to a fault, and of great courage also."

My meal was complete. I paid what was required and stood up. Then the door opened and Tankarville stood there, his face flushed with hard riding in the wind, and with anger as well. "Where is she?" he demanded.

"Gone," I said.

"She took it all! Every last coin, every ring, every candlestick!"

So that was what was in the bundle! How she had managed it, I did not know. And yet...when we were fighting, Tankarville and I, where was she then? Was she gathering up the more valuable jewels and hiding them on her person?

"We are fools, my friend, for she has duped us both and is away, gone three hours or more."

He slammed his fist upon the table, then dropped into a chair. "Give him a mug of cider," I said. "And I shall have another. She's gone, my friend, so forget about it."

"Forget about it? There was a fortune there! A king's ransom, if you will! Not the gold so much as the gems! A full dozen of them!"

He gripped the handle of the mug and swore, then looked up at me and suddenly grinned. "Ah, what a handy wench! She will fare well, that one!"

"Where did you come upon her?"

"You may well ask. She is anything but a lady, though who she is I do not know. I will not say how or where we came upon the treasure, but we came upon it. She was also in the process of helping herself so we had no choice but to carry her off—at least far enough so she could not inform upon us."

We talked no more, but finished our cider. I went to my horse and Tankerville followed, muttering in his anger.

When I swung to the saddle, I held down a hand to him. Enemies we had been but he was a fine hand with a blade, and a daring rogue, withal.

"If you will," I said, "go to Henry of Navarre. He needs good fighting men and I think he will be generous. Tell him Tatton Chantry sent you, though it may or may not help."

With that I was off to Rouen, with England just down the river and across the channel. It was in my thoughts that after nearly four years I would be close to my homeland again, home from captivity in Spain, from meeting with Henry and all that had transpired between.

And what of my ventures? What might have become of them after four years?

And what of Rafe Leckenbie?

CHAPTER 27

THE ROUEN INTO which I rode, coming down a winding trail from the plateau above, was a bustling port, crowded with shipping from the sea and with boats and barges down the Seine from Paris. There were numerous inns and drinking places, and sailors everywhere, mingling with soldiers and civilians.

I found an excellent hostelry close enough to the waterfront to observe the ships. There I stabled my horse and entered the inn.

The room I had was small and neat and absolutely clean, which was a pleasure. Water was brought to me and I bathed, taking my time about it while considering my next move.

To find a ship to England or Scotland, and one leaving at the earliest possible moment, was my most immediate goal. There were many here friendly to England. And once again I must forget my Irish ancestry and consider myself a native of the Hebrides.

The keeper of the inn directed me to a nearby tailor and I ordered four suits, head to heels, one of them for travel.

While they were being made, I went to my horse. He was standing in a fine stall, munching very good hay, and seemed content to be there, but he took his nose from the manger and nudged me with it. I patted him on the shoulder, talked to him a bit, then walked out into the street, going first to the Quai du Havre where I strolled along, examining the shipping.

Several of the vessels were Flemish, and at least one was from the Mediterranean—a dark, low vessel that lay quietly alongside the quay with no visible activity amid the bustle and confusion of the other ships.

Some seamen loitered near a bollard and I paused. "Hear you aught of a ship loading for England?" I asked.

They looked at me and made at first no reply. Then the smaller of the lot, a slim, wiry fellow, answered. "Little enough for there this fortnight," he said. "Mostly they are loading for the Baltic or the Mediterranean. Is it passage you seek?"

"Aye, and if you hear of aught I am Captain Chantry at the Hotel des Bons Enfants, in the street of the same name. And there's a bit of silver for him who brings me a true word."

"It will not be one of us who decides you may go," the man said.

"Of course. Just word of a ship. I shall do the rest if it can be done."

My street was a bit of a walk from the quays but the masts of the ships could be seen from my window, and it gave me a feeling of nearness, at least. Back at the inn I seated myself in the common room and ordered an omelette and a bottle of wine.

It was the custom to eat but two meals, one at ten and one at four, but travelers such as I ate when hungry, and that I was. The omelette was excellent, and followed by a potpourri composed of veal, mutton, bacon, and vegetables.

Suddenly a man loomed over me. Glancing up, I saw a big, swarthy young man with rings in his ears. "You seek a ship for England?"

"I do."

"For yourself alone?"

"Myself and my horse, and the horse is a fine one. Do you know of such a ship?"

"It may be. I shall speak to the master. It is to London we sail."

"Bespeak a passage then for myself and a horse. The name is Chantry."

He stared at me. "Be you Tatton Chantry? The swordsman?"

"I am Tatton Chantry, and I have a sword."

"Ah, the master will be pleased!"

———

THE PASSAGE BACK was rough but short. When I led my horse down the gangplank to the London dock he could have been no more pleased to reach land than I. Mounted, I rode at once to the house of Emma Delahay.

For a moment I could only sit my horse and stare. The house was partly burned, the windows boarded over. Emma Delahay was gone! I asked a passerby for news. He merely shrugged and walked on. I walked my horse up the street and stopped at a familiar sign. There a man named Holmes had a small shop where he sold clothes to sailors and the like.

"Emma Delahay, you say? Been gone for four years, Cap'n. Seen nothing of her, all that time."

At my next question, he nodded. "The *Good*

Catherine? Aye, she came back, and many a time since. Good ship! Due in again soon."

My further inquiries concerning Emma Delahay went for nothing. She had simply disappeared...vanished. And my money with her!

At the old inn Tom showed me to my old room. "I'll care for your horse, lad." At my question, he shook his head. "Jacob? Been three...almost four years. But he's a wandering man. No telling where he's come to by now. Sooner or later he'll come back."

He brought me ale and sat down across from me. "Quiet it is," he said. "All is quiet now." He looked at me sharply. "You did him in, you know."

"Who? Jacob?"

"Not Jacob! Oh, no! Never him! I mean Leckenbie. That last piece of yours, it destroyed him. It angered the Queen and she had hard words for some of her people. They hanged a dozen of them at Tyburn and put a few others behind bars. But not Leckenbie! Oh, never him! He got off, skipped out—and is a wealthy man, they say."

"And Tosti," I said, "what of him?"

"I have not seen him. For a while, he was much about, a lonely man, I think. Yet all has changed here. Robin Greene is sunk far into drink and all the talk now is of Kit Marlowe, Thomas Kyd, and Will Shakespeare."

London *had* changed. Or perhaps it was I who had changed, for does a man ever remain the same? My voyage to sea, my captivity, mild though it had been, my experience of other lands and other peoples, had had their effect upon me.

When Tom had gone about his business I sat long

over my glass. I was older... four years older, and nigh onto five. The months had passed quick in Spain, and in the wars as well. Now, looking back, they were a blur of confused images with only a few moments standing out, stark and clear. Often they were the inconsequential moments, or what seemed so.

In my pocket were a few gold coins from the purse given me by Henry; beyond that I had nothing. I was a man alone, without home, without estate, without family, and at this point, without friends.

What was I to do? Find Emma Delahay? Then how? She may have died, for the plague visited London often. My small fortune was gone and my gold would not last long. Should I return to writing? But I was no writer, merely a man with some facility with words. Still, I had a story of the wars, perhaps several, and so, until fortune smiled again, perhaps...

To sit idle was never my way. Somehow I must be doing.

The England of Good Queen Bess was a country on the march. Merchants and tradesmen, once despised, now often held positions of honor. Some of them were acquiring coats of arms and being ushered into the gentry. Yeomen had become nobles, and all was changing. Of the old families who had come with William from Normandy, few remained in any kind of power. A new order of men was rising, yet there was no lasting place for me in England, for sooner or later questions would be asked and my identity discovered.

Richard Field... I would seek him out. With that in mind I went to my room. At my small table I began to compose a firsthand account of the battle of Arques. To flesh it out I included a brief account of Henry of

Navarre. It was no obsequious, flattering picture, but a straightforward account of the man, his character, and his capabilities.

Most of the night I worked, driving swiftly ahead, caught up by the excitement of my own narrative. It was not the picture from the long view as so many were, but from the standpoint of the soldier in the field, of hand-to-hand combat, the clash of blades, the blood, the dying, the waiting, and the occasional flashes of humor.

Next day Richard Field greeted me as an old friend, for he at least had not changed except that he was now risen in the world. His print shop was twice its former size, and he employed a dozen workmen and apprentices now where there had been but two before.

Alone in his private chamber where he conducted his business, he stood back and looked at me. "Ah, but you have changed! The boy has become the man! And that scar on your cheekbone?"

"It was single combat, at Ivry, between the armies. With a lieutenant of the Duke of Mayenne. I fought two such fights."

"And what have you here? Another manuscript?"

"A firsthand account of Arques."

"Good! I think we can use it. Do another on Ivry." He glanced over the sheets of manuscript. "Hah! A picture of Henry of Navarre! That will hold much interest here!"

Seated over a glass of wine I explained that I sought Emma Delahay.

Richard Field shrugged. "Who can say where she is? London is a vast place and people come and go.

She was a woman alone, and there are many murders—most of which go unpunished and the murderers unfound.

"It might be that. Or she might just have chosen to disappear. You spoke of the *Good Catherine*. Her master may know something that would help you."

For hours I wandered the streets of London but saw no other familiar face. Tosti Padget, had he been here, would probably have known all, but he had disappeared. Then, at night in my chamber, I worked at telling the story of the battle of Ivry, and noting down several others, one a tale of Spanish treasure I heard while there.

When I saw him again, Field commented, "You who are forever trying foreign ventures should go to the Levant Company, lately chartered to carry on trade with Turkey, Venice, and all the eastern Mediterranean. It has the smell of a good thing, indeed.

"Besides," he added, "it were well to be free of London now, for the plague is such that soon all feasting must cease, and the theaters may soon be closed."

We talked on various subjects, drinking our wine the while, and he told me much that had obtained whilst I was away to the wars. Despite what I had heard heretofore he said he thought Robert Greene was dead, and that Edward Alleyn, the tragedian, had married Joan Woodward, stepdaughter to Philip Henslowe, a theater man himself.

"There was great scandal, too, about the taking of the great Spanish ship," he continued. "A rich prize she was, and all who came aboard her made off with some thing, and none of them trifles. The Queen, they say, is furious. My lord of Cumberland is he who finally laid her aboard and deserves the most, but some others, Raleigh among them, are much discontented."

Late it was when at last we parted, and I started back through the streets alone. Yet I had two pistols, well charged, and my blade with the silver hilt.

Emerging from the door, I saw a carriage drawn up down the street, all silent and standing, and I liked not the look of her, with two powerfully built men on her box. As I started past, the coach came forward, following me.

"You're daft, Chantry!" I told myself.

Yet it was coming up, moving more swiftly now, and I drew warily to one side and stepped into a doorway to have my back against something. The coach drew abreast and stopped, and a woman's gloved hand emerged from the curtained window.

"Young man!"

Holding myself ready, I replied, "Is there something you wish?"

"Are you not the gallant Captain Chantry?"

"I am Captain Chantry." I glanced to left and right. "These are black streets, milady, and were I you I should make the best of my way home. Thieves do hunt the streets about here, and no man is safe, let alone a woman."

"Will you not share my carriage? Come, do not be afraid. See?" She opened the door. "I am alone."

Curious and intrigued, I moved a step from the building. Indeed, she was alone, and as for the two men on the box, I counted myself quite their equal.

"What is it you wish?"

"Come, get in, and we will drive you to your inn.

Oh, yes! I know where it is. A strange place, too, by all accounts. One wonders if the handsome young captain is as guileless as he seems."

Curious indeed, I stepped into the carriage and seated myself opposite her.

She laughed. "What! Is the noble captain afraid then? Will you not sit beside me, Captain?"

"If I did so I could not see your beauty half so well, milady."

She laughed again and leaned toward me. She was masked. Her perfume was delicate and suited her. She was clad as for a ball, her white shoulders but barely covered, her hat riding upon a blond coiffure.

"Come, Captain! Do you so soon forget old friends? I have cause to remember you, who were so gallant, and such a magnificent swordsman! My! I who have seen the best was amazed! And quick to act, too! Never a second's hesitation!"

She leaned back so that her face was half in the shadow. Suddenly her bantering tone changed. "Captain, I have long ears, for I have discovered that information is ever the price of victory, and I understand a venture upon which you depended much has failed you."

"It is the fortune of trade, milady."

"Indeed it is, and my informers tell me that while you ventured but little, your ventures were marked with success."

"Small success! And the woman I trusted disappeared, taking with her what little I had."

"But you trusted her? Some men would think you a fool to trust any woman, particularly in a business way. Was she your mistress, too?"

"She was not," I replied stiffly.

The coach had come to a halt. Looking out, I could see that she had indeed returned me to my inn. I moved as if to depart but she put a hand on mine. "Stay, I would talk a minute.

"Look you," she said. "Who I am or where I come from does not at this time matter. You trusted a woman and she failed you, or seems to have. I needs must trust a man and I know no other who seems so likely a risk."

"I thank you. If there is anything—"

"There is, indeed." From a bag beside her on the seat she took a smaller sack. "Take this. Count it well, and when you have done so, think how it might be invested.

"In the sack you will also find a name and a place. You are not to try to discover who bears the name, nor go near the place until the venture is complete. Nor even then unless in dire emergency.

"Do you, if you should leave England, return to this same inn. I shall find you."

"But, milady, I—"

Her hand pressed mine. "Take it. I trust you. Indeed, there is no other I can trust. Even you may fail me. But as you are alone and without family, so am I . . . Do for me what you can.

"This that you hold may seem much, though it is not enough for what I need. Not enough for what you need, either, although it is a step.

"Take this, and of the profits from the venture, you may keep half. That is all. Now go."

Swinging down, I turned. I saw her face for a moment, but masked with a domino such as women sometimes wore at masquerades or when they wished not to be known. Her chin I saw, and her mouth. It was a firm little chin, and the lips were lovely. The eyes behind the mask seemed beautiful.

She waved, and then the carriage began to roll. In a moment it had whipped around a corner and was gone.

A moment I stared after it, then went into the inn and to my room. I put the sack upon the table, doffed my hat and coat, and bolted the door.

Then I drew the string on the sack and dumped the contents upon the table.

They fell in a dazzling heap, and one, rolling free of its companions, fell upon the floor.

For a moment I could only stare. Gems . . . rare and beautiful gems! Not less than a dozen of them.

Stooping, I recovered the one from the floor. It proved to be a ruby, and a fine one, too.

With one finger I separated them. Three rubies, all of fair size, four diamonds, an emerald, three pink pearls, and a pendant of gold set with amber and onyx.

I sat down on the bed. I was perspiring freely. For a few minutes I simply sat and stared, stunned by the enormity of it.

Nor was I mistaken. My father had owned a few fine gems and had begun teaching me about them when I was very young. These were, as nearly as I could see in the light I had, excellent stones. Several had obviously been removed from their settings, losing a part of their value, no doubt.

There were also three gold coins. They were all

alike. Taking one, I examined it close to the light, but the inscription was in a language strange to me.

Again I stirred the gems with my fingers, slowly pushing them together. Ten thousand pounds? Closer to fifty. And I was to have half . . . of the profits!

CHAPTER 28

WHEN I HAD completed my account of the battle of Ivry and took it to Richard Field, he greeted me with the news that the *Good Catherine* had come up the Thames only hours before, and was even now about to discharge her cargo.

Taking my payment from him, I left at once. The *Good Catherine* lay but a short distance away.

The captain was a square, solid man and he watched me board. I went to him on the quarterdeck. "I am Tatton Chantry," I explained.

"I know you. You've become a famous man."

"It is not fame I seek, particularly that kind. Two things I need to know: the success of my venture and the whereabouts of Emma Delahay."

"Your ventures," he put emphasis on the plural, "have been successful. I am a cautious man, Captain Chantry, not a gambler as many in the trade have become. I trade in staples, in established items. I do not look for gold or gems, just profitable trade.

"I was instructed to continue to reinvest what you ventured, and have done so. Come below to my cabin and you shall see."

We went below and he took from the grate a small pot. "Hot chocolate," he said. "It is something learned from Mexico."

"A habit I acquired in Spain," I said.

He glanced at me under his thick brows. "Spain, Captain?"

"I have been a prisoner there." Briefly, I explained the circumstances of my capture.

"Good! You are a man after my own heart. There is a time to fight, and a time to talk. You saved your crew, and you saved yourself. The ship was already lost to you."

From a drawer he took a small book. On the cover was pasted a small square of paper. *Accounts of Captain Tatton Chantry*.

Opening it, he showed me in neat columns of figures the sum and total of my investments and how each bit had been invested. I glanced at the total, then I had to look again from surprise. He noticed it and smiled complacently. "That is it, Captain, nine thousand four hundred and sixty-two pounds.

"I might add that having your money with which to work has made it easier for me. There is no need to seek more adventurers to include their bits. I hope you will not see fit to withdraw all you have here."

"On the contrary. I wish to draw one hundred pounds now, and a bit more later. However," here I paused for a moment, "I think you will have no need to look for other venturers. I have lately been asked to invest quite a large sum, more than enough to supply trade goods for several ventures."

"You wish to venture my entire cargo?" He shook his head. "I would not advise it, Captain. You know the old saying about putting all one's eggs in one basket. Much as I appreciate your confidence, I would suggest you place your investment in several ships. I can recommend—"

"I was coming to that. I wish at least four other good, substantial men, such as yourself. And," I hesitated a moment, "although you may not approve, I would like one other, one who is daring, one who is shrewd, but one willing to take risks if they offer a substantial profit."

Before him I placed the largest of the rubies. "Do you know gems, Captain?"

He picked up the stone and took it to the stern light, turning it slowly in his fingers. Coming back, he placed it on the table between us. "I know something of gems. My estimate would be around five thousand pounds."

I sat back in my chair. "Several such stones were entrusted to me, Captain, and I am to invest them as I see fit. The lady who entrusted me professes to know nothing of ventures or the like."

"But something of men," the captain commented dryly. "You have known her long?"

"I do not know her at all."

He shrugged. "I have been at sea all my life, Captain Chantry, and have been in many ports and foreign places. I am surprised at nothing."

He got to his feet. "Very well. I shall make a list of the cargo I have in mind and will bring it to you. In the meanwhile I will think of other ships' masters who might be the sort of whom you speak."

We walked out on the deck, and at the rail he said, "These other ventures? Must they be to the New World?"

"Not at all. In fact, I have heard of the Levant Company, who will trade to the eastern Mediterranean, largely in raisins, currants, and such."

"I had something of the kind in mind. This other man, the gambler. He has been wishing to chance a voyage around the cape to India. He has the vessel, he has the crew, and he is an excellent seaman. I will arrange a meeting."

After a moment, he said, "This woman? Would she prefer you not to gamble?"

I shrugged. "With you and the others whom you will find the chances are much in our favor. I think she would be willing to take a flyer ... she certainly took a chance on me."

"Not so much of a chance, Captain Chantry. She was a good judge of men."

I wondered afresh. Who could she be? I knew so few women, but obviously at least one knew me.

Could she have been Emma Delahay? This woman seemed much younger, and more slender. Moreover, Emma Delahay could make her own ventures.

"Captain," I said, "who do you think she can be? I mean what kind of woman?"

He stared at the crowds along the river front. "I have been thinking on that. She may be a noble woman who wishes to be wealthier, or one who fears the future. She may be a mistress of some great man who has been given gems and is wise enough to know that beauty fades but gold does not. Or she may be a thief using this method of turning her stolen jewels into cash. She may also be some fashionable bawd who realizes that youth fades and with it her stock-in-trade."

He paused a moment. "Or it may simply be someone who wishes to establish a tie with you. And there is another thought. It may be that some enemy of yours has deliberately given you stolen goods, planning to have you caught in their possession."

He turned and looked right at me. "Chantry, to be caught with stolen goods could mean hanging!"

Suddenly, and with awful clarity, I saw it all. It was a trick! Not by Rafe Leckenbie, who seemed to have vanished, but his mysterious supporter, the man with the white hair and the cold eyes!

The rest of the gems were hidden in my room! Even now the villains might have come seeking them, and me!

"I do not think that is the case," I said, "but for safety's sake, I think I will accompany my venture to the New World with you."

"I'd be pleased, but do you not return to the inn without looking about."

Indeed I would not.

Two more rubies and three diamonds were in my sash, sewn into the material only that morning. The emerald, three pink pearls, and the pendant were in my room, but well hidden.

One day, years ago, I had been leaning out the window watching what went on below when a gust of wind slammed the window at me and I jerked back quickly, my fingers clutching the edge of the shelf on which I had been leaning.

My fingers had given a sharp tug at the bit of board that trimmed the window ledge and it had swung out, revealing a cunningly hidden compartment beneath it. From the dust I gathered nobody had opened it in years, and may not have even known of its existence. Possibly some mechanical-minded guest had contrived it himself for the purpose of hiding something.

Into that compartment I had put the remaining gems, closing it carefully and scattering dust along the edge. The window was rarely opened, I knew. The chances were that nobody now alive knew of the place. I had planned to leave the gems there but a short time. Now I knew it might be long before they were removed, for I had decided to remain aboard the ship, and said so to the captain.

"Let me take the other gems," the captain suggested. "I will have our friends here to speak with you within the next few hours."

Hidden in my clothes was the slip of paper on which was written the name and the place where I could communicate with the mysterious lady.

"You go ashore, Captain?"

"There is much to do, Chantry. Much."

"I wish to send a note ashore with you. Can you deliver it to Saint Paul's Walk?"

"Aye, I shall be nigh to it."

From my sash I took a bit of paper brought from the table in the cabin. On it I wrote: *All is begun.* "Tell him who sent it, that is all."

A week later, I was at sea, bound for the New World.

CHAPTER 29

A HAND PRESSED down on my shoulder, and lips whispered, "Ssh! Not a sound!"

Confused, I lay perfectly quiet. The man beside me was Silliman Turley. Slowly, my mind sorted out the pattern. I was ashore in the New World. The *Good Catherine* had sailed off without me. Close by was the camp of the party who had seized the Spanish people of whom one was Guadalupe Romana.

I lay still and I listened. At first there was only the faint rustle of leaves overhead, the breathing of Turley, and then a sound of voices, not too far off. I could smell the damp earth, the rotting leaves. Near me on a piece of bark, an ant struggled with some tiny bit of fodder.

The voices came again, and they were very close by. "I tell you, there is nothing! She's hard aground in the river and it will take high water to float her free. She's made a little water and it looks like somebody has gone through her. Things scattered about like a search was made of what must have been the woman's quarters."

"Nothing at all?" The voice was faintly familiar. "I can't believe it."

"Like I say, somebody's been through it. But then she never got where she is by herself. Look, Cap, that passage through the outer island is narrow, and you can bet all you've got that somebody steered through."

"There's nobody aboard?"

"Not so much as a rat. We went over her, stem to stern. The current's not strong in that river this time of year and she had some tide behind her and the wind. She went into the river and jammed herself into the sand, hard and fast aground."

"No sign of the crew?"

"Like I told you. I found a camp ashore. There'd been some men camped there but they'd been attacked. Savages, it looked like. We found eight dead men, dead three or four days. They might have been a part of her crew."

"Why savages?"

"One had an arrow in him and the bodies were stripped and mutilated."

There was a silence. "Say nothing of this to anyone. You can find the ship again?"

"I can." Again there was a pause. Finally the second voice said, "Cap? Looks to me like you had it pegged. The sinking ship was a trick to get them off her and ashore while she was looted, only something went wrong.

"I think those men I found dead were supposed to get back aboard her but they never made it. Savages killed them first. Then the tide, wind, currents, whatever, moved that ship. Maybe somebody helped."

Leaves rustled. They could be no more than twenty or thirty feet away.

"Do you believe that story about the other man? The one who was fixing their boat?"

"The boat is gone, you said. If there was not such a man, what happened to it?"

"Savages?"

"Mayhap. I like none of it, Andrew. There is much going on. The ship gone through, the boat missing—"

"Aye," Andrew replied gloomily, "and the vessel of Don Manuel is soon to be here, if the stories be true. We must be ready for them.

"Cap, I say slit the throats of this lot, or take what they have and leave them to the savages. Then take Don Manuel's vessel, strip what's worth having from the *San Juan de Dios,* and be off. We are short of hands as it is and no need to lose more fighting the savages."

"Andrew, I want those chests! Our information was good. Part of it was the girl's dowry, part was to the King of Spain. It was placed aboard the *San Juan de Dios.* It was seen to go aboard. The vessel has stopped nowhere until now. If it is not aboard then it is here, and I mean to have it!

"Andrew, much is at stake. I mean to go back—"

"They will hang you, Captain. Sure as you set foot in England again, they will hang you."

"Gold can buy much, Andrew, and the Queen needs gold. By the time we return the way will be smoothed, and when we proffer a gift here and there...do not worry, Andrew. I know whereof I speak."

"We kill them, then?"

"When we have milked them of all they know. Someone knows where the chests are, and I think it to be one of these."

"You would kill the woman, too?"

"Though she knows where Inca gold may be, what is that to us? They can move about in Peru, as they are Spanish, and perhaps they can find it. We could not move freely there, for we should be discovered and killed. Unless she knows something of the chests she is of no use to us, and could be much trouble."

"You are still thinking of England?" Andrew said gloomily. "I still say you should find another place, an island of our own from which we can sail our ships. Even a place on the shores of France. I know a—"

"Talk no more to me of that! England is my home and it is England where I would be." They moved off, talking still.

Turley lifted his hand from my shoulder. "I was afeared you'd come awake, noisylike. They was right over us."

"We've got to think of something, or they will kill them all."

"Aye," Turley agreed, "a bloody lot they are! But there's two of us—not enough to do much."

We waited and watched, yet nothing offered us a chance. We must do something, alarm them, create a diversion . . . Ideas came and were discarded, yet there had to be a way.

Guadalupe was alerted, for I was positive she had seen me, that her signal had been based on something she knew. There must be some reason for our holding back. I saw Conchita bring a cup of something, coffee probably, to Guadalupe. They whispered together, I was sure, although they did not seem to do so. Conchita left, carefully not looking toward us.

Soon Armand, the Basque, came to the fire and squatted beside it, taking a piece of meat that had been broiling. As he ate he looked across the fire and up at the slope where we were hidden.

Conchita had gone back to where Guadalupe Romana was sitting, and was straightening some clothes she had washed, folding them, taking her time.

Armand straightened up from the fire, wiping his hands on his pants. At that moment Felipe came from the trees bringing an armful of firewood. He dropped it, dusted off his hands, and walked away toward the woods past the two girls. Armand followed.

"Turley!" I touched his arm. "Look! They are going to try to escape! Can you create a diversion? Distract the others?"

He glanced at the camp, and then like a ghost he was gone into the woods.

How he moved so swiftly I could not guess, but suddenly, at least two hundred yards off, I heard the cry of a wolf. A long, quavering howl that rose, quivered in the still air, then died away. It was such a howl as made the hair stand on the neck. Even I who knew—or suspected—that the wolf was Silliman Turley, was startled.

An instant later a large stone suddenly landed in the very center of the fire, scattering burning logs and embers. A series of weird whooping calls came from the woods.

And below in the camp, all was turmoil. Some of the captors ran for their muskets, which had been left rather carelessly stacked against a tree. Others drew their swords, rushing to the edge of camp.

A quick glance toward where Guadalupe had been showed that she, Conchita, Armand, and Felipe had vanished.

Moving quickly, I took a route that I calculated might intersect theirs. I was not as good in the forest as Turley, but even the few days I had been there had taught me a little. I ran—as swiftly and silently as possible.

They had run into the thickest of the woods and now I came upon them. Without doubt their captors were already searching for them. I must get them far away, or into some kind of hiding. Turley's place was best, but I knew I could not find it, nor could I find him, so I must trust him to find us.

Leading them through a shallow stream and up the opposite bank, I turned downstream as swiftly as possible, weaving a way among the close-growing trees.

All the while my mind raced ahead. The captors would be able to put no more than a few men to hunting for us. Some of their people must be left to guard Don Diego and his party. Nonetheless, they could be upon us within minutes.

We came into a thick stand of what Turley had called chestnut oaks, fine, tall trees growing very straight and thick. There was little brush there and we ran more swiftly, yet I kept looking around at the girls to see how they came. Despite their skirts, which they gathered in their hands and held high, they both ran well.

I saw an opening between the trees and led the way off along the hillside. Glancing back, I saw that Conchita had fallen, but was getting up. I could see Guadalupe's breast heaving with effort. "I am afraid...I cannot..."

"We will go slower," I told her. Then we went over

the ridge into the forest beyond. That we were pursued I had no doubt.

Suddenly I was face to face with Silliman Turley.

"How far is it to your place in the swamp?" I asked him.

He hesitated suddenly uneasy. " 'T'aint far, only—"

"Only what?"

"Don't think I'm backin' off, but a place that will hide one man who does mighty little movin' around mayn't hide all of us. The savages never found that place o' mine, but surely as I take so many in, they will. Be no use to me more, an' it's a tidy spot."

"You won't need it much longer, Turley. You'll be coming away with us."

"Don't cal'clate on it. This here's a good land. I been thinkin' a sight since you showed up and I ain't a-tall sure I want to leave. Maybe they'll fetch my scalp sometime, but this here's a good country.

"There's plenty of fish, there's game in the woods for the takin', an' you know, back to home a man could get hanged for killin' a deer or even a rabbit. All the game back there belongs to the Queen or the gentry. Here I got only to kill it and butcher it. Then there's roots, nuts, fruit about, whatever a man could want. Of course, I do miss the bread, and I miss settin' over a glass with friends. I do miss that."

"There will be settlements here," I commented. "It won't be long."

"*Here?* You're mad. Who'd want to leave all that behind and come out here where there's nothin' to drink but branch water? Maybe a few wild ones like me, but—"

"Let's go to your place, Turley. We don't have any choice. They'll be finding us soon."

"All right," he agreed reluctantly.

The brush was thick the way he went, and he wove an intricate pattern, turning back and forth, doubling on his way, occasionally returning to straighten up grass and conceal the trail.

After a half-hour of steady travel, we paused. Glancing at Turley, I said, "Where are you taking us? This way doesn't ever seem to have been traveled."

"It ain't been. That's why the savages can't find me. I never use the same route twice."

We walked on and now he seemed to be seeking something along the river's bank. He turned abruptly and walked into the water. Halfway across he said, "Walk right behind me. But take a step wrong right or left and you'll go into thirty feet of water."

Two feet below the surface of the water were two logs, side by side, a bridge hidden under water and virtually invisible.

One by one we crossed, following him closely. Had he not guided us, we could never have found our way.

Almost two-thirds of the way across, he stopped. "This here is pretty fancy. You see that blaze on the tree? The one over on the point?"

"I see it."

"When that blaze is faced right toward you, stop. Then feel underwater on the side toward the blaze. You'll find more logs. Track turns at right angles there. Then you got to count. Take ten steps, no more, no less. Then you feel on the side nearest the nigh bank an' you'll find the rest of the bridge. Once a body knows his way you can just about run it if you're surefooted."

When we reached the bank he led us into the swamp. Here and there were hummocks of earth, usually carrying a stand of cypress. Turley still twisted and turned. Most of the time we were on dry ground, occasionally wading through thick patches of reed, often a tangle of trumpet vine.

We came at last to a narrow hummock of earth and a narrow path through thick brush. At the end of the path was a body of deep water. Beyond the water lay acres upon acres of reeds, growing very tall. Turley went past me and moved off to the left a dozen feet, then put his hand in the water alongside a rotting log. When his hand lifted it held a rope which arose from the water across the narrows. Water fell dripping from the rope as he held it; then he gave a tug and a log slid from among the reeds. He reeled in the rope, pulling the log across, and when the end of the rope reached him he guided it into a notch in the rotting log where the rope had lain.

Then, he walked out on the log and we followed, balancing as best we could, to reach the far side of the water. Once there, he drew the log back into the reeds.

He led us through the reeds along a muddy ridge we had not seen from the opposite side, until we reached a raft of logs moored in an open place among the reeds. On the raft was built a crude circular hut of branches and slabs of bark, and close to it a lean-to. On a rack nearby a hide was stretched—deer, I presumed.

Under the lean-to were baskets of chinkapin and hickory nuts. Turley had told me the Indians used them not only to eat as they were but to make bread from the meal or thicken their soup. We tried it that night and a very wholesome thing it was, and goodly to eat.

Once upon the raft we rested, for all were weary from much walking up and down dale and through swamp and brush. Nor were we free from fear, for our enemies would not soon give up their chase.

The big man, their leader, had been abroad searching for the *San Juan de Dios*—or else our escape might have ended in disaster. He had taken a number of his men with him. My own treasure worried me, for hidden though it was, they might come upon it. I reflected how a man cannot be free until he has possessions—and then he is no longer free but bound by them.

Now I had but one desire—to be free of this land, to secure my treasure and escape to sea where we might come upon a ship, even the *Good Catherine,* for their intent was to trade along this shore.

Guadalupe Romana looked upon me with cool eyes. "You have freed us from them," she said. "Now what do you propose to do?"

"Get away to the sea. Find there a ship that will take us to England or some foreign land. Once there we can be secure and arrange for our futures."

She raised an eyebrow. "You would plan *my* future?"

"Nothing would please me more," I said, surprising myself at the words, but adding very hastily, "yet I would hesitate to more than suggest. Safety in England would give us time to plan, and perhaps we can arrange for you to return to Peru."

She shrugged. "I was not safe there before. Why should I be again?"

"Perhaps to return to one of those hidden places still maintained by the Incas," I suggested.

"I escaped from there, too," she admitted, "nor can I well return."

"All this can be decided at another time. Now it is enough to bring you alive into England, and with our friends."

For a moment there was silence and then I said, "Señorita, I, too, know what it means to escape. I had to flee my own land. Even in England, if they discovered who I was, I would be in danger. I would say this to none but you, but I wish you to know that I do understand."

We rested, then ate, then rested some more. Silliman Turley and I talked, and from time to time I translated for Armand and Felipe, although the former, having been a fisherman, had picked up some words of English.

The original plan of the *Good Catherine* had been to trade to the south as far as the mouth of the Savannah River, avoiding any contact with the Spanish, and then to turn about and come back up the coast. This she might already have done, although I'd been but a few days ashore and doubted there had been time. There was every chance she might come again along the coast.

She might and she might not. In any case, I must recover my boat and its treasure!

CHAPTER 30

BEFORE THE FIRST light," I suggested, and they agreed, content now to rest.

Over a slight fire, built upon a bed of flat stones, Turley with Conchita's help made a gruel and some cakes, using the nuts for meal. There was smoked fish as well, and we were hungry.

It was a tidy place he had here, and it spoke well for Silliman Turley. He was no idler, but a workman competent with many skills.

"I have a boat," I said, "a ship's boat. It is loaded but will still carry us all if we can reach it."

With the fire out the night was very dark, yet bright with stars. We heard vague sounds, and a sort of *whoosh* as some great bird, an owl no doubt, swept by on wide, slow-moving wings. The girls could have slept in the house, if such it could be called, but they preferred the cooler outside air.

Guadalupe was no more sleepy than I, so we sat together listening to the sounds of the night and watching the stars.

"Where was your home?" she asked. "I mean, when you were very young?"

I told her, choosing my words with care, and without naming places, of my boyhood. I told her what little I remembered of my mother, and of my father and his teaching, of his sharing with me those things he loved, the beauties of the wilder world and the love of learning and of pleasure in the word.

"You loved it, and yet you left?"

"My father was killed, part of my home was in flames. Whether it was the house or the stables, I know not. I escaped, and they pursued."

"But you did get away."

"That I did, but only because my father had expected that day and had taught me well. Each possible route we might take, and what I must do if alone, where I must go."

"If you go back will they know you?"

"I think not. The name I shall use now is another name, and I shall return to the place from England. A few about may know the look of me, but the ones who know will never speak. There I shall go, and there I shall live."

She sat close to me in the darkness and told me of her Andes mountains, and of the far land beyond those mountains where she had lived, but she, too, mentioned no names. And it pleased me that she was wary, although she had others to protect, and I did not.

At last she went away to lie near Conchita and to sleep. And I slept, too, awakening, shivering, in the first chill moments before the dawning.

Turley was awake also and he brought the canoe around. A dugout canoe it was, but good enough. We loaded into it what we required and pushed off. There was a soft rain falling and no great visibility, which was helpful in avoiding our enemies—or would be, if they appeared.

We held close to the southern shore of what was obviously a large sound, a place of only brackish water, affected by the tides and also by the fresh water flowing down from several rivers that rose somewhere far inland.

Turley sat in the bow, as it was he who knew the way, and Armand held the steering oar, guided by gestures from Turley. I sat amidships, keeping my weapons dry under my blanket ... or so I hoped.

We had been moving an hour before day came, only a vague graying of the mist about us. We glided through the still water like a ghost boat, shielded or at least screened by the mistlike rain.

We had far to go. We crept from the swamp into open water, holding up for just a minute close against a wall of reeds to study the sound. All was still. We could see less than a hundred yards. Felipe and I now took up our paddles and the canoe moved forward, gaining speed. Water dripped from our paddles when we lifted them.

A huge old snag lifted suddenly from the water like the head of some primeval monster, and Turley's gestures guided us around it. Ahead there were patches of outlying reeds and we went between them.

We saw nothing, heard nothing but the occasional lonely cry of some gull overhead. The sky above was clearing. The rain ceased. Yet suddenly the sky was darkened again, and looking up, we saw an immense cloud of birds.

Turley looked around at me. "Passenger pigeons," he said. "The savages kill them for their oil. Knock 'em down with a long pole when they are roosting. I've seen 'em killed by the thousands. Good eatin', too."

"Turn in toward the shore," I said, "toward that lightning-struck pine."

We eased in toward shore. Stepping off to a log which lay half-in, half-out of the water, I told them, "I'll not be long!"

Swiftly I moved, holding to solid ground when I could find it until I was safely among the trees, mostly cypress and swamp gum mingled with a few pines. Walking the log again, I got back to the narrow, sandy islet where my boat had been hidden.

It was still there! A hasty check showed me that nothing had been changed. Taking in the painter, I shoved off with an oar, pushing the boat back out of the narrow waterway in which it had been snugged down.

Once clear of the islet I settled the oars in place and pulled strongly, with a glance over my shoulder from time to time to maintain the proper heading.

Yet for all of that it was nearly an hour until I came alongside the canoe. The boxes were covered by a tarpaulin brought from the ship.

Despite the heavy load the boat carried there was plenty of room for the others. Silliman Turley got out and with Felipe's help got the canoe ashore and turned bottom-up.

There was no sign of the big man or his followers, no evidence of Don Diego or Don Manuel. Yet I doubted I had seen the last of them and was eager to be away.

Once in the boat we wasted no time but hoisted our sail and moved off. Guadalupe came aft to sit by me in the stern where I held the tiller.

She indicated the tarp-covered mound in the boat's center. "What is it there?"

"Some food from the *San Juan de Dios,* some of my things and some of yours."

"*Mine?*"

"I was aboard the ship. I found some of your clothing so I bundled it up to bring to you."

"May I have it?"

"Not yet. I don't want to loosen that tarp, and the less moving around we do, the better."

A thought came to me. "Turley? There's several muskets under that canvas. They'd better be checked, but I left them charged. There's powder and shot there, too."

He dug under the canvas and got out the muskets. He looked them over with satisfaction. "All shipshape, Cap'n!" His eyes swept the horizon. Nothing in sight but the distant shore. "Where we headin' for?"

"South by a little west, right down the sound. There's an inlet runs through the bank there into a little cove behind Cape Lookout. That's where we're going."

After a bit I said, "It's a chance we have to take. The *Good Catherine* should be beating back up the coast by now. The skipper told me he sometimes used that cove to lie up in. Anyway, it's our best chance of sighting him."

Turley was quiet for a moment. "What we don't know was where the pirate ship is—if they are pirates."

The clouds were low and the wind held fair. Off to our left now we could see the long yellow line of the inner side of the bank that broke the force of the sea. It was a long, narrow island stretching away for how many miles I knew not, but fifty or sixty miles of which I knew. The Atlantic side was straight and smooth, offering no inlets, no passages for most of its length. On the inner side facing toward the sound, the shore of the bank was broken by many small, sandy islets and shoals.

An hour passed. I glanced at the sky. Only clouds, broken here and there now, showing patches of blue. We could not see the Atlantic across the dunes of the outer banks. Had a ship been there we would have missed it.

"Who were those men?" I asked suddenly, of Guadalupe. "How did they come upon you?"

"I know not. Suddenly they were all about us, and we had no chance. Yet they seemed to know who we were and where we had come from, and they addressed both Don Diego and Don Manuel by name. They said Don Manuel had a ship soon to be here."

"Aye, I heard them speak of that. The *San Juan de Dios* was never in danger of sinking. She had only made water, I do not know how, and somehow they managed to frighten Don Diego."

"He knows nothing of the sea. He is much thought of as an administrator, but he has crossed the sea but once and knows it not."

She watched the sea for a moment, then said, "There was one among them ... not much older than you, I think, who seemed a not bad man. He would have helped us had he been able, and I believe he intended to. He said their captain was interested only in money ... and power. They were all Englishmen, I believe."

The wind seemed to be picking up. I eased the tiller to bring us a little closer to the outer island. On the chart I had been shown the cove behind Cape Lookout and the narrow inlet that led to it from the sound. Turley glanced at the sky, and then at me. The clouds were building up and the southeastern sky had a yellow look that I did not like.

Turley and Armand were taking in sail. Suddenly Turley seemed to stop all movement, looking back over my head. "Sail, ho!" he yelled then.

Turning, I looked aft. A pinnace by the look of her, three masts, and a good ship under sail. She was crowding on all canvas, trying to overtake us.

Obviously she had come from behind one of the shore-side islands and was no more than a half-mile off and closing fast.

Another glance shoreward told me we were coming up to the coastal banks and fast ... but none too fast. Yet the pinnace drew more water than we and would not dare, or so I hoped, follow us much further.

Guadalupe leaned closer to me. "Tatton," it was the first time she had called me that, "don't let them take me. Those men ... the way they looked at me and talked about me. I'd rather die."

"I won't," I replied grimly. "I'll see them all in hell first."

My words were brave but the pinnace was coming on swiftly. When I glanced at them again they seemed to be making ready with a bow gun.

Yellow was the sand on the long isle eastward, yellow under the dull gray sky where the winds lurked. There was a distant flash of lightning and a roll of thunder, and I could hear the beat of the waves upon the outer shore. Salt spray spattered my face and from behind me I heard a dull boom that was not thunder, and then a *whishing* from overhead and a shot plunged into the sea some twenty yards beyond us— too close to give me pleasure.

An island, a small, sandy cay, loomed on our right. We slid behind it, with the outer bank closing on our left. I glanced back. The pinnace was coming on, although under shortened sail. There was a shoreline ahead of us too, not much more than a mile away. The pinnace fired again, but again the shot passed overhead.

"We will need the muskets," I said to Turley. He nodded. He had shortened sail because of the wind. Now, sheltered by the islands, he raised the sail again and we moved more swiftly. The gun boomed again, and again it was a miss, but closer, much closer.

"Cap'n?" Turley said.

I glanced around. The pinnace was hove to and lowering a boat. Men were getting into it.

Guadalupe said quietly, "I can fight, Tatton, and I can shoot. And I'd not mind shooting any of them, for they are a bad lot . . . except for Tosti, that is."

Something within me stopped cold. *"Who?"* I said.

"Tosti," she replied. "Tosti Padget."

CHAPTER 31

THAT ONE WHO had been lying on the ground! No wonder he had seemed familiar! Tosti Padget here, and a pirate! Yet, why not? He had been drifting, at loose ends, with no destination in view. Yet, how had he come to this?

The wind had fallen, for we had glided into that narrow channel that led into the cove, and the sandbanks and trees on either side cut the force of the wind. Armand and Felipe were bending to the oars, but ours was a lost cause. Glancing back, I saw the ship's boat clearing the side of the pinnace with at least a dozen rowers.

Again I looked ahead. Turley was rowing also, but with a musket by his side. I recovered my own from beneath the tarp and looked to its charging. Then the pistols.

The wind touched my cheek, but it barely filled the canvas, helping us not enough. Mentally, I made the calculation, and if my judgment was correct we would reach the cove on the other side just about the time they came up with us.

Yet what had I to expect at that haven which we sought so desperately? Exactly nothing.

Ships used it for shelter from the storms, and one such seemed to be building, for the clouds were swelling into great masses off to the southeast, and the wind blew in fitful, spiteful gusts. The *Good Catherine* had used this place...but that she would be there was unlikely, or that she would take part in a fight that seemed to have nothing to do with her. Unfortunately, I had been given up for dead long since.

"Guadalupe," I said, "can you steer a boat?"

"I often have."

"Here, then. I think some shooting is in order."

If the wars had taught me anything it was something of muskets. Beyond a hundred yards their aim was a chancy thing, yet it was worth a gamble, and with a little elevation...

Putting my back against the boxes covered with the tarpaulin and settling myself down, I lifted the musket. "Lie down!" I told her.

She did as she was bade, as did Conchita, and I took a careful sight, then touched off my shot, tilting the gun to get proper elevation. I had no great confidence in the weapon, but my shot landed among them—although with what damage I knew not. Yet they fell off for a moment, and seemed none too anxious to provide me with a second chance.

My second was a clear miss, yet not by much, for it hit the gunwale and bounced off into the sea. Shooting at such a distance was unheard of, yet I had noticed the balls carried further than expected although without accuracy. I deduced that given proper elevation, a ball would drop among them.

The pinnace itself was now coming, slowly, taking soundings as it came.

Suddenly we emerged into the cove, and wonder of wonders, a ship lay there at anchor.

It was the *Good Catherine*!

I stood up and whooped loud, waving my hat vigorously. But although somebody seemed to be watching us through a glass, I doubted they could see much. Spyglasses were found on some ships now, but few were of much value.

Turley shook loose the sail and we made for the *Good Catherine*. Heavy-laden as we were, we made but slow time and the boat from the pinnace closed in swiftly.

It was Guadalupe who got off the next shot, and it struck matchwood from the gunwale. Turley rested his musket on the tarp-covered cases and fired. His shot also scored. We saw one man drop his oar and rise up, and my ball took another.

The boat swung off and we saw the big man rise up, sword in hand, gesturing at the others. More afraid of him than of us, they set to work, but we had gained a little as we had our sail and they had none.

Suddenly there was a shout from Felipe. He was pointing, for the pinnace had cleared the inlet and was coming straight for us.

"Can you swim?" I asked Guadalupe. "If you can, you and Conchita head for the *Good Catherine*. Tell the captain you're friends of mine and he will stand by you."

She looked at me for a long moment. "And you?"

"We will keep them busy," I said. "I got these lads into this and I'll not see them suffer alone."

By then I'd recharged my musket. Armand and Felipe had taken up theirs. "Take turns," I advised. "Don't let them catch us with an empty gun."

We were still moving, and now there seemed to be

action aboard the *Good Catherine*. Armand fired toward the boat and missed; Felipe did not. His shot was well aimed but the boat was drawing closer. His ball hit the man at the tiller, for he had gotten a good shot. The man leaped to his feet, clawing at his chest, then tumbled into the water. The boat swung wide and lost distance.

The *Good Catherine* was moving now, moving to cut off the pinnace. Suddenly a gun boomed and we saw a round-shot skip the waves across the bow of the pinnace. The pinnace promptly replied, and the master of the *Good Catherine* proved himself. He let go a broadside of four well-aimed guns. The first holed the pinnace a point abaft the beam, and just above the waterline. Another shot smashed the bowsprit and brought down the forestay.

What happened to the other two shots I never knew for at that moment their boat came alongside ours. Turley fired into the boat, as I did. Then, grasping my two pistols, I fired again, once with each.

"Tosti!" I yelled. "You're on the wrong side!"

He leaped to his feet, staring at me, and then the big man lunged from the stern of the boat and I was staring into the eyes of Rafe Leckenbie!

A shout from the pinnace tore his eyes from me. She was bearing down upon us, not answering to her whipstaff, for he who manned it must have been killed.

The *Catherine* was also coming up fast. Sheathing my blade, I ran forward to throw her a line. The pinnace, running blind, sheared into Leckenbie's boat and ran it down just as my line was taken by the *Catherine*.

For a time all was confusion. Leckenbie's men were swarming aboard the damaged pinnace as his longboat sank. Not sixty feet away Guadalupe and Conchita were being helped aboard the *Catherine*.

Armand and Felipe came to help me lash lines around the boxes. One after another they were hoisted aboard, and at last I stood on the deck.

Gesturing to the boxes, I said, "Take them below. To my cabin."

A glance toward the pinnace showed the two vessels were drifting apart. The pinnace was damaged, but nothing beyond repair.

Leckenbie was aboard there. Rafe Leckenbie, of all people! I stared after his boat with almost a hunger in my heart. Never had I wanted so much to fight a man, to meet him face to face. Had he been the man who led the attack on my father's house, I could have been no more eager.

Would this be our last meeting? Knowing the man, I knew it would not. He was never one to give up. I knew that from our first meeting he had meant to kill me, and not for an instant had the thought left his mind.

Nor mine. . . .

Was it that I doubted myself? Was it because he had made me feel fear, knowing the closeness of death? There was a savage hunger in me, a hot desire to cross blades with him, to end once and for all what lay between us.

For with him alive, I would never know peace. Always I must be on guard, certain that he would strike at me in the way I could be most hurt. For

Leckenbie, to kill was never enough. He enjoyed making other men suffer.

And now I was vulnerable, for now I loved...

Yes...in that moment I admitted it. For the first time I confessed it to myself. For better or worse I loved Guadalupe Romana.

Not the Irish girl of my dreams, but a lass from the high Andes, a girl of another blood, another way of life. She I loved.

And neither of us could ever know safety as long as Rafe Leckenbie lived.

Now was the time...

Captain Dabney was on his poop deck and I went to him. "Pursue them," I said. "We cannot let them escape. There is a man aboard there, whom I—"

He interrupted. "Captain Chantry, you are now aboard my ship. Yours is most of the cargo aboard, but the vessel is mine. I shall not risk it in needless pursuit of some reprobate you wish to fight."

He brushed lint from his sleeve. "You were in grave danger, so I came to your help. Now you are safe and I see no reason to risk either the vessel or a single man of my crew in order to follow up a fight that is yours alone."

"Do you think he will lie quietly by, knowing I am aboard and have what he wants? He will not. He will attack at first chance."

"Very well, then. If he attacks, we will defend ourselves. But if we can avoid his attack we will do so. I do not command a ship of war, Captain, nor a privateer. I am a simple merchant seaman and I shall do my best to return the investment of those who ventured with me, of whom you are one."

He turned and looked me up and down. "I would suggest, Captain Chantry, a bath, a change of linen, and a good night's sleep. In the morning you will think better of your insistence."

Ashamed, I shrugged. "You may be right, Captain. I am a fool."

"Not a fool, Captain. No man is a fool who can survive ashore there and come back aboard with a lovely lass and whatever is in those chests. I imagine you have done well."

He gestured toward the pinnace, limping away toward the inlet. "If you are wise in your judgment of that man, whomever he may be, he will come upon us when he can. Better get some sleep."

"The man aboard there," I said, "is Rafe Leckenbie!"

"Ah? The man who was driven from London. So this is what he came to! Well, well! Yes, I think we shall see more of him."

He bowed. "Captain Chantry, a good night to you."

A good night? With Rafe Leckenbie alive? Would there ever be a good night until I had faced him again?

CHAPTER 32

SURPRISINGLY, I SLEPT. Not the night through, but for several hours. The bath I had, and the change of linen lay hard by my bunk and ready for use. Yet when I awakened it was not the clash of arms that brought me from a sound sleep, nor a woman's scream, but the sound of the wind.

Our harbor back of Cape Lookout was a snug one—if any harbor is snug when a hurricane blows. The main force of the wind came, at first, from the south-east and that was the point of our best protection, but even there the land was not high. The waves broke on the outer shore, but the wind swept, almost unimpeded, across the low dunes that made up the point.

The *Good Catherine* was a snug vessel, her crew well chosen and tautly disciplined, the ship herself well kept and secure. Knowing the sort of man Dabney was, I felt secure despite the wind, and so did we all. I heard it from the crew when we went on deck.

For I could not lie abed with the wind blowing at such strength. Awakening, I dressed to be prepared for any emergency and was about to go on deck when the door to Guadalupe's cabin opened a crack. "Tatton? Is the storm very bad?"

"It is bad," I said, "but we're in as good a place to

last it out as there is along this coast, the vessel is a strong one, and her captain an excellent seaman. If there is serious trouble I will come to you." Suddenly a thought occurred to me. "Will you wait, Guadalupe? I have something for you."

Hastily I returned to my cabin where all was battened down and secure and took from among the chests the one containing her clothing. It was the largest of all, but not heavy for one of my strength, and I took it to her.

When she saw what I had she drew back the door, remaining behind it, and I placed the chest just inside the room. I showed her hooks upon the wall, low down. "Lash it, or it may break a leg for you. The lines are there." Stepping out, I went on deck quickly and after a moment heard the door close just as I was leaving the passage.

Sheets of driving rain swept the deck like volleys of grapeshot, and the sky was weirdly lit by continuous flashes of lightning. Grasping the ladder, I went to the poop deck where Dabney stood, his legs spread wide to take the roll of the ship.

He saw me and lifted a hand. When I drew near he shouted above the storm, "She's holding well. I think we may have no trouble."

Several men were about the deck, but no more than would be around on any watch. Dabney was sparing of his men as of all else.

Standing beside him, I watched the rain and spray blow through the rigging and sweep the deck and thought of those far out at sea—or worse, those who had been caught sailing off the shore. Many a fine ship would go down this night, or be beached out yonder, and torn apart by the waves. In such a gale as this the safest place, unless one lay as we did, was far at sea. Often I'd heard landlubbers talking of ancient seafarers staying within sight of land, which was absurd, as it was by far the most dangerous place to be, what with rocks, sandbars, shoals, and contrary winds or unexpected capes on an unmapped coast.

During a lull in the roar of the wind I said, "I thought you might need a hand so I came on deck."

"Kind of you, Captain. But I suggest you go below and have your rest. By the look of you when you came aboard I'd say you need it."

He glanced at me. "How is the lass making it?"

"Fine enough. She heard me in the passage and asked if all was well. I assured her we had a sound ship and a sounder master. I hope she went back to sleep."

"Aye." He seemed pleased at my confidence. "You do the same, Captain. I might add that our trading to date has been profitable, very profitable."

Below I did not lie down at first, being too much awake. Catching hold of the table, I eased myself onto one of the settees against the bulkhead and took a book from the shelf, where they were held in place by a strip of molding. It had been long since there had been time or opportunity to read and I sorely missed it.

The books upon the shelf were not the same as those it held when last I was aboard. Evidently those had been replaced by a store the captain maintained below decks.

One was called *Ta'rikh al-Hind,* and the language was strange to me. I was just replacing it when

Dabney came in, stripping off the cloak he had been wearing on deck.

I held it up. "What is it?" I asked.

"A book about India," he said, "written by Al-Biruni, one of the greatest Islamic scholars."

He draped his cloak over a chair back and dropped to another settee. "My man will have some hot chocolate here at once." He indicated the book. "We do wrong in the Western world to ignore the scholars of the East for they have much to teach us. He was one of the greatest and long resided in India. This book was written about 1030 or so . . . I am not sure of the date. But very good, very good, indeed."

"You have been there?"

Dabney glanced up. "I am well past fifty years of age, young man, and nearly twenty of those years were spent in the Indian Ocean . . . the Arabian Sea, if you will. Men were sailing those seas before ever a Greek prow cut the waters of the Aegean.

"Hippalus, we Europeans say, discovered the monsoon winds that will take a ship across the Indian Ocean from the coast of Africa to India. Alexander found pilots from India who knew all those waters three hundred years earlier. They showed his admiral Nearchus the way to the Persian Gulf."

A man entered bearing a covered pot. Taking cups from a rack, he filled two of them with steaming chocolate.

"The days are long at sea, Captain Chantry, and when one has an efficient crew there is time on one's hands.

"I read . . . I replenish my books often, yet a few I always keep for they are like old friends. Once I read them through; now I dip into them from time to time and read a few pages.

"When I was a lad I went out East on a voyage with my father. Our ship was wrecked there and we remained for many years. First my father and then I myself were masters of ships there."

We drank our chocolate and talked, the ship rolling with wind and sea. At last he returned to the deck, and I to my bunk.

All night long the wind blew hard and strong, the roar of the winds a mighty sound in the night. Then of a sudden there was no wind and the silence awakened me to a yellow, awesome dawn. There was no sound. Suddenly we were caught in a world empty of it, and my throat caught with fear. Then I realized. We must be in the eye of the storm. If so, the winds would return, but from another direction.

I dressed and started for the deck, but Guadalupe was there before me. "I need the air," she said. When I started to explain about the hurricane she told me she understood. She had experienced such storms before.

She stood beside me and we watched the sailors, tightening up all that might have come loose, preparing for what was to come.

"Did you live in Lima?" I asked.

"In the mountains and at the sea, and then in Cuzco. Only at the last was I in Lima. There was much that was different. I remember the bullfights, and I remember once there was a new viceroy or some official and they decorated all the balconies with greenery. We went to a play given by the Society of Jesus entitled *The Prince of Fez*.

"There were many duels, for there was much talk of honor. And scarcely a week went by when someone was not killed, or so it seemed to me.

"My mother died when I was eleven and my father was killed . . . It was said to have been done by thieves but I did not believe so. I believe he was killed by assassins, for my mother had told him much and they thought to find among his papers what he would not tell them."

"And they did not?"

She smiled triumphantly. "They did not. There were papers and maps also. I hid them."

"They may have been found since."

"They will never find them. The house where we lived was very old. My mother had once lived there with her grandmother, who was the daughter of a brother to the Inca. She showed me a secret place."

We went below and Conchita served us breakfast. Silliman Turley came aft, but would not listen to moving aft with us. "I've a good bunk for'ard an' I like it there. What about that Leckenbie? You think he's through?"

"No." I was sure about that. "He's not through."

What would he do? Would he dare an attack under cover of the storm? How badly hurt was the pinnace? She did not seem too badly damaged, but if she were damaged beyond repair he would have a double reason for attacking us. He would need a ship.

What had become of Don Diego? And where was Don Manuel's ship, which was expected at any moment? Had the hurricane destroyed it? Or was it lying up in safety somewhere down the coast?

Rafe Leckenbie knew of that ship, too, and would

be watching for it. Nor could either of us escape from the haven we had chosen until the storm abated. To try to get out now would expose us to all the dangers of a lee shore. Outside of our cove the shore stretched away to the northwestward before curving around to the south, low, sandy shores so far as I could see or remember, and a deathtrap for any kind of sailing craft in this weather. Like it or not we were bound here together until the storm blew itself out.

Dabney came down from the deck once more as we were finishing our breakfast. He listened to my thoughts about Leckenbie and agreed. "The rain is easing off, and as soon as it does so I shall have all the guns charged and ready."

"Leckenbie will try for surprise," I said, "using a frontal attack only as a last resort. He's devilish shrewd, and a daring man."

"We will be ready," Dabney assured me.

Toward nightfall the wind began to die down, blowing in fitful gusts, but the sea remained heavy. Dabney had retired to rest, leaving his mate in command. MacCrae was a Scot and a solid man. Now twenty-six, he had been fourteen years at sea and had sailed with Hawkins and Frobisher before coming to the *Good Catherine*.

He was a tall, lean, no-nonsense sort of man who kept a tight ship, liked most men, and trusted none of them too far. "We've a good lot aboard here," he told me, "and they sail with us because they like it. Most of the crew have been with us three to four voyages now.

"Captain Dabney lets them carry a bit of trade on their own account, so each makes a bit on the side. Nobody does his own trading. The captain does that.

But they can carry up to ten pounds each in goods aboard here. As mate and sailing master I can carry up to fifty pounds, and I do. Translated into goods, that will make a tidy profit for the voyage. So we've all an interest in it."

Alone, I paced the deck, looking off toward the inlet from which the pinnace would probably come. Now I avoided Guadalupe, as I was restless and irritable, knowing attack might come at any moment. If we were caught unawares not one of us would survive. The quality of mercy could not be expected of Rafe Leckenbie.

How had Tosti ever become entangled with him? He had been a decent young man of no particular talent, much knowledge, and a desire to have something and be somebody without any clear notion of how that was to come about. He had sat waiting for the pot of gold to fall into his lap, forever talking of inheriting money, of finding treasure, of somehow coming into wealth without doing anything to bring it about. I had liked him, and he had been friendly when I had no friends, yet Leckenbie may have offered an easy road to all he wanted.

The waters of the cove darkened, the heavy seas abated somewhat, although I believed the tail of the hurricane had still to pass over us. Occasionally stars were glimpsed through the clouds, and the wind had died down although surf could still be heard booming on the Atlantic shore, beyond Cape Lookout.

A gull swung by heading in toward the shore. I went up on the poop, which offered a better vantage point for observing the cove, but all was dark and still. The few stars had disappeared under clouds.

MacCrae came to my side. "You know the man Leckenbie, Dabney says. Is he as bad as they say?"

"Worse. He will stop at nothing, has no regard for people and never did. He is a man who is totally evil because he is totally selfish. Men follow him because he leads them and because of hope of gain or fear. He will use people and discard or kill them without wasting an instant. He is also the finest swordsman I have ever met."

"You fought him once?"

"And was nearly killed. That was long ago and I have learned a lot. I hope I have learned enough."

Again I went below. Dabney was up, his chocolate on the table before him. Guadalupe was there also, tired but awake.

"All is well on deck?" Dabney had papers before him, and was engaged in some problem of navigation.

"So far," I said. "He is at least making us lose sleep."

"Which is probably a part of his plan," Dabney commented calmly. "Being the man you say he is, he will no doubt choose a moment when we least expect an attack. I am sure he knows just what we are doing."

"You mean he has spies here?"

"He needs no spies. He knows we expect an attack, so we must be forever on guard. On the contrary, he expects no attack and he will choose the time. His men can rest, relax, and await the proper moment. That is why I now have but three men on deck. The others are resting."

"But if he should come upon us now?"

"We would have ample warning. How can a boat approach us without our knowing?"

Nonetheless, I was worried. Yet the hot chocolate tasted good as did the scones. "You live well, Captain," I commented.

"Why not? My life is aboard ship. I see no reason for a Spartan existence. One needs the comforts, and I can have them nowhere else."

Suddenly a man appeared in the door. "The pinnace, Captain. She has just come from the inlet, but is not heading toward us."

"Thank you, Samuel. Now alert the men, but have them stay at their posts. See they are served a round of rum. I shall be on deck shortly." He refilled our cups and his.

"You are complacent, Captain."

"Not complacent. Confident. I trust in my ship and my men. Whatever Leckenbie is doing at this moment is not important. He is not planning a direct attack on my ship with his pinnace. His is the smaller vessel with fewer guns, and your Rafe Leckenbie is not a reckless man. He will not see his vessel destroyed until he has another.

"What he is doing now is a feint, perhaps, or he is getting in position for a later attack. For that, one man can watch him as easily as a dozen. We must simply hold ourselves ready. He has the advantage of the attack and the choice of time and place."

He put his cup down. "You have recently been to France, Captain? Did you by any chance meet Montaigne? The man of the essays?"

"I did not. As you know, I was with the Spanish forces, who were waging war against Henry of Navarre. We were defeated and I was taken prisoner. I do know that Montaigne is no longer mayor of

Bordeaux. Not since the plague. He has been, I heard, mediating between Henry of Navarre and Henry III."

"King Henry freed you, you say? And spoke to you in person?"

"He did. I believe," I hesitated, choosing my words with care, "that he knew something of my family."

"Ah? Interesting! Most interesting, Captain! Did you know that you also had a mutual friend?"

My expression must have been blank, for he smiled again. "You do make the right friends, Captain Chantry. The helpful ones. I refer to Jacob Binns."

He looked so smug that I was irritated. "I do indeed know Jacob Binns," I replied. "He seems to have acquaintances everywhere, though when we met I thought him but a simple fisherman."

"No doubt. He has been many things in his time, many things." He paused, listening to some movement on deck. He was aware, I believed, of every creak of timber, every scurry of footstep, every lap of water and strain of rigging aboard his vessel. "If you do not know, Captain Chantry, I must explain. In his own way, Jacob Binns is an extremely important man. There is in the world a secret group, a society, if you will, of men of similar experience and ideas. It is old, older than any other, older than even any religion we now know. It is a society that crosses all boundaries, all lands, and all seas. Its numbers are few but they are everywhere.

"Jacob Binns is an envoy, a messenger or communicator between members. No doubt he or someone close to him knew who you were and where you were."

I did not like the mystery of it, nor the feeling that

forces might be pulling at me over which I had no control, even though they be friendly. Yet, Binns had been a good friend to me.

Suddenly a man was down from the deck. "Captain? The pinnace is heading for the entrance. I think she is going to sea."

Dabney got to his feet at once. "I think she is not." He turned to me. "Shall we go on deck, Chantry? The attack is about to come."

Instantly I was on my feet. Guadalupe started to rise too, but my hand pressed her down. "Stay...it will be safer, and I want not to worry about you in what happens."

The clouds were low and gray still. The sea was ruffled with whitecaps but the swell had lessened. We lay scarcely a hundred yards offshore as the cove was not a large one, but the pinnace had skirted its far rim in reaching the entrance. All eyes were upon her.

Suddenly, she seemed to change course toward us, then her bow swung away again. Puzzled, I looked at Dabney. "What is he about? Is he going to sea? Is he going to attack? Is he—?"

Guadalupe screamed.

Spinning around, I was in time to see them coming over the rail, dripping wet, cutlasses in hand. While all our attention had been taken by the seemingly erratic maneuvers of the pinnace, the attackers had swum out from shore. Over the rail they came, some with cutlasses or knives in their teeth to allow both hands for climbing. They spilled onto our lower deck, in a mass.

They swarmed over the rail ready for attack, and they found the deck was empty!

The Captain and I faced them from the top of the ladders leading from the poop deck.

On the deck below there was only Guadalupe, standing in the doorway of the passage leading to the main cabin, which was under the poop deck.

The attackers halted momentarily, Rafe Leckenbie among them, caught off guard by the empty deck where they had expected enemies. Cutlasses lowered, they stared about them, and at that moment, Captain Dabney fired his pistol.

He shot into the mass of attackers, and a man fell, but instantly on the shot the ship's crew rushed from under the fo'c'stle and from the cabins aft.

Taken from both sides, the surprise of Leckenbie's men was total. They were doubly shocked, first at the empty deck, and then at the attack.

Leaping to the deck, I took a cut at a brawny pirate with a hairy chest and a ring in his one ear. The cut only scratched him and he lunged at me but I thrust low and hard and he impaled himself on my sword. For a moment we were face to face, then I jammed my palm under his chin and shoved him back off my sword.

Rafe Leckenbie stood waiting, smiling. He saluted me with his blade. "It has been a long time since first we met, Tatton Chantry!"

"But worth the waiting, Rafe," I said. "Do you wish to die now?"

He laughed, a great laugh, a fine laugh. "Die? Me? I have just begun to live!"

We crossed blades. His skill, I perceived at once, had grown with time. There was fighting about us, but we ignored it. This was our moment, and I was remembering that awful night on the high moors when he had come so close to killing me.

He fenced coolly, skillfully. He was a man with greed only for power, a man born to dominate—or die in the attempt. If he had one love, this was it. This crossing of blades, the art of the sword. And he was a man created to fight.

For all his great size and strength, he moved with the speed and ease of a dancer, on his toes, poised, smooth. For every move of mine, he had an answer. I felt he was toying with me, and yet . . .

"Ah!" he said, as I parried his blade. "You have learned!"

He feinted for my head and attempted a flank cut. I parried and thrust to the right cheek. He parried the blow easily, again attempted a head thrust and then to the chest. Again I parried and my point tore his sleeve near the shoulder, but touched no flesh.

The fighting around us ceased, but neither of us noticed nor moved except toward each other. He attacked suddenly, coming in fast with a style I had never encountered before, a whole series of thrusts and cuts, baffling in their speed and unexpectedness. It needed all my skill to escape them. His point, needle sharp, touched my thigh. I parried his next blow and with a quick riposte, drew blood from his cheek. For an instant his eyes flamed with anger, then it was gone.

"You are good!" he said. "Very good!"

Yet I was not to be misled. That he flattered me to lead me into taking unnecessary chances I was sure, yet I fenced cautiously, studying his methods, yet careful not to take anything for granted, for he was a shrewd blade and meant to kill me. He was very sure of himself, fencing with the absolute confidence of a man who had never been bested with a blade. Several times he lunged, yet each time I managed to deflect his blade. Steadily I retreated, circled a little, but fell back. He was constantly upon me, and time and again I had the narrowest of escapes. Once he nicked my shoulder, again he grazed my cheek, drawing blood. He smiled at that. On the instant I moved, grazing his blade and with the slightest flexing of the wrist pressing it out of line, then instantly lunging. My point went two inches into the latissimus muscle, reached by a thrust that went between arm and body.

Recovering instantly, I pressed the attack. Blood stained his shirt and ran down his side. And now his coolness was gone. He had been hurt; I had actually drawn blood. In a fury he came at me and for several wild minutes I was hard put to defend myself.

As he came on fast, I circled and stepped in a spot of blood. I slipped. Instantly he was upon me, his sword lifted for a killing thrust.

As he stabbed downward I threw myself at his legs, and he staggered back. Coming up fast, I grasped his sword arm and pressed him back.

He laughed, and deliberately began to force his arm down. The strength of the man was prodigious. He was laughing at me now, laughing with a terrible rage as he forced my arm down and down, bringing his blade closer and closer to my throat. Yet the years had done much for me, and I was no longer the boy he had fought that first time. The long months of fencing with Fergus MacAskill, the climbing in the mountainous crags of the Hebrides, and the years in the wars, all had conspired to make me a different man.

Suddenly I began to shove back. Harder and harder I pressed and my arm ceased to move downward. His blade stayed firm and then inexorably I was pushing him back.

He could not believe it. Nothing in his life of continual triumph had prepared him for what was happening now. My strength was not only equal to his, but was surpassing it. His arm went back, and suddenly he sprang away, jerking his wrist from my grip and striking out with a wild slash that ripped wide my shirt and left a bloody gash across my stomach.

Swiftly he pressed his attack. He thrust hard and I felt the point of his blade in my side. Another twist of the blade and he had cut my cheek. He was a fighting fury now, filled with hatred of the threat I presented to him.

Nothing I could do seemed to stop him. He came on, pushing hard. Suddenly I gave way, and he came in, closing the distance. My next lunge took him by surprise. I risked all . . . but the blade caught him coming in and thrust deep.

For a moment he stared, unbelieving. Then he leaped back. For an instant he swayed, drenched now along his lower side and leg with the red blood of his wound.

He lifted his sword, threw it in the air and caught the blade, then threw it like a spear!

Yet my blade lifted and caught his, throwing it aside. I went at him then, standing close to the rail, and he stood, braced to meet me, no weapon in his hands. Then his left hand went behind his back to his belt and came from under his jerkin with a knife, a sword-breaker such as Fergus had carried!

I feinted, and he moved to catch my blade but I swept it down and then up, ripping the inside seam of his breeches and cutting half through his wide leather belt.

Blood was pooling beneath him. He crouched, teeth bared in anger. Then suddenly like a flash he turned and threw himself over the rail and into the water!

Leaning over the rail, I saw blood on the water. His body had gone down, his blood mixing with the bubbles of the sea.

The pinnace had stopped not fifty yards off. Our guns were bearing on her; our men stood with lighted matches ready for a broadside.

The pinnace held still, and for an instant I believed they might chance it.

Long I stared at the water, yet I saw no further sign of Rafe Leckenbie. He had gone down, bleeding profusely, into the depths. Then, as if impelled by his disappearance, the pinnace began slowly to back off.

We held our fire, waiting.

CHAPTER 33

THE HOUSE OF gray granite sits in the hollow of a green hill with all the bay and the rocks below it. A strong walker may climb to where the old fort lies, its black stones made blacker still by the blood of those who died there, and the burning of the fires that ate away its heart more times than one, yet each time by a son rebuilt.

Ours is a quiet place with the gray sea before us, rarely still, and the black rocks and islets rising from it. Here and there lies a patch of green where the grass grows or a tree.

To this place have I come after my wandering years. My father died somewhere near but where his body lies no man knows. It matters not, for his spirit haunts these gray rocks, resting or moving among them as he forever did. By now he knows that I have come again, bought back the old place and some of the land around. And if my name is another's the hearth at least is mine, and my sons will grow tall from the same deep roots.

You have not failed me, Father, for you gave much, asking only this in return: that I come again and rebuild the old fires that the name and the blood shall live.

Guadalupe is here, and my firstborn, and a fine lad he is, named for you, my father.

The chests I brought back from America were fatly filled, and the Irish folk know me for who I am and say nothing, but greet me gently as they pass. The English whom I also love, although it seems traitorous to some, think of me as a sailor from the days of the Armada, a sometime prisoner in Spain, and a wanderer come home.

My fine Irish horses graze on the salt green grass, and there are cattle here, and sheep. The chests are not empty although I have bought lands here and some in France. And we live quietly but well, going only now and again to Dublintown or Belfast, and mayhap to Cork or London.

Long ago there was a lady left money with me. She has never returned and when I tried the name she gave me and the place, nothing was known, but someday needing it, she will seek me out. She will find lands she owns and a house here and there, and each year I study the money and judge what must be done with it, for she was a woman who trusted at least one man and shall not regret it.

Yet when the gray geese fly west for Iceland, bound on to Greenland and then to Labrador, there is sometimes in the heart of me a longing for distant shores and the beat of waves upon the long golden sands, and the distant view of mountains, far and blue against the horizon, and always the winds that whisper of enchantments beyond the purple ridges.

I shall not go. Guadalupe is here, and my son. My destiny lies here. Like my father before me I shall walk these old paths with my son and show him where the Skelligs lie and old Staigue Fort and the ruins of Derryquin Castle. I shall speak to him of Achilles,

Hector, and Conn of the Hundred Battles, of the old kings who lived at Tara and mayhap of a bloody man who went over the rail into the waters behind the cape at Lookout.

Of Jacob Binns I have seen no more, but my door stands open always for him, or for Fergus MacAskill or even for Tosti Padget.

Kory comes sometimes, with Porter Bob and Porter Bill, and we trade a little and lie a little and talk of the old days that are better gone.

Of Emma Delahay I have no word. Gone she was and gone she is, and some small money with her, although most was accounted for by Captain Dabney of the *Good Catherine*. Was she murdered? Fled? I know not, although sometimes I wonder.

Last year in London a lovely girl crossed the floor, holding out both hands to me. "You are Tatton," she said, "and I am Eve Vypont, and I wish you to know that our horse came back, and you may walk in my forest when you will!"

Silliman Turley keeps a tavern in Ballydehob and sometimes when the *Good Catherine* sails into Roaring Water Bay, we meet there to share a bottle and a loaf with Captain Dabney. So all things at last come to an end.

Guadalupe beside me wears her golden medallion that I took from the deck of a long-lost ship in a far place beyond the sea.

Now I shall go back from the hills to sit beside my fire in the house my own hands built, and sometimes I shall lift my eyes to see the firelight play upon the silver handle of a sheathed sword that hangs there above the fireplace. And when the fire crackles upon the hearth I shall look down from the window to where the gray ghosts of the rainstorms sweep across the distant sea, like veiled women to their prayers.

I have come home again, and I go now to where love lies waiting....

About Louis L'Amour

*"I think of myself in the oral tradition—
as a troubadour, a village tale-teller, the man
in the shadows of the campfire. That's the way
I'd like to be remembered—as a storyteller.
A good storyteller."*

IT IS DOUBTFUL that any author could be as at home in the world re-created in his novels as Louis Dearborn L'Amour. Not only could he physically fill the boots of the rugged characters he wrote about, but he literally "walked the land my characters walk." His personal experiences as well as his lifelong devotion to historical research combined to give Mr. L'Amour the unique knowledge and understanding of people, events, and the challenge of the American frontier that became the hallmarks of his popularity.

Of French-Irish descent, Mr. L'Amour could trace his own family in North America back to the early 1600s and follow their steady progression westward, "always on the frontier." As a boy growing up in Jamestown, North Dakota, he absorbed all he could about his family's frontier heritage, including the story of his great-grandfather who was scalped by Sioux warriors.

Spurred by an eager curiosity and desire to broaden

his horizons, Mr. L'Amour left home at the age of fifteen and enjoyed a wide variety of jobs including seaman, lumberjack, elephant handler, skinner of dead cattle, miner, and an officer in the transportation corps during World War II. During his "yondering" days he also circled the world on a freighter, sailed a dhow on the Red Sea, was shipwrecked in the West Indies and stranded in the Mojave Desert. He won fifty-one of fifty-nine fights as a professional boxer and worked as a journalist and lecturer. He was a voracious reader and collector of rare books. His personal library contained 17,000 volumes.

Mr. L'Amour "wanted to write almost from the time I could talk." After developing a widespread following for his many frontier and adventure stories written for fiction magazines, Mr. L'Amour published his first full-length novel, *Hondo,* in the United States in 1953. Every one of his more than 120 books is in print; there are more than 300 million copies of his books in print worldwide, making him one of the bestselling authors in modern literary history. His books have been translated into twenty languages, and more than forty-five of his novels and stories have been made into feature films and television movies.

His hardcover bestsellers include *The Lonesome Gods, The Walking Drum* (his twelfth-century historical novel), *Jubal Sackett, Last of the Breed,* and *The Haunted Mesa.* His memoir, *Education of a Wandering Man,* was a leading bestseller in 1989. Audio dramatizations and adaptations of many L'Amour stories are available on cassettes and CDs from Random House Audio publishing.

The recipient of many great honors and awards, in

1983 Mr. L'Amour became the first novelist ever to be awarded the Congressional Gold Medal by the United States Congress in honor of his life's work. In 1984 he was also awarded the Medal of Freedom by President Reagan.

Louis L'Amour died on June 10, 1988. His wife, Kathy, and their two children, Beau and Angelique, carry the L'Amour tradition forward with new books written by the author during his lifetime to be published by Bantam.